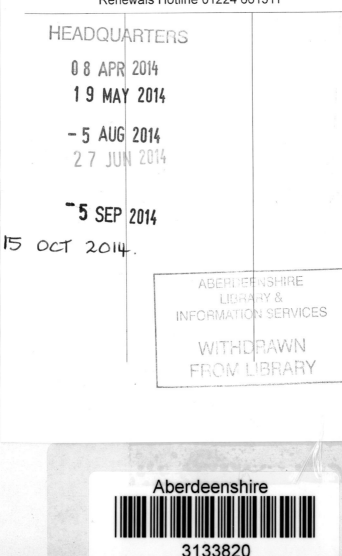

NOVELS

Chosen (Tindal Street Press 2010)
Losing It (Sandstone Press 2007)
Nina Todd Has Gone (Bloomsbury 2007)
As Far As You Can Go (Bloomsbury 2004)
Now You See Me (Bloomsbury 2001)
Sheer Blue Bliss (Bloomsbury 1999)
Easy Peasy (Bloomsbury 1998)
The Private Parts of Women (Bloomsbury 1996)
Partial Eclipse (Hamish Hamilton 1994)
Limestone and Clay (Secker and Warburg 1993)
Digging to Australia (Secker and Warburg 1992)
Trick or Treat (Secker and Warburg 1990)
Honour Thy Father (Secker and Warburg 1990)

ANTHOLOGIES (as editor)

Are You She? (Tindal Street Press 2004)

LITTLE EGYPT

Lesley Glaister

SALT

CROMER

PUBLISHED BY SALT

12 Norwich Road, Cromer, Norfolk NR27 0AX United Kingdom

© Lesley Glaister, 2014

The right of Lesley Glaister to be identified as the author of this work has been asserted by her in accordance with Section 77 of the Copyright, Designs and Patents Act 1988.

This book is in copyright. Subject to statutory exception and to provisions of relevant collective licensing agreements, no reproduction of any part may take place without the written permission of Salt.

Printed in Great Britain by Clays Ltd, St Ives plc

Typeset in Sabon 10/14

This book is sold subject to the conditions that it shall not, by way of trade or otherwise, be lent, re-sold, hired out, or otherwise circulated without the publisher's prior consent in any form of binding or cover other than that in which it is published and without a similar condition including this condition being imposed on the subsequent purchaser.

ISBN 978 1 907773 72 3 paperback

1 3 5 7 9 8 6 4 2

For Andrew, once again

PART ONE

Spike's a thin streak of a boy, American, with silver studs in his face and ears, pale matted snakes of hair, and a distinct whiff of the vegetable about him. He hitchhikes when he needs to travel, or else he walks. He doesn't believe in *money* – marvellous!

We met when he sprang from a skip and landed right in front of me in a tumble of rolling oranges. I screeched and clutched my trolley handle, frightened half to death. He was all solicitation and apology – charm, I'd go as far as to say. We were in the service area behind the supermarket and I'd caught him 'dumpster diving'.

U-Save throws out huge quantities of perfectly good food just because it's out of date. A sinful waste and shame, I say, and have said, but do they take heed? Once I'd regained my composure, Spike showed me his haul and offered me a caramel doughnut – delightful. And then he climbed back into the skip and called things out:

'Carrots? Hummus? Tiramisu?' and if I said yes he passed them to me and I added them to my trolley. I've seen him regularly since then and the same has happened, which does save money, but really the fun is in the sport of it, don't you know? If I could climb and spring about like Spike I'd do it myself. The beauty of it is that you never know what's coming next. I've been introduced to all sorts of new delights that way: panacotta, globe artichokes, sushi, chicken satay on most useful pointed skewers.

Spike became a friend to me – like an angel, you might say – and it was Spike who set me free.

We were sitting on a doorstep in the service area sharing a tub of Kalamata olives. (Not the most salubrious place. Here they keep the bins and skips and bales of flattened boxes. Here the dual carriageway roars above you and occasionally a hubcap or paper coffee cup or strip of rubber tyre flies down. Here stray cats yowl and prowl – there's plenty of vermin to keep them fed. And here too, the smokers among the U-Save staff emerge to puff on their cigarettes. I've spotted I'm Doreen how may I help you?, the sourest faced person I've ever met, puffing away there. Seeing me with Spike caused her orange-pencilled eyebrows to shoot into her hairline. Most gratifying.)

It was a late September day, still quite warm, and I'd rolled up my trouser legs to sun my shins – flaky and crinkled and mapped with veins. However did they get like that? Each time he finished an olive Spike ejected the stone forcefully from between his lips, aiming for an empty beer-tin, but overshooting. I told him he was blowing too hard; he demonstrated that if he blew more softly the stone simply dropped onto his legs. 'Well, move the tin further away then, dear,' I suggested, but he merely frowned and desisted from his game.

We turned to the subject of dreams – in the sense of

ambition. His I found grand but disappointingly vague: peace, love, equality, and so on. Visions of the world as it could be. As he waxed lyrical I watched the nervous fidget of his hands – fingers young and straight but stained from smoking, painfully bitten nails.

When the olives were gone, he rolled himself a cigarette. 'What's your dream then, Sisi?'

(You see how I reverse my name? How much more comfortable it's made, by such a simple flip.)

'To leave,' I said, nodding towards my home.

'And go where?'

'Sunset Lodge. Once I've sold up.'

He snorted his derision, but I indulged myself once more in describing the luxury I'd seen in the brochures: reclining armchairs, vast televisions, tempting menus, alternative therapists, a dedicated 'friend', parties, seasonal entertainment and a 3-star suite for visitors.

Spike ground out his cigarette and fiddled with the packet of tobacco. 'Don't give in to the fuckers now,' he said.

'You asked my dream,' I pointed out.

We sat in a silence that almost approached the prickly for a while, until he broke it.

'They still hassling you?'

I shook my head, which was a lie. Stephen, the latest of the developers' representatives, waits for me twice a week in the U-Save café where I go each morning for my coffee. I conduct all my business in the café rather than let anyone into the house. (Osi would go berserk at such an invasion.) The U-Save Consortium propose to buy Little Egypt – the last remnant of the family property – to raze to the ground and erect what they call a 'mega-homestore' and it's Stephen's task to win me over.

From the scattered litter, Spike picked up a glossy leaflet advertising this week's special offers and skimmed it, scoffing. 'Thirty-six fishy nuggets – buy two get one free – that's 108 fishy nuggets. The oceans will be fished-out before they're finished.'

'And think of all those fish without their nuggets!' I jested, but he didn't laugh.

'What if,' I said, 'now don't go getting on your high horse, dear, but what if a person *did* want to sell a property to someone like, say, U-Save.'

'Then they'd want their fucking heads examined.'

He moved to a crouch as if about to spring away, but I caught his arm. 'But what if, for instance, there was something there, something hidden that got uncovered, dug up, say, during the building work?'

He cocked his head at me and squinted. 'Like Roman ruins and stuff?'

'Mmm,' I said, 'or a corpse, something in that line?'

There was a chink of silver against tooth as he puffed out his lip. 'Huh, they'd cover it up and you'd never know. Think they'd let anything get in the way of profit?'

Though he was not to know it, these were the magic words that freed me. It was a thought quite new, a revelation. Ever since . . . well for all the years, all these years I've supposed that we could never leave, that once *it* was discovered we'd go to prison; Osi, certainly, and perhaps me, too. That's what Victor believed and left me believing.

I needed to be back home to test the thought. To be alone. If Spike was right, then we could sell and go. Could it really be so? But what of Osi? I flailed about until Spike hauled me to my feet. (My knees are really dreadful, the left in particular.

You can get new ones, I hear, though not, so far, at U-Save.)
　'You really think so?' I asked him.
　'I fucking know so,' said he.

I

Isis wandered into her parents' bedroom, stretched out on the stripped, stained mattress and stared at the ceiling. She could hear a faint stipple of birdsong from outside and Mary banging round the house with her broom – she was always in a temper when Evelyn and Arthur left, till she got things ship-shape. Apart from that it was quiet, except for the usual creaking and settling of the house, as if it too breathed and shifted into another mood with the departure.

From where Isis lay, the wardrobe mirror reflected only a dull blue swatch of cloud. Crushed in behind it were all the gowns and frocks that Evelyn shunned, preferring trousers – often Arthur's own. When she was small, Isis had sometimes crept in to watch her parents dress. They hadn't cared and went on just as if she wasn't there at all. As they'd talked – usually about bloody Egypt – Arthur would stride about, hair stamped across his chest like two grubby footprints, thing jiggling and sometimes jabbing out like a fried sausage. Evelyn's bosoms were like empty socks, her belly hair a puff of mould. The hard muscles in her long shins reminded Isis of the fetlocks of a horse.

Sometimes Isis pictured her mother as a horse, of the thin haughty variety, and Arthur as a big whiskery dog, trotting obediently at her heels.

They had left in high spirits, convinced more than ever that *this* time, after all the years, all the false trails, all the disappointments, they would find the tomb of Herihor. Evelyn said she felt it in her bones, and Arthur always expressed great faith in her bones. Besides, they had a new guide now, a Mr Abdullah, a topping fellow who really knew his onions.

Their leave-taking had been the usual kerfuffle of luggage and lists and last minute panics, the scrunching of wheels on gravel – and swearing this time, when Arthur broke the tread of the third stair while lugging down a trunk. And then the quiet. Only now a trapped fly began to buzz and bat itself against the window and Isis roused herself to let the poor thing out.

She paused to finger the ornaments on the sill – a shiny black scarab, its base covered in minute columns of hieroglyphs; an ankh of lapis lazuli, and her favourite, Bastet, a cat-headed woman, gold inlaid with turquoise and lapis and carnelian. This last really belonged in the British Museum in Arthur's opinion, but these were Evelyn's special treasures.

Once the house had been full of Grandpa's collection of Egyptian statues and ornaments, even an enormous gilded mummy case at the turn of the stairs, but over the years Evelyn and Arthur had sold almost anything of value to raise money for their quest.

Snarling through the quiet came the sound of an engine and Isis peered out of the window in time to see the drawing up of a low, bright yellow motorcar. Once it had stopped, the figure inside, like a gigantic insect in hat and goggles, sat motionless staring up at Little Egypt.

'It's Uncle Victor!' Isis cried as she pelted down the stairs.

For days, Victor, Evelyn's twin, had been expected back from the nursing home, where he'd been ever since the war. He was still unfolding himself from the motor as Isis launched herself at him, rubbing her face against the stiff twill of his jacket, 'Oh I'm so glad,' she said, 'so, so glad.'

'Steady on,' he said. 'By God Icy! You've grown!'

"Well we haven't seen you for *years*!' She stepped back from him. *He* seemed smaller than she remembered and rather old and stooped. 'We'd almost given up on you,' she added.

He took off the goggles and helmet and tilted back his head. 'Good to see the old place again,' he said. 'Didn't always think I would.' He blinked. 'Where is everyone?'

'They've only just gone,' Isis said, '*literally*. This morning. Evelyn hated to go without seeing you – but they had to catch their boat.'

'But she wrote they'd be here till the 27th.'

'That was the day before yesterday,' Isis said. 'Our *birthday*, we're thirteen now,' she reminded him.

Before the war, when they were small, Victor had never forgotten the twins' birthday, always sending something silly and expensive – and nothing to do with Egypt. As the only other person in the family who wasn't obsessed by Ancient Egypt, Victor was her ally.

'Blast,' Victor said in a dwindling voice. 'Not much of a hero's welcome then.'

There was a pause and Isis shifted awkwardly, wondering what to say to this man who looked so different now, and so cast down. The lines on his brow and around his eyes were sharp as knife cuts and his skin was grainy grey.

'What a lovely motor,' she offered and it was the right

thing, for Victor brightened and patted the bonnet as if it was a horse.

'Yes. Bugatti. Quite a stunner, eh?'

The interior was upholstered in pale lemon leather and the dashboard was a glamorous glossy wood, intricate with complex whorls of grain. 'Walnut,' he said. 'Pigskin. 16-valve engine.'

'It's beautiful.' She stooped to sniff the leather interior. 'It smells of money.'

'Dear little Icy.' Victor reached out to give her a proper hug. '*Thirteen*,' he said. 'I don't believe it.' Squashed against his chest, she saw the two of them reflected, in grotesque distortion, by the curve and shine of chrome, and below her ribcage felt a pang, a qualm, and pulled herself away.

Mary came out drying her hands. The sunshine lit up her fair curls and she was smiling. 'Welcome back,' she said. 'You've missed Captain and Mrs Spurling. Will you be staying? Only I'm not set up for visitors what with the laundering and them only just gone.'

'You're looking well, Mary,' he said. 'Does a chap good to see those dimples again.'

Blushing, Mary dipped her head. 'I'm tolerable. It's only soup. I expect I can eke it out and we've got a bit of ham.' She slid Isis a look. 'You can help by laying the table, Miss.'

'I've only just had the tablecloth off,' Mary grumbled. 'If I'd known I could of stretched it for another day. He'll have to make do with second best.'

'I don't s'pose he gives a fig.' Isis took an embroidered cloth from the sideboard and, together with Mary, flapped it over the table.

'And I had that ham lined up for your tea,' Mary said, straightening the cloth.

'But don't you think it's nice to see someone else?' Isis said. 'And he *was* nearly killed, you know.'

Mary nodded and went out and Isis wished she could bite her tongue off. Mary had been married briefly to a Gordon Jefferson. They'd tied the knot in July 1914 before he went off to the front. They'd had one weekend together in Hastings, and then he'd sailed off and got himself shot at the Marne. There was a photograph of the wedding day beside her bed, Mary with a smaller, sharper face clutching the arm of Gordon Jefferson: short, uniformed, bespectacled and stern. Mary still wore the ring, a band of gold, thin as wire, embedded in the work-worn puffiness of her wedding finger.

After she'd washed her hands and combed her hair in readiness for lunch, Isis found Victor standing in the hall, a blank look in his eyes. She paused on the stairs to watch him; he stood as if lost, hands hanging limply at his sides, mouth a little open as if he was stupid, which he most certainly was not.

'You'll never guess what we got for our birthday,' she said extra brightly, bounding down to take his arm.

Victor flinched.

'Come and see.' Isis pulled him towards the drawing room. She flung open the door to reveal a cage dangling from a stand and inside it, two bright budgerigars – one blue, one green.

'What beauties,' Victor said. 'Bit lost in here though, eh?'

The drawing room was only used when Evelyn and Arthur were home and Mary had already swathed all the furniture in dustsheets so that the poor creatures were surrounded by nothing but hulking white shrouds.

Isis made kissy noises through the bars and the birds moved away from her with disconcerted chitters and huddled together in a puff of feathers. 'I hate to see birds in a cage though,' she said. 'You'll never guess what Osi's gone and called them.'

'Something Egyptian at a wild stab?'

'*Rameses* and *Nefertari*,' Isis said. 'Have you ever heard anything more ridiculous?'

'*You* could call them something else,' Victor pointed out. 'They're hardly going to know the difference.'

'Mary was livid,' Isis told him, and mimicking Mary's voice: '*What we need's a new tutor for the twins, someone else to help about the house, a lad to help George in the garden and what do they come up with? A couple of blasted budgies!*'

'Fair point,' Victor said.

'Thing is, Uncle Victor . . .' Isis took his arm again. She didn't know how to put it, not quite. 'I worry that Osi . . . that he might . . . *get* them.'

Victor frowned. 'Don't catch your drift.'

But Isis stopped. One of the budgies and then the other began to cheep, hard chips of glassy noise that rattled against her teeth.

'Lunch,' called Mary.

'Coming,' Isis yelled back, sending the birds into a frenzy.

She knew she should not worry Victor. Anyway, she had a plan to keep the budgies safe.

At the table, Isis noticed how the spoon shook in Victor's hand, and as he moved his head, the silk cravat slipped down to reveal a scar, like a livid bacon rasher sizzled to the side of his neck. Dizzied, she put down her spoon. The soup was too thin with the water Mary had added to make it stretch. Peas and cubes of carrot floated on the surface. It was a grudging soup – you could always tell Mary's mood from the way her food came out.

Victor was trying to have a conversation with Osi. 'Been out and about?' he said.

Slurping, Osi shook his head.

'Have a fine time when the folks were home?'

Osi nodded eagerly and opened his mouth to tell him all about Herihor, but Victor held up his hand and grinned at Isis, almost like his old self for a moment. 'No Egypt over lunch, if you don't mind old chap?'

'Hear, hear,' said Isis.

Osi scowled at her. 'Have you got your medal with you?' he asked Victor. 'Why aren't you wearing it?'

'Prefer to leave all that behind me.'

Isis saw that the tablecloth was jumping where he sat. He saw her looking. 'My bally leg,' he said, a note of panic in his voice. 'It jerks and jumps, I can't . . .' He was leaning on it and pressing with all his weight.

'It's all right,' Isis said. 'Have a slice of ham, Cleo's having kittens, perhaps you'd like one? There's dates in the pantry, Mary makes a lovely date and walnut loaf but she says there's enough dates there to last us till judgement day . . .'

Victor snorted dryly. 'It's all right,' he said. 'No need to gabble.' But he continued to press down on his leg and pushed his soup aside. He said nothing more and they sat in silence except for Osi's terrible slurping.

'Don't take any notice of me,' Victor said at last. 'Didn't mean to be so sharp.'

'It's quite all right! After luncheon perhaps we could go for a walk? Or perhaps a drive? It's a lovely motor Osi, you should go and look.'

Mary came in, pushing the door with her hip and carrying a bowl and jug. 'I've resurrected a bit of stewed apple for you, and there's cream,' she said. 'And I expect you'd like some coffee.'

'And a spot of brandy,' Victor added.

'Very good, *Sir*.' The door banged a little too emphatically as she went out and Isis darted a look at Victor to see if he minded, and saw that his eyes had gone lost again, and cloudy.

'It seems unfair of Evelyn not to wait and see me,' he said. 'It was an arrangement.' His leg began jumping again.

'They'd booked their passage,' Isis said. 'Will you take some apples? And she really was upset to miss you.'

'Nothing's as important as their blessed expedition though,' said Victor.

'No,' agreed Isis. 'Never.'

Osi pulled a gruesome face at her. He was eating with his mouth open as usual and she saw the churn of apples on his tongue. 'Don't be so putrid,' she said.

'Don't be so stupid then.'

'I'd rather be stupid than putrid and anyway I'm neither.'

'Are.'

'Not.' This was unspeakably childish but Isis could not help it. 'You bloody idiot,' she said.

'Now then.' Victor's face had gone ghastly grey. He picked up a spoon but it dropped from his fingers and clattered to the floor. He bent to retrieve it but couldn't reach. He was half under the table, contorted, arm stretched out towards the spoon, panting with frustrated exertion – as if it mattered!

When she bobbed beneath the edge of the tablecloth to retrieve it for him, Isis saw how his leg was jumping and caught the awful frightened tang of his sweat. 'Forget the blasted spoon,' she said as she emerged. Her heart flowed out to him, this ruined man, her uncle. 'Oh Victor I'm so sorry about your neck,' she blurted. 'About your leg, poor Victor.'

He gulped, jaw twitching, his whole being trembling with the effort of control, but it was too much. Something in him broke apart and he began to shake. Tears spurted shockingly from his eyes and Isis darted a panicked look at Osi, but he was concentrating on spooning up his apple.

'*Osi!* Wake up you *fool!*' she shouted.

Victor began to jerk all over now as if he was having a fit.

'Mary!' Isis yelled. 'Mary!' and she ran towards the kitchen where she collided with Mary who was carrying a coffee tray.

'Lord above, what's got into you!'

'Quick. Victor's gone berserk.' Isis took the tray so that Mary could hurry.

'Mr Carlton,' Mary said, having to shout above the noise he was making now, a frightful, inhuman yowling. '*Captain* Carlton. You're upsetting the twins.'

She got hold of one of his hands and when she got no response, his shoulders. 'Captain Carlton!' She shook him until he met her eyes, his all red and flinching. 'Come now,' Mary said. 'Come to the kitchen with me and we'll see if we can't get you calmed down.' Victor was gasping as if he couldn't get his breath, but he consented to go with Mary and she flicked a look of alarm at Isis as she led him out.

'Osi!' Isis went and shook him.

'Not my fault,' he said, staring at his empty bowl.

'No of course not but . . .' *Sometimes I could kill you*, she thought. 'How can you just carry on eating? Don't you *care*?'

'Finished now,' he said, got up and left the room.

2

LATER, ISIS CREPT along the corridor to listen at the door of the Blue Room where Mary had settled Victor for a rest, but there was nothing to hear and she went down to the kitchen.

'Is he staying the night?' she asked.

Mary was whipping butter and sugar together as if she was punishing it. 'Can't send him off in that state, can we?'

'You making a cake?'

'He'll have to have something for his tea.'

'What kind?'

'Guess. What's he doing visiting just when they've gone? That's what I want to know, and if you ask me he's in no fit state to be out and about.'

'Date loaf?'

Mary harrumphed.

'It's my fault,' Isis said.

'You can break a couple of eggs for me,' Mary said. 'Your fault? How do you make that out?'

Isis picked up an egg and tapped it on the side of a basin.

'Harder than that.' Mary took the egg from her hand and

gave it a sharp crack so that it split obediently, its contents slithering into the bowl. 'And don't be daft. It's the war that sent him, not you!'

Isis went back upstairs and listened outside the Blue Room. In hospital Victor had had treatment with electric shocks, but now he only needed to take pills when he had an episode. Mary had made him dose himself and he was sleeping it off and mustn't be disturbed.

Isis wandered along to the nursery door and there was Osi with his books. He didn't even look up. I might as well be a ghost, she thought, and imagined skimming over the worn carpets and the creaky floorboards. There must be ghosts here, of the people who'd lived in the house before – maybe of people who lived here before the house was even built – but they were discreet ghosts and never bothered anyone.

Little Egypt was miles from anywhere – ten from the nearest village. Isis dimly remembered when they used to go there – the grocer's, the church, a pub, stocks on the village green where people had been pelted with rotten vegetables in the olden days. But now that Evelyn and Arthur were so set on their mission they were always away and the outings had stopped. Mary, left in charge, didn't allow the twins to stray from the grounds of Little Egypt where she could keep her eye on them. A good school was too expensive and Evelyn wouldn't dream of letting them be educated with common children. And even the last tutor – a straggly, limping French man, grandly called Monsieur de Blanc – had gone away last year after a row about his pay. Arthur had promised, next time he was home, to hire another tutor. Once they found Herihor, they would be rich, of course, and able to send Isis to the best school in the country. She wasn't so sure how Osi would get on. Maybe a school would turn him normal?

In her parents' room it was cold, the sun had gone round to the other side of the house and the papyrus scrolls on the walls, with their men and animals and gods, gave her the creeps. She opened the wardrobe and sniffed Evelyn's most glamorous dress: green chiffon, sewn with thousands of sequins. The fabric under the arms was whitened with sweat and the sequins were cold as fish scales against her cheek.

She had only one memory of Evelyn in the dress. When Grandpa died it turned out that he'd left Little Egypt to Evelyn, and Berrydale, thirty miles away, to Uncle Victor. Evelyn had been livid because Berrydale was worth more and she needed funds for her expedition, while Victor was bound to fritter his inheritance away.

To raise money for the excavation, she'd sold most of Grandpa's precious collection of paintings – he was still whirling in his grave according to Mary – and held a ball before they left. Four-year-old Isis and Osiris had been dressed up as their namesakes in long white robes with black kohl caked around their eyes and great tall head-dresses, to be cooed at by all the ladies and gentlemen. Evelyn, the horse, had paced about in the slithery frock, smoking and neighing with Arthur panting faithfully at her heels.

Despite a stab of disloyalty, Isis grinned. If only she could draw, what a funny picture it would make. And after all, Egyptian gods could be people or animals, so why not her parents? She shut the wardrobe and wandered back to her bedroom where she found Cleo crouching on a fallen dressing gown, tail lashing from side to side, quietly yowling.

Cleo was forever having kittens, which vanished overnight. Mary used to claim that she'd sent them by coach to a stray cats' home, which, at first, Isis had believed, until early one morning she'd found a wet and heavy sack outside the kitchen door.

Years ago, and it still made Isis sicken to remember, she'd discovered Osi with a litter of dead kittens in the nursery. The tiny creatures, all hard and stiff, their tabby fur dried into spikes, had been lined up on the floor as if for some kind of ritual, and his eyes had been bright, cheeks rosy with excitement.

Isis had shrieked for Mary who'd spirited the kittens away, muttering about disgusting, morbid little boys, and Osi hadn't spoken to Isis for months. But he had never stopped being obsessed by anything dead and the nursery windowsills were cluttered with the skeletons of birds and mice.

Kneeling down now to stroke the cat, Isis was just in time to see a neat wet purse slither out from under her tail on a trickle of pink water. The purse twitched and squirmed and Cleo twisted round to split the silk with her teeth and extricate the first kitten.

Isis cried out with a pang of pleasure. She'd caught her! This time Mary could do nothing about it; Isis would protect the kittens and Victor would back her up. In fact, a kitten might be just the thing to lift his spirits.

Cleo nipped through the little string that came from the kitten's belly and rasped it with her tongue until it opened its toothless mouth and gave the tiniest squeak.

'Clever Cleo,' Isis said, settling down to watch and stroke and give encouragement. After the kitten came something frightful, wet and red that Cleo ate, and then there was another kitten, and another two. Four kittens, though the last never moved when Cleo freed it from its purse and its mouth stayed sealed despite a frenzy of licking.

The three blind kittens found their way, with a little nudging, to Cleo's teats and, kneading with their tiny paws, began to feed, their pipe-cleaner tails twitching with the rhythm of their suckling.

Once she was sure that all the kittens had come, Isis went to tell Victor the good news. Of course, she shouldn't disturb him, but surely tapping softly on the door wouldn't wake him if he really were asleep. There was no answer. She opened the door and peered into the dim, smelly room. The curtains were drawn and Victor a hump beneath the eiderdown. Drawn by curiosity, she crept inside.

He was facing away from the door and she skirted the end of the bed to see his face. His eyes were closed, face sagging to one side, peaceful. The scar showed on his neck, shiny and raised and so much like a rasher that she almost expected the smell of bacon, but there was only the whiff of brandy and an empty glass on the bedside table beside a phial of pills. She leant very close to look and was startled to see his eyes open.

'Icy,' he said groggily.

She jumped back. 'Sorry,' she said. 'I came to tell you that Cleo has had her kittens and I thought you might like one?'

He drew himself up so that he was half sitting against his pillows, and patted the mattress. He was wearing a pair of Arthur's pyjamas, dark red paisley, and his skin was the colour of raw pastry.

'There's one black and two tabby I can't tell if they're girls or boys and one dead, I'm afraid.'

'Come here,' he said and opened his arms. Isis hesitated. She didn't want to touch the scar or to be too close to the smell of brandy and something else, stale and unappealing, but afraid of offending him, she leant forward awkwardly into his arms. 'Dear little Icy,' he mumbled into her hair and his arms were tight around her.

'Isis!' Mary came in with a tea tray on which sat a slice of date-flecked cake.

Isis jumped from the bed, blushing hotly. 'Cleo's had kittens and I was telling Victor and saying he could have one,' she said. 'I didn't wake him, honestly.'

'Kittens! Whatever next! I'm sorry.' Mary put down the tray. She swished open the curtains, her expression unreadable. 'As if Captain Carlton wants anything to do with kittens!'

'I will have to decline the kitten, I'm afraid. But it's perfectly all right.' Victor added to Mary. 'She's quite a tonic, don't you know?'

'We'll leave you in peace,' Mary said, and yanked Isis through the door. 'Whatever were you thinking? Going into a gentleman's room on your own!'

'He's my uncle.'

'And him not well in the head.'

'He didn't mind.'

'Lord above.' Mary rubbed her hands through her hair causing it to stand up madly. 'And where *are* these famous kittens?'

Isis led the way to her room. Cleo was giving the black kitten a vigorous licking and the two tabbies were suckling. 'That one's dead,' Isis pointed out.

'That's one small mercy,' Mary muttered.

'Aren't they beautiful?' Isis knelt down. 'Clever Cleo.' She stroked the cat's head, and she arched her neck for more.

Mary tutted. 'Well, you can't keep them here for a start.'

Isis clutched Mary's sleeve. '*Please* don't drown them.'

'They'll have to come down to the scullery.'

Isis scooped up the dead kitten, took it down to the kitchen, wrapped it in a duster and, muttering an apology, pushed it in the stove before Osi could get his hands on it.

She left the kitchen quickly before the flames crackled round the little corpse. Now was the time to carry out her plan for the budgerigars.

'Don't worry,' she whispered to the panicking birds as she dragged the cage across the hall to the ballroom. That the ballroom was a vulgar extravagance, out of kilter with the rest of the house, was Arthur's oft stated opinion. In his heyday, before the twins were born, and in a fit of grandeur, Grandpa had had it built on to the back of the house, along with the adjoining orangery, but for years there had been no parties and no need for it at all. Now its tall mirrors were dull and spotted and the windows looked through to the broken orangery with its wizened fruit.

Isis closed the door behind her and unlatched the cage. At first the budgies took no notice and then the blue one hopped through the entrance into thin air, and with a frightened screech wheeled out into the room on unpractised wings, clumsily looping round the ceiling and bashing itself against its reflections before finding a perch on the chandelier. The other bird soon followed, sending a squitter of droppings down onto the parquet and shrieking until at last it found its mate and they huddled together amongst the startled tinkling of the crystals, crooning and preening.

They were way out of reach up there and they could have the ballroom to themselves – they'd only need seed and water.

Cleo and the kittens would never catch them and nor would Osi.

Thinking she caught a glimpse of movement in a mirror, Isis turned to catch her own white face, her hair in its awful childish pudding-basin cut, her face a plain, pale pudding too. She tore her eyes away, went out quick and shut the door.

I HAVEN'T SET EYES on my brother for years. But I know there's something wrong because the bucket system's broken down. I will go up today. I've said it before, but today I really will. Those broken stairs – it's like contemplating Everest. But really it's the fear that stops me; I'll admit it.

Yes, I admit it. I'm scared of what I'll find.

The bucket system came about when we stopped talking, which was, I believe, 1992. Ten years! Gone like a flicker. Before that we used to eat together and have some sort of stunted conversation. Even in his heyday (did he have one? Did either of us?), Osi was never any good as company, not like a real person in the world. He's *not* a real person in the world. He hasn't left the house for decades or been seen by a single soul. The only person to whom he counts as anything is Mr Shuttle, the solicitor, for whom he exists as an occasional ragged wobble of ink on a dotted line. Mr Shuttle knows nothing and cares less about us. We are a task on his list of tasks, faceless. He pays his bill himself from our investments – easy money, I should say. Our scant and intermittent communication is conducted perfectly well by Royal Mail.

Ten years ago he wrote to advise me that in order to remain solvent, we would have to sell another parcel of land, informing us that he'd had what he called 'feelers' from the U-Save Consortium.

It was Grandpa himself who set the ball rolling by selling the land off to the railway board, before we were even born – around the turn of the last century, I believe. And then, in the 20's, Victor sold the nut grove for the A road. And later we sold off the meadow, and after that parcels of land for the dual carriageway, which cut the estate in two. Those arrangements kept us in funds for years. Then U-Save bought the meadow on the other side of the road to build their supermarket with car park and petrol station. I saw no objection myself, and in fact it was a bonus, making shopping so much easier. But Osi refused to sign the contract, would only stick his fingers in his ears and hum like a demented hornet when I tried to tell him that we had no choice. So, of course, I had to forge his signature in order to sell the meadow, which is now my lovely spanking great big shop.

Osi has never set foot inside U-Save; and even when we still spoke, he maintained a ridiculous pretence that it wasn't there. But how *I* love it!

If it weren't for U-Save I would be stark staring mad by now.

Once he'd removed his fingers from his lugs and saw from his window that the bulldozers were ripping up the land, Osi sealed his lips to me forever, rarely even venturing down the stairs again. But there was absolutely nothing else I could have done. What else did he think we were to live on, the stupid, stubborn bugger?

Isn't *bulldozers* a lovely word?

Since U-Save arrived, my life has been arranged like this: each day I push my trolley across the bridge to lose myself in that sweet brightness, the million choices that there are. The store is open 24/7, as they term it, and in the middle of the night, if I can't sleep, I go across the bridge and wander in the aisles, counting things. In Home Laundry for instance – I have counted 54 ways you can wash your clothes. There's liquid and there's powder and there's capsules, there's bio and non-bio, special stuff for coloureds, whites, blacks – (and that doesn't count conditioning or stain removal.) However does a person make a decision like that? And that's just one decision out of – perhaps hundreds. I'd love to hear Mary on the subject.

Or I ride the moving pathway that sweeps you up to Clothing, Household and Electrical. They have a pharmacy, a Post Office counter, a bank machine, even a dentist who does a weekly clinic. I do my ablutions in the Ladies; eat and conduct my business in the café (with its panoramic view of Little Egypt); buy my food and clothes there (I have training shoes with flashing lights [£6.99], meant for children I know, but such a lark, how could one resist?); I buy books and batteries for my radio; even find my friends there – take Spike as a for instance.

I devised the bucket system even before Osi and I ceased to talk, because he was such a lazy blighter and wouldn't always deign to come down to eat, as well as the fact that my knees were getting bad. Besides, the stairs were becoming too risky for daily traverse – downright dangerous, to speak the truth. Osi would put a note in a bucket rigged to the banister, to indicate what he wanted. In actuality, there was little need for he ate the same thing almost every day – water biscuits and liver

paté or Dairylee cheese triangles, and bars of blackest chocolate. And once we ceased to talk we simply carried the system
on and it became our only communication. (Though occasionally I'd hear the distant rumble of the lavatory cistern.) From
the deterioration of his handwriting I've charted his degenera-
tion, but as long as the bucket was going up and down, I knew
he was alive at least, and eating.

I've never sent a drink up there so I must suppose he drinks
from the tap in the bathroom, as he did as a child, angling his
head over the basin and suckling on the steel. (I am partial
to a Gin or a lovely drink called a Bacardi Breezer. And of
course I like a cup of tea. Coffee I take in the café in my shop,
where they make it better than ever I could.) Sometimes for a
lark I'll send Osi something unexpected, once a tin of squid
(courtesy of Spike), which remained in the bucket travelling
up and down for days until I took it out to try it for myself. (I
wouldn't bother.)

It was a few weeks ago now that the bucket system began to
become erratic. A note with nothing on it; a failure to haul
it up; a failure to send it down; the bucket lowered but with
contents untouched. Once there was a dead pigeon inside, and
once something much, much worse that compelled me to dis-
card the bucket and buy a new one (plastic, red, £3.99).
I fear he's lost his mind.

I really, really must go up.

3

It was weeks since Evelyn and Arthur had gone. Isis pictured her mother cantering through the desert, Arthur nose to the ground, hot on the scent of Herihor. When they found the tomb, he would raise his snout and howl. There would be a telegram, of course, and then what celebrations! A party in the ballroom, school, *friends*, perhaps a finishing school in France. And Isis would become tall and slim, she would bloom and win a heart or two, no doubt.

The gate banged and shook her to her teeth. She was supposed to be helping Mary search out the last of the peas, but instead she was riding the gate – pulling the rusty wrought iron thing open as far as it would go and swinging back on it, a lurch of a ride that ended in a sickening jolt.

She got off and leaned over the gate, wishing someone would drive by, or at least a person on a horse or a bicycle to say hello, but it was a quiet lane, leading to nothing but a scatter of cottages. George's cottage was a mile or so away, and she had dared walk to it once or twice. But it was a dull walk to a dull dwelling – not worth the tongue lashing if Mary missed her. The only regular excitement was the trains, but none were due.

She shut her eyes and listened to the high trill of a skylark, the faint swish of breezy leaves – and at last there was the sound of an engine and Mr Burgess' grocery van came puttering along. Mr Burgess was very proud of the vehicle, though Isis was sad not to see his horse anymore. It had been a funny horse, mottled like a rainy pavement, with a hot velvet nose that would nuzzle in her pockets for biscuit crumbs. The motor van, which Mr Burgess boasted could do 25 miles an hour, was painted with beautiful swirly letters: Burgess and Son, General Provisions.

Isis held open the gate and Mr Burgess saluted as he drove through. She began to call 'Mary!' but Mary was already approaching, a bowl half full of peas in her arms, her hair all snarly, cheeks pink and dimpling.

Mr Burgess doffed his hat. 'Mary.' He was beaming so hard that his moustache quivered as he went round to the back of his van to fetch the carton of groceries.

'Any letters?' Isis asked. Mr Burgess' wife ran the village Post Office and Mr Burgess delivered the post to the far-flung customers on his round. Not that many letters came to Little Egypt. There were bills of course, but Arthur and Evelyn rarely sent anything except a hasty postcard.

'Not today,' Mr Burgess said and yelped as Dixie, the black kitten, ran up his leg.

'Isis, shut that little beggar in the scullery and finish picking the peas.' Mary put the bowl in Isis' hands. 'Fill it to the brim, there's a dear, while I get Mr Burgess his cuppa.'

Isis unhooked Dixie's claws from Mr Burgess' corduroy trousers, and snuggled her face in his silky fur. His body was tiny as a bird's and he never stopped moving. She carried him out to the scullery, where Mary tried to keep the kittens shut up, and then she crept to the kitchen window and climbed onto the pile of bricks she'd constructed as a vantage point. Mary was laughing as she put cups and saucers on the table, and her hands went to her hair, patting and smoothing.

Isis got down and sat on the bricks. With her thumbnails she popped a peapod and ate the five green peas, starting with the biggest, and then she crunched the pod between her teeth and spat out the stringy bits. Eventually she dragged her feet to the vegetable garden to pick more peas. She sneaked past the potting shed – there was no sign of George, for which she was grateful. Mary didn't especially like George either, not because he was idle and ancient, but because he was half mad and most dreadfully rude. Though Osi would sometimes trail him round the garden, oblivious to the snapping and snarling and outrageous cursing this provoked.

The garden was a scandal, Mary was always saying, but mention it to George and you'd get your ear bitten off. Arthur was supposed to be hiring a lad to help, but no lad ever arrived and now there was bindweed clambering over everything, quite smothering the raspberry canes, and dandelions and nettles between the rows of beans and peas. Isis stung her wrists trying to reach the pods. She soon gave up and went back inside.

Mr Burgess' hat was on the table but he was in the pantry with Mary and they were laughing. His was a pleased sounding chortle and Mary's a high false trill. There was a fly crawling on his slice of cake and she let it.

The kitchen door opened and Mr Patey, the coalman, put his head round. 'Hello, there? Anyone home?' He was holding an iris, just one, dark blue and splashed with yellow.

Mary stepped out of the pantry, cheeks aflame. 'Wilf!' she said.

'Mary.' He handed her the iris and she smiled at it, at him, and at the floor. Though he had a dirty neck, Mr Patey was far more handsome than Mr Burgess, and younger too. His hair was dark, his skin smooth, his eyes warm and toffee brown. He had what Evelyn would call a common accent, while Mr Burgess, Isis grudgingly considered, spoke quite well for a grocer.

Mr Burgess stepped out of the pantry, pinching his moustache.

'Patey,' he said in a chilly voice. He glared at the iris as if it was a snake.

'That wants water,' Mr Patey said. 'How's the wife?' he added to the grocer.

Mr Burgess picked up his hat. 'Well, I'll be off, Mary,' he said.

'And the kiddies?' Mr Patey added. 'They doing well? Only Mrs Burgess was telling me your nipper had a cough.'

'Next week as usual,' Mr Burgess said. He put on his hat, picked up the empty box, and giving Mr Patey a wrathful look, left, slamming shut the door behind him. Isis sat down on the low stool by the range and ran her tongue along the row of white bumps the stingers had left on her wrist that were fizzing like sherbet. From under her lashes she watched how Mary carried the drooping iris to the sink, Mr Patey close behind her.

'Get on with them peas,' Mary said, catching her looking.

Isis picked one up and stuck her thumbnail in the green ridge. She liked the noise the fresh ones made when opened, a tiny sound between a click and a gasp, but the old ones made no sound at all and the peas were hard and floury. She rolled a pea for Dixie who sprang for it comically, and they all watched for a moment and laughed.

Mr Burgess had promised to take the two tabbies when they were old enough to leave Cleo, but Mary had said Isis could keep Dixie if she must, if it was all right with Captain and Mrs Spurling. Dixie was entirely black but for three white hairs on the tip of one ear and his eyes were lantern yellow.

'Come on Wilf, I must get on,' Mary said now.

'No time for a cup of cha?' Mr Patey said.

'Oh well! You are a terror.' Mary's dimples flickered as she cleared Mr Burgess' cup away and put out a clean one.

The coalman put his flat cap down just where Mr Burgess' bowler had been. His hands were washed but dirty with the deep-down graininess that comes from handling coal, each fingernail outlined as if with ink.

'Blooming mice in the pantry,' Mary said. 'Mr Burgess was helping me set a trap.'

'Why don't you put the cats in there?' Isis asked.

'You ask me in future,' Mr Patey said. 'Any little jobs want doing.'

Isis watched and listened, noticing how different Mary was when Mr Patey was around, how she tilted her head and constantly lifted her arms to her hair, which made her chest lift too.

The next pod contained not bright green peas but cottony mush and a tiny waving maggot. Isis shrieked and threw it down. 'A bad 'un,' she explained.

Mary smiled at her. 'You can run off and play.'

'You forget my age,' said Isis.

Mary continued to look at her until she dragged her feet out of the kitchen and went upstairs to the nursery. When she opened the door, Osi looked up, dazed from his books.

'The train will be coming soon,' she tempted, but he just sat in his stupid baby armchair, finger in place in his book, waiting for her to leave. Once he'd liked to watch the train as much as she did. They would hold hands and scream when it went past. She banged the door on him and hurried down to the end of the garden, past the orchard and the vegetables, past the potting shed, past the icehouse and the compost heap, along the path she'd trodden through the weeds, to wait, face pressed against the fence, for the thunder of the train.

One day, she vowed, she'd travel on the train to London, moving past this very spot, looking out of the window at the place where a girl stood waiting through the long, tedious ache of her childhood. Once she'd poked a stick through to touch the train, but it had been ripped from her hand with terrifying force. Today the train chugged sluggishly and the grey steam hung and sank in its wake, leaving Isis covered in smuts.

She walked back in time to see Mr Patey leaving and ran to open the gate for his pony and cart. He saluted as he set off at a clip, shedding nuggets of coal as he went. She listened till the rattle of the cart and the trotting sound had faded away and then she swung herself on the gate, from which the black paint was flaking leaving orange patches of rust. Once, when she was younger, she'd licked the rust – it tasted nothing like oranges but rather how she thought the war might taste, deep blood and gritty metal.

4

ALMOST AS SOON as the sound of Mr Patey's pony had died away, I heard another motor approaching. The third vehicle in one morning! It was Uncle Victor in his canary bright Bugatti, with a lady by his side. He had taken to visiting once every week or two, often with a companion – never the same once twice – and always no better than they should be, in Mary's opinion. Isis opened the gate for Victor to drive through, which he did much too fast in a spray of gravel. She pelted after him up the drive.

Victor took off his goggles, grabbed and tickled her. Though it was much too babyish, she squirmed and giggled. The lady unwound her scarf to reveal hair so fair it was nearly white. She wore the sort of make-up that Isis recognised as common, though it was still rather pretty, on her lips and cheeks and round her eyes, which were hard and miniature as grape pips.

Uncle Victor stopped tickling and helped the lady step down from the car.

'Isis, this is Mademoiselle Mignon.' He drew out the name as if it was comical. Mademoiselle Mignon was small as a doll with a tiny narrow waist and dainty, pointed, child-sized boots that made Isis feel like a clodhopper.

'Bonjour, Mademoiselle.' Isis raked her mind back to her French. 'Comment allez-vous?'

Mademoiselle squealed out a laugh. 'Oh, no need for that, French by name but not by nature.'

'Don't know about that,' Uncle Victor said, and she squealed again, revealing that her top teeth were chipped.

'But very well all the same, thank you, dear,' she said. 'Your uncle's told me all about you twins. And,' she patted Isis' cheek, 'you can call me Mimi, if you like.'

Isis breathed in the sharpness of her scent, glamorous yet not quite pleasant.

'I'll take Mimi in to tidy herself up,' Victor told Isis. 'You run along and tell Mary there'll be another two for luncheon.'

Isis hurried to the kitchen with the news, but Mary had heard the motorcar arrive and was already scrubbing extra potatoes, her chest wobbling up and down with indignation.

'There's only the three chops,' she said. 'I can't work miracles.'

Isis looked at the chops, already laid out in pan – three small shards of bone with hardly any meat.

'They won't stretch,' Mary said. 'That means no chop for me nor you, and you children need your meat.'

'What about a cheese pudding instead?' Isis suggested. She knew for a fact that there was cheese.

Mary frowned, considering, and blew out. 'We can put them chops aside for tomorrow. Good girl. If they don't like it, they can blooming lump it.'

Each time Victor visited he seemed a little better, Isis thought, though still his leg jumped when he grew anxious for the slightest reason. He'd taught her the story of how he got his Military Cross, saying it was more seemly for another party to tell the tale, which, with all due modesty, he couldn't keep on trotting out.

Isis washed the smuts from her face and called Osi to the table. When he'd finally trailed down, all crumpled and inky -fingered, Mimi clutched his face between her hands, squashing his features like a cod-fish. 'And aren't you the dead spit of your uncle?' she said.

Mary had made the cheese pudding, a humble nursery dish, into something wondrous to behold, a quivering yellow dome garnished with chives and curly sprigs of parsley.

'That's a sight for sore eyes!' Uncle Victor said, rubbing his hands. 'Another drop of sherry, Mary, if you please.'

'Where do you come from, Mimi? Isis asked.

'Shepherd's Bush,' Mimi said. 'We drove up last night and stayed in a dear little country pub, didn't we, Vic? We're on the way to Scotland for a wedding.'

'I've always wanted to go to Scotland,' Isis said, 'but isn't it terribly cold?'

'Lucky I've got Vic to keep me warm.'

Mary snorted.

'My auntie lives in Glasgow,' Mimi said, and Isis was shocked that she spoke with her mouth full so that you could see a curd of pudding and a squashed pea on her tongue.

Osi was eating steadily with his eyes on Mimi. He always stared at Uncle Victor's ladies. He too ate with his mouth open and no amount of telling would stop it; even Evelyn and Arthur noticed and ticked him off, but still there was the visible churn of food you had to look away from.

Victor nudged Isis under the table and raised his eyebrows.

'Did you know that Uncle Victor has a Military Medal?' she said in response. She looked apologetically at Mary, hating to stir up memories of Gordon Jefferson.

Mimi put her tiny doll's hand on his sleeve, 'I know, but he won't tell me about it, poor dear.'

'Don't much like to talk about it,' Uncle Victor looked at his plate. The edge of the tablecloth trembled along with his jumpy leg.

Mary went out, the door shutting smartly behind her.

'Go on,' Mimi urged Victor, and when he didn't speak she turned to Isis, 'You shall have to spill the beans, dearie.'

'All right. He was at Gallipoli and his regiment was all killed by the Turks, he risked his life for them by drawing fire, not his fault that they all got shot to bits and then he went to the Somme and got shot himself,' she abbreviated, all in one breath.

'My, my, Victor,' Mimi breathed.

'Thought I was a gonner too,' he said and when he raised his eyes there was a ghastly sheen to them. 'Never thought I'd be here again, at this table.' One hand went to still his leg and one to the scar on his neck. 'Enough,' he said, voice cracking. 'Icy, tell Mimi about your kittens.'

Before they left, Victor showed Mimi round the house, and Isis trailed after them with the kittens dancing along behind. Mimi was impressed by the ballroom, despite the budgies in the chandelier and the dead trees in the orangery, and went straight to the piano to play a jingling waltz. No one had touched the piano for years and the first few notes were bleary with dust and the droppings down between them, but the tone soon brightened and Isis began to dance, twirling alone, then

Victor took her in his arms and swept her round and round until she was breathless and giggling.

When Uncle Victor took Mimi out to the garden, Isis shut the kittens in the scullery and followed them, but when they neared the icehouse, Victor shooed her away. She wandered back through the orchard where the apples and pears were still hard and green, though the plums were nearly there. She picked one and took a bite, but it was viciously sour.

The icehouse was her special place and she should have been the one to show it to Mimi. It was the location of her clearest memory of Grandpa, who had died shortly after. He had ridden her on his shoulders down the bright green mossy steps to the icehouse door. She could even remember the clutch of her thighs on his hairy neck, and the grip of his hands on her ankles. When they got to the bottom, he stooped to let her climb down in front of the small door with its silver padlock the size of a Bath bun.

'Now look at this.' He took a key from his pocket, unlocked and removed the padlock and swung the door open till she was enveloped in cold black breath. Grandpa's huge hand reached down for hers and he stooped to take her in through the low doorway. Inside was a thick hush like fur, broken only by the sound of dripping. She shivered and Grandpa said, 'Of course it's cold, girly, it's full of ice. See?' He pointed down into a shallow pit and as her eyes got used to the darkness she made out a dim grey gleam.

'Wait,' he said. He let go of her hand and with a great huffing and creaking got down on his knees and reached over for a lump of ice. Outside in the warmth she'd studied the ice, which had a fleck of leaf frozen into it and something wiry that might have been a daddy-long-leg's leg. Her hands had ached with cold

Now Isis pulled up a stalk of rhubarb. If she could beg a bit of sugar in a cup, she'd take her book upstairs and dip the rhubarb in the sugar and read away the afternoon. And then it would be suppertime, and maybe a game of cards, or patience at least. And then time for bed, and that would be another day gone, and they would be another day closer to the return of the horse and hound.

She heard Mimi squeal and crept back down the garden to where Victor was sitting at the top of the icehouse steps with Mimi on his lap. She could see nothing much of Mimi but her legs sticking out on either side of Victor, the skirt ridden right up, pale stockings and even paler legs. Isis' eyes were riveted on the milkiness of the bare skin. Mimi was making a sort of mewing noise and Victor sounded as if he was choking. Isis gripped her rhubarb stalk and felt a pang in her lower abdomen, a queer sensation, strong and wrong, she knew that much, dirty and provoking. She had a sudden need for the WC and ran back to the house before Victor could turn and accuse her, as he had once before when he'd had a lady there, of being a mucky little spy.

THREE DAYS AND the bucket, with its Dairylee, its chocolate and its water biscuits, hangs heavy at the foot of the stairs. Of course, I must go up. I can't sleep for knowing that, for worry about my brother. I strain my ears for evidence that he's moving about up there – but my ears are too duff to believe what I hear, and besides, the house has a language of its own: shiftings, mutterings and creakings, to speak nothing of the infiltrating wildlife.

Pulling the rope causes a fossilised bell to croak and I have done it time and time again, for hours on end, making the pigeons panic and feather fluff come puffing down the stairs. But all to no avail. The truth is, with stair number three almost completely gone, and four and five in a perilous condition, I dare not risk the climb alone. Not with my knee – and what if my foot went through? What if I got stuck?

The truth is, I'm afraid that he is dead.

Dead or raving mad.

I am afraid.

I do not want, alone, to find him.

I would go up. But first – or instead – I went to feed the spudgies in the ballroom. As I opened the door I caught sight of something curious, a red flash and shiver in a mirror. It was a fox with a dead bird in its mouth. A fox! It slunk quickly through a hole – new, or at least one I'd never noticed – in the skirting below the window that gives out to the orangery. And then I caught an awful glimpse of an old woman, a stranger, shrunken, stooped and white, with gaping mouth.

The spudgies came down in a shriek and twitter, greedy for their Trill; perhaps it was a few days since I'd been in. In truth, I can't remember. I shut my mouth and crunched across the floor, avoiding the reflections, to sprinkle seed on the mantelpiece and then I stood for a minute, birds on my arms and shoulders, and in my hair those little scratchy claws.

A fox! No, I could not go upstairs today. Perhaps it was a sign? I could not go up alone. I needed help. In all my life I've rarely asked for help. Full of a new resolve, I bade the flock goodbye and went to the scullery to don my anorak.

I pushed my trolley up the ramp and onto the bridge. They had to build this bridge for me; it was a condition when I sold the meadow. The bridge provides the only access to Little Egypt since the dual carriageway was built and that is how I've liked it. To get onto the bridge you have to unlock the gate. There's a key and a padlock and three bolts – top, middle and bottom. The bottom's a devil to stoop to, and stiff, but once I'm inside, after my daily forays, I lock us in, safe and sound. The gate was a further condition of the sale. It's a good, stout barrier of meshed grey steel, spiked along its top to deter clamberers. It keeps out the vandals and the nosy parkers and the developers. We are cut off, like survivors in a castle; the roads and railway make a sort of moat around us. We're unassailable and I keep Osi safe inside. Safe and hidden. The postman trudges across the bridge and puts the post in the steel mailbox by the gate. And there's the Post Office inside U-Save, and a public telephone should I want one, so you see I'm not cut off from the real world. I like the real world, would love more of it, more and more.

So, I locked the gate behind me and stood on the bridge, praying, pleading rather, that Spike would be there today. He would be the one to help me, the only suitable person since he lives outside what he calls 'the system'. If anyone else came in, Osi might be discovered, the authorities would be called, and who knows what would ensue.

I like to stand on the bridge, traffic streaming between my legs. It's a thrill. It's like a river. At night, a river of light; in the daytime it's the colours of the roofs – cars, coaches, lorries – the pattern of overtaking, sometimes a gridlock. Sometimes an accident with police and ambulances, sirens and flashing lights. I bring my tea out on those days and have a good old gawp.

Sometimes I go out in the small hours when the traffic is sporadic and listen to the surging, the receding of engine sounds, separate enough to hear instead of lost in the constant roar and think *none of you would be travelling this way if it wasn't for me*. If I hadn't sold the land for the road, all the people on business or off to funerals, going to their lovers, mothers, children and all would have to go another way. It makes me proud, the difference to the world that I have made.

It was a drizzly day and the road was sizzling, spray hanging in the air, and I didn't linger on the bridge but hurried across, down the far-side ramp, through the gate, past the petrol station and into the service area. Two young men were smoking by the door but neither acknowledged me. If it were not for me, they wouldn't be there either, smoking and smirking, nor would the shop itself. (Sometimes I approach the staff and point this out. But not today.)

I went to the skips, but Spike wasn't there. I was feeling a little frantic, I will admit, thinking of Osi all alone: either dead or in some predicament. Thinking of a fox, slinking in the house, thinking of the feathers between its teeth. I looked back at the lads in their turquoise and orange livery. Could I ask them if they'd seen Spike? I started towards them, but as if with one mind they threw down their cigarette stubs, ground them underfoot and went back through the doors.

A person properly in the world would summon the police. But a policeman nosing around is the last thing that I want.

From underneath a pallet I saw a half-grown kitten prowling and pouncing. So light it was, so springy, it made me feel earthbound, heavy, though in truth there's nothing left of me. (I buy all my clothes from Kiddies.) The kitten made me feel old and I am old, I know, by any reckoning; 93 if you want to know, but still, no need to wallow in it. I stood there, old and damp and getting near despair, a feeling of helplessness billowing up around me, so that when Spike came round the corner, I could have wept with gratitude.

'Hey, Sisi,' he said, 'how's it going?' All dear and cheery. The damp had settled on his felted locks, glittering like sequins. I would have kissed him, but I think it may have scared him off.

'Very well, dear, thank you,' I said. 'Despite the inclement weather.'

He looked ruefully at the damp knees of his jeans, then,

light, almost, as the kitten, jumped up onto a skip and disappeared inside.

'There's a shitload of cheese,' he called. 'You ready?'

I stood there with the trolley trying to catch but mostly dropping Brie and Camembert, Gouda, Edam, Wensleydale with chives (I love the one with cranberries best). Of course it was a pleasing haul, but my mind wasn't on it. Mangoes and pork pies, cheesecake and pitta breads, sour cream and sausages, bags of rocket, punnets of cress, the packages just kept coming. At last he finished with a pair of pineapples.

'Would you like to come to Little Egypt?' I asked, once he was back on solid ground.

He was sorting out the goods for the trolley, leaving some for me, packing the rest into his haversack.

'My house,' I prompted.

He hoiked the bag onto his back and pulled a face. 'You never asked me before,' he pointed out. He unwrapped a pork pie and took a bite.

'I could make you a cup of tea,' I said. I hesitated. Should I mention Osi now? 'A nice cup of tea on such a miserable day.'

Spike looked up at the sky and hugged his arms around his thick jumper; in the wet it was reverting to the smell and texture of the originating sheep.

'Sure,' he said. 'Why not? You lead the way.'

He finished his pie and offered to take the trolley for me, but I need it for my balance. I admit to nervousness, some sort of shame, simply at the idea of someone else being, *seeing*, inside Little Egypt. One person could never hope to keep it clean and in truth, lately, I haven't even tried. There's room for me to walk beside the kitchen table to the stairs and to the ballroom. I sleep in my chair with my feet on a box and do my ablutions in U-Save, using the WC in the scullery otherwise, so you see, there's been room for all wrappers and catalogues and so on and no need to put them out. No dustbin lorry could get here since there isn't an access road. Acres of space inside the house are stacked with packaging, and I believe the cardboard and the polystyrene act as insulation, which is ecological and green and all the rage. It's all right for me. I don't care. Osi hasn't been downstairs for years and in any case, he wouldn't even notice. I didn't think that Spike, who called himself an anarchist, would judge me for the mess.

'Jeez, that it?' We stood on the bridge and looked at the roof with its slipped and missing tiles, a rowan tree hailing from a chimneystack. 'Oh my God. It's huge.'

I could stop now, I knew. Once Spike stepped inside, a spell would be broken. It would be an ending – or the beginning of the end. At that moment, just as I was wavering, the rain came on more heavily, hissing down, turning to hailstones, stinging where they hit. I could not send him away in such weather and so we trudged across. I took the gate key from my pocket and let him through into the grounds of Little Egypt. Was Osi watching from a window? He always used to watch me come and go. He thought I didn't know, but I'd catch his figure at the window. Checking up that I came back and that I was alone.

5

ONE MONDAY MR Burgess took the two tabbies away. He knew a widow who would like them, he said, and they were going to live the life of Riley. Mary found a box, poked holes in the lid with a knitting needle and tore up newspaper so they should be comfortable on their journey. Isis kissed each on its nose before they were stowed, with a lot of twisting and hissing, into the box, and she stood watching the van diminish down the lane.

Cleo sat at the backdoor licking her paws and seemed not the slightest bit disconcerted – perhaps she had a streak like Evelyn's in her. 'Not a natural mother,' Isis had once overheard Mary say, and though she'd minded on Evelyn's behalf, she could hardly disagree.

Once the sound of Mr Burgess' engine had dwindled, she went to search for Dixie whom she hadn't seen that morning. There was no sign of him in or around the house and she combed the garden, calling his name. She went past the ice-house, down to the potting shed and opened the door. George was sitting in his chair, legs wide, in a dense cloud of pipe smoke.

'Clear off,' he said, his voice a thick, phlegmy gurgle.

'I'm looking for my kitten. A black kitten.'

'Boy then girl what do they think I am?'

'Just a tiny black kitten,' Isis insisted. 'Have you seen him?'

'Clear off, blasted hun,' he said. He took his pipe from his mouth and shook it at her. 'Blasted animals, bloody liberties, bugger off with you.'

She squinted through the pall at the grim twist of his face, the smoke-yellowed eyebrows jutting forward like filthy tufts of shaving brush.

'You're the one taking the liberties,' she said and quickly shut the door.

She searched the end of the garden, stirring the weeds with a branch. She looked round the icehouse, safely locked, and right through the vegetable garden and the orchard, and she found a toad, old birds' nests, the china arm of a doll and a broken saucer, but no sign of Dixie.

Once more round the house, she tried every room that wasn't locked. Osi stood defensively at the nursery door but swore he hadn't seen the kitten. In the ballroom she was spooked by shivers in the long bleary mirrors that seemed to wobble and bulge as if the glass was melting. The birds had settled very happily onto their glassy tinkling home and now there was a crusty white patch on the floor beneath the chandelier, fluffed with tufts of fallen feather and down.

She looked in the bathroom under the great tub and behind the pipe. She searched around the shrouds in the dining room and went up the attic stairs to peep into Mary's room.

Only when it was starting to get dark did she give up. 'You *must* have seen him,' she said to Mary, who was sitting by the stove with her favourite book – *December Roses* – on her lap, having five minutes before she got on with the tea.

Mary shook her head. 'He couldn't of got in the van with Mr Burgess?' she suggested.

'*No*, I was watching.'

'Or shut in George's shed?'

'I looked.'

'When did you last see him?'

'Not today at all. He'd gone out already before I came down. Someone must have let him out.'

She stared at Mary, whose face was pink from the warmth of the stove. There was a basket of darning by her feet and the book with its flagrant, tragic cover was splayed on her knees.

'He's probably gone on an adventure,' Mary said. 'He'll be back tomorrow right as rain, you see.'

Isis squashed down the wave of helplessness that tried to rise in her. Mary looked so comfortable there, so warm and dry and complacent.

'I wonder how many kittens you've killed in your life,' she said.

Mary tilted back her head and narrowed her eyes. She didn't speak for a moment, but when she did her voice was low and tight. 'Listen. I'm left alone here and have to use my judgement in all sorts of difficult things and I'm scarcely ever paid. Stay here, working my fingers to the bone and worrying myself into an early grave just for love of you – and your brother.'

The word *love* was like a flickering tongue of light. No one ever used that word, not in connection with Isis. 'Sorry,' she mumbled.

'I haven't done anything with that wretched kitten and nor would I, not now you're attached. Dare say I'm quite fond of the little scamp myself.'

'Sorry,' Isis said, 'I *know* you wouldn't really.'

'Any more of that sort of remark and I'll think myself at liberty to leave,' Mary continued, 'and then where would you be?'

'Please don't.' Isis sank down beside Mary and put her head against her knee as she had when she was small. She felt a great big fool now, crouching on the floor, and it was a few moments before she felt Mary's hand on her head, but it was just a grudging pat, as if she was a dog.

'Can't all sit about all day.' Mary got up, slapped her open book face down on the kitchen table and picked up a knife. There was a scatter of vegetables waiting on the table and she picked up a carrot and began, in quick deft movements, as if she was sharpening a pencil, to peel it. Isis watched the golden shavings coiling on the table.

'Don't go,' she said urgently. 'Don't go and marry Mr Patey.'

The knife fell from Mary's hand. 'Whoever said anything about that?'

'I promise I'll be good.'

Mary sighed. She went to the drawer, fetched another knife and handed it to Isis. 'Make a start on them spuds then,' she said.

Mary was upstairs with one of her heads. Weeks had passed with no more sign of Dixie and Isis had at last given up hope. Sometimes foxes take kittens, she knew, and there were foxes around, and badgers. And even hawks and owls will take small furry prey; Mr Burgess said he'd seen a kestrel. It was one of those things, and one of the dangers, Mary said, of getting yourself attached.

It was only early October, a shivery day that felt like a premonition of winter. Evelyn and Arthur hadn't come home when the excavation season was over – and now it had begun again. It cost too much to keep travelling back and forward across the globe, and they needed to keep the money to unearth Herihor – if they ever found the tomb. It seemed to Isis that they really didn't like to be at home at all. Even during the war, when all archaeological work in Egypt had come to a full stop, they had both stayed in London, Evelyn driving ambulances while Arthur, too old for the front, had had a desk job in the War Office.

At last Mary came down and into the kitchen, white faced, her hair all pillow squashed.

'I thought you were staying in bed,' said Isis.

Mary threw Cleo off the stove, stoked it up, filled the kettle, and then sank down, fingers pressed to her temples.

'I'll make you a cup of tea,' Isis said. Sometimes the word *love* would flicker in her memory like a flame and she would want to show Mary that she was also loved. 'You just put your feet up,' she was saying, when there was a perfunctory knocking at the door and Mr Burgess was standing there, blowing like a grampus, a box piled high with groceries in his arms.

Mary nodded at him but didn't shift herself.

'I don't know what you want with all the salt,' Mr Burgess grumbled as he put the box on the table. 'Sure you didn't over-order?'

'We do seem to run through it,' Mary said.

'I've never known anyone get through so much.'

Mary shrugged. 'Did you put the brandy in?' she asked.

'You seem to be running through that, too,' Mr Burgess said. 'Gentlemen callers?'

Mary pressed her lips together. 'Go along outside now,' she said to Isis.

'Are the tabbies all right?' Isis asked the grocer.

'Dandy.'

'What's she called them?'

'Don't know. Little black 'un turn up?'

Isis shook her head and Mary frowned as if to say, don't get her started. 'Do you good to get some roses in your cheeks,' she said.

'Who for?' Isis said. 'Who cares if I've got roses in my cheeks?'

'Mind your manners.' Mary used the cross voice she never used in front of gents. Mr Burgess' face was stiff. He reached into the box, brought out a liquorice pipe and shoved it at Isis.

'Run along,' he said.

'Besides, it's beastly cold out there,' she said, risking a scolding by taking the pipe without saying thank you. It was, after all, a very childish gift. How old did he think she was? She went out through the kittenless scullery, clambered up the bricks and stuck the pipe in her mouth. It was a thick stubby one, decorated with scarlet hundreds and thousands to denote burning tobacco. Childish or not, she might as well enjoy it. It would last her for weeks if she could remember to suck and not to bite. Peering through the window she saw that the groceries were still in their box. Usually Mr Burgess would help Mary unpack as she checked off the items on her list. But Mary hadn't moved and Mr Burgess was sitting with his hands on the table instead so that you could see the missing fingers where he had been injured in the war, just an ordinary war wound, nothing heroic.

Isis could hear the rise and fall of Mary's voice, though not the words. Mr Burgess listened expressionlessly before he shook his head. He began to speak and she could nearly hear him, she tried to get her ear against the glass . . . but she toppled and slipped off the wobbly bricks, grazing her knee. It didn't really hurt too much, only a little scrape, but she limped back into the kitchen as Mr Burgess was saying: 'If you knew what I know.'

'I told you. I'm not interested in your blasted gossip,' Mary snapped, and then turned to Isis. 'What have you done to yourself?' She sat her down and went at her knee with a cloth and stinging iodine. There was an awkward silence in the kitchen, till: 'Why don't you feed the budgies?' Mary suggested.

Isis took some crusts and stomped her way to the ball-room. While she was there she ran her forefinger up and down the piano in great crescendos high to low and low to high until it hurt and then she pounded and pounded with her fists, foot on the loud pedal till the birds screeched and flew about in a panic and the chandelier was ringing.

Mary came raging in. 'What is the matter with you today?' she said. 'You might have a bit of consideration for my head.'

Even after Isis stopped, the noise stayed in the room, bouncing between the mirrors where Mary was reflected with her hair all wildly standing out, and the dark, wounded look of a migraine in her eyes.

'Sorry,' Isis said. 'But I don't know what to do with myself.'

'Oh Lord,' Mary muttered weakly.

'I love you,' Isis said, the phrase jumping from her mouth and opening Mary's in surprise. They stood looking at each other reflected over and over back into the hungry mirrors and the birds settled back amongst their crystals, tiny pastel feathers fluttering down.

Mr Burgess came blundering in. 'My goodness, this wants sweeping,' he remarked. He went to the window and peered out at the wreck of the orangery. 'And this wants bringing down.'

Mary turned from Isis. 'I never stop,' she said.

'I didn't mean . . .'

'I've had enough. Isis would you show Mr Burgess out?'

'No, Mary . . .' he said. 'Don't go getting all het up. Let's have another cup of tea.'

'You should be getting back to Mrs Burgess,' Mary said wearily. 'Oh, and by the way, I hear tell you're expecting a happy event?'

'A *baby*?' Isis was incredulous. He was so *old*.

'Patey,' he said. You could hardly see his mouth move under the droop of damp moustache.

'I would of heard anyrate,' said Mary.

'I was meaning to say,' Mr Burgess bluffed. 'I would of said.'

'I should congratulate you and Mrs Burgess,' said Mary. 'Now I need to lie down.' You could tell from the sogginess in her voice that she really was at the end of her tether. 'Show Mr Burgess out, please. The list's on the table as per usual.'

Mary went out, hand groping along the wall as if she'd gone blind, which was part of the migraine, and Mr Burgess and Isis returned to the kitchen. 'She does gets real humdingers,' she explained. She stared at his face. Above the beige moustache his cheeks were scrawled with red and blue, tiny veins that looked like scribble.

'Are you *really* having a baby?'

He gave an irritated puff. 'Patey been round and about much?' he asked.

'Now and then.' Isis was cautious. Mary hadn't said another word about the coalman, but after he'd visited she would be especially bright and cheerful, almost glittery, making jam tarts, and even finding time for a game of gin rummy at the kitchen table.

'There's things she should know about her precious Patey,' Mr Burgess said. 'Any chance of a cup of tea?' He looked towards the kettle.

'You can have water,' Isis said. 'And I dare say I could stretch to a biscuit.' She took the last one from the tin. It was soft and only fit for the birds, but he chomped it as she ran him a cup of water. '*What* should she know? I don't want her getting married either,' she added.

'Married!' The word barged out of him on a spray of crumbs.

'There's been no talk of it,' she soothed. 'Just me wondering where it will all end.'

Mr Burgess sat down at the table, putting his bowler in its usual place. He cleared his throat. 'Well, for one thing, did you know he was a shirker?' He left a pause for her reaction, which was none. 'A *shirker, a slacker*. Meaning he never fought. He left it to others to do his dirty work and most of 'em never came back.' He looked down at his mangled hand, and his voice mangled along with it. 'Lost both my brothers in France.'

'Oh dear,' Isis said. His moustache flopped lifelessly over

his lips and his eyes filled up. She left a decent interval before she said. 'Mary does know he didn't go to war.'

'Nay, but I don't reckon she can know the whole story.'

'What is the whole story then?'

'He worked at the pits.'

'I know. He was a miner before he was a coalman.' It seemed to her a perfectly logical progression.

Mr Burgess sent out his big wet tongue to fish a crumb from his moustache. 'He didn't have to go, mining being what they called a reserved profession, but he *could* of gone. Most of his fellows went. He's a coward, that's what he is.' He leant forward, 'And worse.'

'What's worse?' Despite herself, Isis was intrigued. 'Did you know Mary's husband died at the Marne?' she added.

'Aye.' He shook his head. 'And now she's consorting with a coward.'

'But what did Mr Patey do that was worse?' she urged, fascinated.

'He had to get married, if you catch my drift.'

She didn't but nodded sagely.

'Though there's those that say she tricked him into it. Lost the babe and her looks with it. Then,' Mr Burgess leant towards her, a repellent gleam in his eyes, 'he started carrying on with Mrs Burke, widow of the coal merchant. Well, his missus goes and dies, doesn't she, terribly convenient that, and before she was cold in her grave, he ups and marries Mrs Burke, though she had a good ten years on him. More.'

'So he's married?'

Mr Burgess sat back, swollen with significance. 'That's the best of it. No sooner are they wed than she pops her clogs too. What do you say to that?'

'How terribly, terribly sad,' Isis said. 'Poor Mr Patey.'

'It's blasted fishy, that's what it is.'

Isis stared at him. Surely he couldn't mean that Mr Patey killed both his wives?

'I've said nowt,' Mr Burgess said. 'And you never heard nowt from me neither. But . . .' he let the word hang significantly, 'if Mary should happen to find out . . .?'

'She probably *does* know. She knows him quite well, after all.'

He exhaled noisily. 'She can't know the ins and outs. I can't think that of her. And she should be careful, don't you think?'

'He's a Quaker,' Isis said. 'That's partly why he didn't go. She told me. He was brave enough, standing up to all the insults, if he got one white feather shoved at him, he must have had a hundred, that's what Mary said.'

'Brave!' Mr Burgess stood up abruptly and seized his hat. 'Brave! *Quaker!* Exactly. Couldn't have put it better myself.' He wobbled his hand. 'Quaker, shaker, trembler, coward.' His cheeks had gone dark as beetroot. He buttoned his jacket with fumbling fingers. 'Well, time I got on. Tell Mary there's a gift in there.' He nodded at the box. 'Lemons. Only a bit spoiled.'

'I'll tell her,' said Isis.

'You think on what Mary should know for her own good,' he added, picking up his hat.

'But it's gossip,' Isis said uncertainly. She began taking groceries from the box – a huge bag of salt, a string of onions, a slab of lard and six or seven shrivelled greenish lemons.

He jabbed a finger stump at her. 'Forewarned is forearmed,' he said, snatching up next week's list.

6

HOWEVER BAD HER head, Mary would usually drag herself downstairs in the morning, but today, even by the time the morning train juddered past, there was still no sign of her. Isis ventured up to her room and found her lying with the curtains drawn, a chamber pot with sick in it by the bed.

'Mary?' she whispered, but the only response was a groan. Isis took the chamber pot away, tipped the contents down the WC, and then sat with Mary, wiping her brow with a dampened flannel, the way Mary did for her when she had a fever, that cool dampness so terribly soothing.

'Don't fret,' she said. 'I'll see to our lunch and so on.'

'Wilf might come,' Mary murmured. Isis' eyes went to Mr Patey's iris, quite desiccated now, on the bedside table.

'I'll send him away.'

Softly, Isis closed the door and stole downstairs. She stood on the landing listening to the quiet of the house, not quiet really, always a squeak or a creak or a gurgle of pipes as if the house kept up its own mumbling story. Idly, she wandered into Evelyn and Arthur's room. On the dressing table sat the scarab and the ankh – but there was no sign of the cat goddess.

When was the last time she'd seen it? Not for a while, certainly. Perhaps Mary had put it away? Or Osi had it?

Isis opened the nursery door onto an empty room that stunk of unwashed boy and goodness knows what else. It was very rare for her to be there when Osi wasn't. Though it had been the playroom for the two of them when they were small, it had become entirely his domain, a small dank outpost of ancient Egypt. Like a trespasser, she entered, holding her breath against the smell. The tree-of-life rug was ruined with a dark stain of ink or paint. The walls were scrawled with hieroglyphs and pinned with layers of scrolls. Books were piled everywhere, with tongues of bookmark sticking out in all directions, and there were brushes and paints and stacks of exercise books and papyrus scrolls; the vast brow and nose of some broken sandstone god propped against the wall, and on every surface a clutter of Osi's ornaments – or artefacts, as he insisted on calling them – wooden dolls and animals, shards of broken pot and faience, stones with scratches. But there was no Bastet. Shutting the door behind her, she went downstairs and outside to look for her twin.

After the stuffy peculiarity of the nursery, it was a pleasure to be outside. The sun was hot and the air fresh, with just the first twinge of autumn. She stooped to pick an apple from the tangle of long grass in the orchard – there were plenty of windfalls. Soon they would gather them and Mary would start to turn out her chutney and apple cheese and apple cake – which at least would make a change from everlasting date. Munching the apple – too hard and sour and with seeds that were still white – she noticed a wasp's nest on the wall, a clever papery thing, empty now? She put her ear against it and was startled to hear a grumble, a rustle, life still there amongst the fragile cells. Jumping away, she scrubbed her ear against the ticklish fizz of sound.

Osi wasn't in the orchard, or the vegetable patch, or down by the fence. Passing the icehouse she checked that the padlock was secure before she went round to the potting shed. As she opened the door she was saying, 'Sorry to disturb you, George, but,' and then she stopped, hands crammed to her mouth. George was on the floor. He was lying neatly, hands on his chest, eyes open, quite plainly dead.

As if to make up for his stilled heart, her own set up a hard, fierce clamour. She would have to do something, tell someone, disturb Mary; and then there was a sound, a creak, as if someone else was there and, despite the heat, the hairs on her arms rose stiffly.

'Hello?' she said with a sudden dizzying whoosh of dread, thinking it might be Mr Patey. There was only one place the person could be, and that was behind a projecting shelf of flowerpots. She swallowed. She had never fainted in her life but wondered if she might be about to do that now, the edges of her vision melting and a sort of buzzing inside her skull.

And then Osi stepped out, clutching a book. 'He's passed on, Icy,' he said.

She exhaled dizzily. 'I can see that, you clot.'

They both stared down at him.

'What are you doing out here?' Isis said.

'I found him.'

'When?'

'He was just sitting there with his pipe in his hand.'

The deckchair was empty, the pipe was on the floor, a scatter of ash beside the bowl.

'Did you put him on the floor?'

Osi knelt by the body and had his face about an inch away from George's, which looked just as bad tempered in death as in life. It was disappointing how much the same he looked.

'Move back,' she said.

He looked up at her, baffled. 'Why?'

'Why didn't you come and tell me?' she said.

'I wonder how old he was.' Osi poked George's cheek.

Isis crouched beside Osi and grabbed his hand. 'Don't touch,' she said, peering at the body. The skin was waxy, the pale blue of the eyes dull. Flecks of dust or tobacco had settled on their surface, causing her to blink in sympathy.

'We'll have to tell Mary,' she said. 'But she's having one of her heads. Even Mr Burgess would have been a help today.' To her own mortification she began to cry, getting up quickly so as not to splash George with her tears.

'We don't have to tell her.' Osi followed her out of the shed and caught hold of her sleeve, his nails catching and scratching.

'Of *course* we do!' She got hold of him by both arms. 'Osi, be normal,' she pleaded. His eyes were exactly the same greenish dun as Evelyn's and were acutely focussed, as if he was really here, tuned in to this moment, and not in ancient Egypt for once. He looked not so much a child as a shrunken old man with his pallid indoor skin and stringy hair. The volume clutched to his chest was *The Egyptian Book of the Dead*.

'We could send him on his journey, Isis, to the next world, with his spade and trowel pipe and food and –.'

'Don't be ridiculous. Don't be so . . .' she struggled to find the word, '*grotesque!*'

After the bright sunshine, Isis was hardly able to see inside the house, and as she hurried upstairs to Mary's attic, her sight was swimming with pallid after-images of George's face. She tapped on Mary's door before she opened it to find Mary lying in exactly the same position as before, eyes shut tight.

'Sorry to disturb you,' she whispered, hating herself for feeling a sort of pride to be the bearer of such momentous news, 'but George has passed on.'

Mary opened her eyes, squinting against the light.

'Are you sure?' she murmured.

Isis nodded. She strained against the wail that wanted to come out and made a strangled gulping sound. Her cheeks were itching with the tears and she scrubbed them away. 'What shall I do?'

Mary tried to sit up, clutching at her skull. 'Oh Lord above,' she said.

'No,' Isis said. 'You don't have to move only I don't know what to do.'

Mary lowered herself back down. 'Just a minute,' she whispered. She lay thinking. 'I'll have another dose of powders.'

The doctor had been called out to Mary years ago, and had diagnosed migraine. The powders he'd given her didn't help much, but Mary liked them and sometimes, she confided, took one when she didn't have a headache so that she could enjoy it more.

Now, Isis unfolded one of the little paper envelopes and tipped it into a beaker of water. Mary sipped it slowly, eyes shut, grains of powder sticking to her lip.

'You're *sure* he's gone?'

'He's on the floor with dust in his eyes and they're open,' Isis said, scrunching her own eyes against the sensation.

Mary handed Isis the empty beaker and lay back down. 'Wilf'll be here soon – he'll take charge.'

'We don't want *him* here.'

'Don't be silly.'

'But . . .'

'He'll help.'

'But, but Mr Burgess said . . .'

'Blast Mr Burgess,' Mary muttered.

'Well I for one don't trust Mr Patey,' Isis said stubbornly, and waited for Mary to ask her why, but Mary said nothing. In the distance there was the sound of a pony's hooves and of wheels on gravel.

'There you see, that'll be him now.'

Mr Patey was already in the kitchen when Isis got down. 'Proper Indian summer,' he greeted her.

'Mary's ill,' she said.

'In bed? I'll go up and see her.'

'*No.*' Isis stood in front of the door, though he could easily have thrown her aside. 'She can't see you today, but she wants you to help us with something.'

'What?'

'George.'

'That old bugger.' He'd taken his cap off and was smoothing his glossy black hair. There was a smell of clean sweat and coal dust coming off him.

'Mary said you'd help us.'

'Did she now?' He narrowed his bright brown eyes – they didn't look like murdering eyes – and she was struck by the thick sootiness of his lashes.

She turned her back on him and went outside. He followed

her to the potting shed where Osi was sitting at the threshold muttering over his book.

'Get out the road,' Mr Patey said. Scowling at Isis, Osi inched himself aside.

Mr Patey knelt down and touched the old man's cheek.

'Osi found him, just a little while ago.'

'He's gone all right,' Mr Patey said. 'Mary not been down?'

'No.'

'One of her famous heads, I reckon?' he said and Isis nodded. 'Right then.' He frowned and rubbed his hands. 'Let's get this sorted. Does he have a missus?'

Isis shook her head. 'She died years ago.' She watched Mr Patey's face for a reaction to that, but there was none that she could see. 'Will you get the police?' she said.

'What I reckon I'll do is take him to the village. To the doctor's. No one else around?'

Isis shook her head.

'Then you kiddies'll have to help me shift him.'

'Or we could see to him here,' Osi said.

'*Osi!*'

'Might as well get on with it.' Mr Patey crouched down to get hold of George under his arms, the dead head lolling against his abdomen, and as he stood up the twins each took a leg. He wasn't a heavy man and through the thick tweed of his trousers the shins felt thin and hard as sticks. His boots were like something historical and there was a smell of wet beds about him, and a damp patch left on the floor where he'd been lying. They managed to lug him to the cart and prop him in the back amongst the sacks of coal. Despite herself, Isis was impressed by the efficient, fussless way Mr Patey handled the corpse and trotted it away so briskly in his cart.

'Mr Burgess said that Mr Patey killed two wives,' she said to Osi, once the creaking and clopping had diminished. The statement sounded ridiculous brought out into the light of day. 'Of course, I don't believe him, but I should tell Mary, don't you think?'

Osi failed to reply. He was staring longingly after the cart.

'By the way Osi, do you know where Bastet is?'

Still he didn't answer and, irritated, she swung the gate hard in the hope of catching him with it, but he jumped out of the way, stuck out his bottom lip and stalked off. Riding on the gate, she let her head hang back and it was as if she soared, dizzied, up into the cloudless blue. George's was the first dead body she'd ever seen, human anyway, and her eyes still hurt with the grit in his.

There was a light scrunch of gravel and Mary came out, wraith-white and shading her eyes.

'Mr Patey took him,' said Isis.

'He coming back?'

'Didn't say.'

Mary winced at the rusty grating of the gate and Isis jumped off and hugged her until she struggled free. 'Get on with you,' she said. 'So the poor old boy has really gone?'

'Even dead he looked just as cross as ever.' Isis remarked as she latched the gate. 'Are you feeling better?'

'Barely. Least I'm still here though.'

Isis took Mary's hand and led her back into the kitchen. 'You sit down,' she said.

'The stove needs filling.' Mary sank down onto her chair.

Isis rattled coal from the scuttle into the stove and put the kettle on the hob. 'Have you seen Evelyn's Bastet?' she asked.

Mary blinked. 'Her what?'

'The jewelled cat?'

'Oh that thing. No, not now I come to think of it.'

'It's worth a fortune,' Isis said.

'I expect Osi's got it.'

On the other hand, Isis thought, having strangers like Mr Patey about the place, going up the stairs, well you never knew what might go missing.

'Mr Burgess said Mr Patey killed both his wives,' she said, looking not at Mary but at the blackened kettle as she spoke. But when she sneaked a look, Mary's expression was merely weary.

'Poor Mr Patey's been bereaved twice, and I for one know about bereavement,' she said, and buried her face in her hands.

Isis took two cups and saucers from the dresser and put them on the table. Neatly she poured a drop of milk into each. As soon as she'd been tall enough to reach the kettle, Mary had taught her to make a good cup of tea, which, she'd predicted, would be a comfort to Isis all her life. She tipped out the old leaves, rinsed the pot and warmed it with the nearly boiling water.

'Careful,' Mary said, when she lifted the kettle. 'Always pour away from you.' Her voice was still frail from her migraine and with the twist in it there always was when Gordon Jefferson was in her mind. Isis was sorry to have reminded her of him, but she couldn't quite let the subject drop now that she had dared to broach it.

'Do you know how they died?' Isis spooned fresh leaves into the pot. The tea caddy was nearly empty. 'We need to put tea on the list,' she added.

'There's more in the pantry,' Mary said. 'The second Mrs Patey had the influenza.'

73

'Oh.'

'And the first was to do with down below,' Mary's hand went to her own curved belly. 'That and her nerves, I believe, poor thing.'

Isis filled the teapot and squeezed the knitted cosy onto it. 'That's what he told *you*.'

'Don't you go listening to that bally grocer.'

Isis was silenced. She studied the tea cups, chipped along their rims and faded inside from years of Mary's scourer. All right then, he didn't do for his wives. Of course he didn't. Not with that kind brown light in his eyes. She'd never *really* thought he had.

'He's still a coward though,' she said, in an effort to retain some grudge.

Mary gave a sort of yawning sigh. 'He's a Quaker and them's pacifists. You know that. He's entitled to his beliefs.'

Isis knew she should drop the subject, but she was in a fidget of irritation at Mary's refusal to hear a bad word about Mr Patey. 'Uncle Victor's no pacifist, he's a hero with a medal,' she said.

'And don't we all know it,' Mary muttered, adding, 'Give it another moment to brew,' as Isis lifted the pot. 'There's heroes and there's heroes.'

'Even Mr Burgess went to war,' Isis said. 'Did you know he lost his brothers as well as his fingers? What if everyone in England was a pacifist? Where would we be then?' She was proud of this argument, that she'd once heard Evelyn voicing. 'A colony of Prussia,' she added more uncertainly. 'Ruled by the blessed hun.'

'Get on with you and pour that tea,' said Mary.

It WAS SO peculiar to take another person into Little Egypt, I cannot tell you. It was like opening a door in my skull and letting someone into my brain to tramp their boots and jab their elbows, to spy and judge the murk. I nearly changed my mind, but Spike was right behind me, eager to get in. The hail was rattling down, he was wet and I needed help, I did need help. And so did Osi. I had to put him first.

So I opened the door into the scullery, left my trolley there, and led Spike into the kitchen. And I saw it through his eyes, dim and cold with all the rubbish, my brown toothbrush on the table beside the sleeping Nine, who was curled up on a dirty plate; an old game of patience (arrested halfway through and stuck forever by food spills to the table); a slither of papers; a puff of hair pulled from my brush adhering to spilled egg yolk; a mouldy jam jar crawling with flies, and indeed yes, now that I was tuned in to it, quite a drone of flies. You get used to such sounds in your own place until they do not register. In any case they sound like thoughts, the thoughts that happen as a backdrop to your mind; passive thinking they would call it nowadays. Yes, that has the drone of flies.

Spike stood with hailstones melting and dripping off him. 'Jeez,' was all he said. He reached out to stroke Nine, but she spat at him and he withdrew his hand.

'Not used to company,' I said. 'I call her Nine, really she's Cleo number nine, the ninth generation or dynasty, but I keep clear of anything Egyptian.'

Spike eyed me warily.

'Perhaps a cup of tea then?' I suggested. I saw him looking at the stove top where sat the heavily encrusted kettle. My hands were trembling as I filled it. Behind me Spike had cleared a space on the table and was putting my groceries there. 'Where's the ice box?' he said.

I thought he said icehouse, and I started, dropping the caddy so that it bounced away.

'Refrigerator?' he supplied, sensing my confusion.

'Just put it in the pantry,' I told him, hiding my face as I bent to grope for the ruddy caddy.

'Jeez,' he said again when he went inside the pantry.

Now, I know there are things in there that have gone vastly past their sell-by date. I expect that's where the smell comes from – and the flies. Curious how I hadn't noticed the flies, but now that I was aware I saw that there were piles of them on the windowsill, dead or dying, and plenty more buzzing wirily around. It was all rather embarrassing. And it struck me like a blow: what on earth would Mary say that I had let her kitchen get in such a state?

'What about a Bacardi Breezer?' I suggested, hand not steady enough to deal with tea.

'Sure,' he said, lifting his eyebrows – studs and all.

There were two bottles of the blue variety in the pantry and he had the caps off in no time and was taking a copious swallow.

After I'd retrieved the caddy I straightened up and looked at him. Within the setting of my kitchen he appeared smaller, diminished, you might say, younger and rather pale.

'Are you quite well?' I said.

'Not used to being . . .' He waved his hand around. 'Inside.' He spoke as if he was trying to avoid breathing through his nose.

'Where do you sleep then?' Curious that I had never thought to ask.

'I have somewhere,' he said. 'A bender in the woods.'

'A bender?'

'Tent,' he said. 'Kinda like a tent, made of branches and carpets – hey, you don't have an old rug or two to spare?'

'Take what you like,' I said.

'Sure?' He looked dubiously about him.

'You can't sleep outside all winter, dear, surely?'

'A couple extra rugs would be good.'

'What do your parents think of your life-style?'

He flinched and seemed to shrink still further. Next to the virulent blue of the drink his eyes were drained of colour.

'My folks are on a different planet,' he began. He told me that his parents were tight-assed Republicans, how all they cared about was money and appearances. They had sent him over to grad school before he joined the family firm. He'd argued with his father on the phone, dropped out of his course and been living outside of all the shit (his word) ever since. He began to trot out his anarchist manifesto, which I'd heard before, but I could scarcely listen. My heart was like a grasshopper in my chest and my breath thin and thread-like. It was a worry that I might go first and then where would Osi be? Keeping him safely tucked away had been my life's work

77

and I could not let him down now, not so near the end.

'Drink up,' I said. I forced in some air before I added, 'Oh by the way, I'm not alone.'

He paused mid-swig.

'I am a twin,' I said.

He eyed me cautiously.

'I have a twin brother,' I elaborated.

He nodded, taking this in. 'Is he still . . . I mean, where?'

'Upstairs.' I had to steady myself against the table. 'Would you like to meet him?'

He finished the drink and banged the bottle down. 'That's OK,' he said, as if about to take his leave.

'No,' I said. 'Don't go, not yet.'

'Got to get on the road,' he said (by which he meant stand by the road and stick his thumb out till some 'sucker' as he called them, picked him up. I thought that an ungrateful way of putting it. But anyone who lived in 'the system' was a sucker to Spike and I'll admit to being flattered that he didn't count me amongst their numbers. But now he'd seen the conditions in which I lived, I could see that he was shaken. Even operating outside the system, it seems he had his standards!).

'No,' I said. 'Let's go and find you a carpet for your bender.'

But we both stood motionless looking at the floor.

'Where is your brother?' he asked.

'Oh, Osi? He's upstairs.' I aimed for a gay and carefree smile. 'We'll pop up and see him, shall we?'

Naturally, I didn't want to alarm Spike with the mention of a possible corpse. Now I had him here, another person, another heart, young and strong, beating in the house, driving round its circulation, I felt braver, I told myself, able to tackle whatever we would find.

7

IT WAS A few days before Mr Patey returned, and when he did he brought his toolbox to fix the sticking pantry door, which had been driving Mary demented. Osi was in the kitchen for once, and Mary was grating lemon rind for curd so that the very air made your mouth water. Osi was crouching to examine the neatly packed hammers, chisels, saws, all clean and gleaming in their stout pine box. The pantry door was off its hinges and Mr Patey whistled as he planed the bottom; the smell of wood shavings blending with the scent of lemons. It was warm in the kitchen with fingers of dusty sunlight coming through the window and the stove roaring.

'A cup of tea would go down a treat,' said Mr Patey. He'd taken off his jacket and rolled up the sleeves of his blue striped shirt so that you could see the muscles in his arms and the dark hairs that curled against his skin. Isis had never really noticed a person's arms before, not like that, not the way you could see the glide of the muscles under the skin, and she watched entranced. She would definitely give him the benefit of the doubt.

'When you've got that door back on,' Mary said with a grin and stuck her tongue out at him. 'And you can stop gawping and fill the kettle,' she added to Isis. 'And then you children can run along,' she added.

'Not *children*,' said Isis.

Obediently, Osi got up from the floor and went upstairs.

'And it's nice in here,' Isis added. 'Anyway, Mr Patey, what did the doctor say about George?'

'His ticker gave out,' Mary said.

'Not very nice for you kiddies.' Mr Patey stopped and wiped his brow.

'Good job you turned up,' Mary said, 'or I don't know what we would of done.'

'Turned up like a bad penny,' said Mr Patey. There was a special sort of fizz in the air between them, smiles like promises. He flicked a glance at Isis and raised his eyebrows at Mary.

'What about bringing in a few apples?' Mary suggested. 'And then you can have a scone and lemon curd. I don't expect you'd like one?' she said to Mr Patey with a dimple.

'You mean, will I leave you alone,' Isis said and heard a muffled snort from the coalman as she went to collect a basket from the scullery.

The Indian summer was going on and on. The sky was a splintery blue between the branches, the apples jaunty amongst the golden leaves. Most of the fruit was too high and so she gathered windfalls, flicking away the tiny yellow slugs that clung to the rosy skins. And then she lugged her haul back to the kitchen window and climbed the bricks. The room looked dim inside and the glass was rippled with condensation so she could not see as clearly as she liked, but Mary had propped the window open at the bottom, so Isis could hear their voices and smell the lemons.

'You know he does for all the widows in the county,' Mr Patey was saying. 'Least them that's under 40-odd and don't look like a barn door.'

'You can't think I care about him?' Mary gave a shrill laugh that didn't sound like her at all. 'And he doesn't "do" for me, Wilf. He's sweet on me, that's all, and it oils the wheels with the tab and where's the harm in that?' There was quiet for a moment and then a clatter. 'This is nearly done.'

'There's a dance in the village, Friday.'

'You know I can't.'

'Mary. You're throwing your chances away.'

'Oooh, it's a bit sharp. Nice, though. Taste.' There was silence for a moment. 'Nice? Can't leave them twins, can I?'

'They're not babies.'

'No?'

Isis bristled.

'Remember they're not *yours*,' Mr Patey said and there was silence until Mary said:

'Can you get them warmed jars out?'

After a shuffle of movement, Mr Patey said, 'Mmm, that's tasty, that is.'

'You can take that jar.' There was quiet and then: 'We haven't heard from them for weeks. Not a postcard to the twins, not so much as a penny payment. No nothing. And then there's his lordship turning up, never any warning, expecting to be fed, and the company he keeps! We might as well be a brothel. And Mr and Mrs, well they might of dropped dead for all we know.'

'Hand in your notice, Mary,' Mr Patey said. 'I'll look after you.'

Isis held her breath. It went quiet and through the steamy

window she saw their two dim shapes blend into one. She jumped off the bricks and made a clatter going through the scullery and by the time she got into the kitchen Mr Patey had his cap on. 'Well, must be off.' He popped half a lemon curdy scone in his mouth, lifted his hand to Isis and went off whistling.

Over the days that followed there was still no letter and the Indian summer ended in a gale that blew the rest of the apples off the tree, along with a slate or two from the roof. Osi retreated more into himself than ever and Mary was cross and snappish. Even Victor hadn't visited for weeks.

On Mr Burgess' day, Isis hung over the gate, shivering in the mean and pesky wind, straining her ears for the sound of his van. She was aware of how pathetic she was, so desperate for some sort of diversion that she yearned for the *grocer* to come. One day I'll look back on this and laugh, she thought, and sent her mind into a future of school and friends and beaus and marriage and babies. Into the proper sort of life that surely soon must start.

At last the van arrived, and she opened the gate and ran beside it back up the drive.

'Any letters?' she asked Mr Burgess as he emerged from his van. 'And, by the way, Mary knows all about Mr Patey and he certainly *didn't* do for his wives. He's actually a decent chap,' she added.

'I hope you haven't been spreading gossip?' He straightened himself up with the heavy box and she heard the click of vertebrae.

'But you said –'

'No letter,' he interrupted. 'But good news. Have you heard? Is it them?'

'What?'

'You don't know!' His scribbled cheeks bunched up in a smile and his moustache quivered.

'What? What? What?' she asked as she followed him round to the kitchen, but he would not answer. Mary was at the sink with her back to them, her whole body jiggling with the vigour of her scrubbing at some stain.

'Mary?' said Mr Burgess.

She turned, drying her hands on her apron, but failed to treat the grocer to a smile.

'*What* news?' Isis said.

'Leave Mr Burgess alone,' Mary said wearily. 'And run along now.'

'But what news?' Isis pestered. 'He's got some good news.'

Mr Burgess waited for both of them to be riveted to him before he gave an answer. 'Only a big tomb found in Egypt. Heard it on the wireless.'

Isis felt her mouth open, stiff and gasping as a fish. For a moment she couldn't speak. Mary was gaping at Mr Burgess too and he was fairly glowing, as proud to be carrying the news as if he had turned up the tomb himself.

'They've *never* gone and found it?' Mary said, dimpling with disbelief. 'Oh my giddy aunt. I don't believe it.'

'Mary!' Isis grabbed her. 'Oh! If only we had a wireless. Is there no telegram? What shall we do?'

Distractedly, Mary squeezed Isis tight before she pushed her away. 'Are you *sure*?' she said.

'How shall we find out?' Isis couldn't keep still. There was a surge in her like a pulsing light and she wanted to yell or sing and she needed to move.

'I reckon there'll be a telegram any minute,' Mr Burgess said. He gave Isis a poke of toffees. 'You go out and watch for the boy.'

Isis took the toffees but pelted upstairs. 'Osi, Osi!' she shouted. 'We think they've found it! They've found it!' Her voice would hardly come out loud enough. She hurled herself into the nursery before he could stop her. His hands were yellow with paint from the model he was making.

'Go away,' he said.

'But they've found the tomb.'

He stared at her. He had paint on his face too and looked grotesque otherwise she would have kissed and hugged him. 'It's over!' she said.

'What?'

'The *wait*.'

'Is it true?' he said. 'Who says?'

'Ask Mr Burgess if you don't believe me!'

The actuality of Osi and his peculiarities threatened to take the shine off her elation and she ran downstairs, forgetting to avoid the broken step so that her foot went through the tread, ripping the side of her shoe, but it didn't matter one bit because soon there would be new shoes and the stairs would be mended and life would really start and this was *really* happening. She ran through the kitchen where Mr Burgess was accepting a cup of tea and outside to hang over the gate, mouth crammed with toffee, awaiting the telegram.

But two days went past with no news and then Mr Burgess came back, moustache adroop, bearing a newspaper. It seemed it had been a false alarm, nothing to do with Herihor at all; the news was about the Carter fellow – though not even *he* had actually found his Tutankhamen. Evelyn and Arthur must be mortified, Isis thought. They must be livid.

The disappointment, after the elation, brought a pall down over Little Egypt, darker than ever before. Mary moved slowly through it looking crushed, and Isis tried and tried to cheer her up by being helpful and with games of cards, afraid that she might up and leave, but was so miserable herself that she could scarcely drag herself out of bed in the mornings. With no tutor and no school there was nothing for her to do. There was a whole world going on out there but still they were held in Little Egypt, suspended as if in souring aspic.

She was surprised to find that she felt cross and sorry on her parents' behalf about blasted Howard Carter and blasted Lord Carnarvon, and blasted Tutankhamen. She hoped they might come back. If only they would at least write. If only they would give up the whole beastly business and come home and put an end to this awful wait.

Both Evelyn and Arthur were atheists, but Isis sided with Mary, who knelt to pray to her English God before she went to bed each night. Isis began to do the same, kneeling on the knobbly rug beside the bed and pleading for them to be brought safely back, or at least for a sign or messenger. And whether it was the prayers, or whether it would have happened anyway, Uncle Victor arrived a few days later like a ruined knight, come to release them from their spell.

8

MARY SHOOK A clean sheet over Isis' bed and Isis helped by smoothing and tucking it in, neat and tight at the corners as Mary had taught her. As they started on Osi's bed, Isis heard a motor drawing up and ran to the window to see the Bugatti.

'Uncle Victor!' she cried and pelted down the stairs to find him already in the hall.

'Icy,' he said. 'Thought I'd drop in for a spot of lunch.'

Mary came hurrying down, primping her hair with her fingers. 'Me and the children were only having cold,' she said.

'Splendid, cold will suit me admirably.'

Victor's cheerfulness seemed as out of place in the house, where gloom had been ruling for the past few days, as if someone had walked in speaking in a foreign language. 'What have you been up to, Icy?' He grabbed and tickled her and she squirmed obediently, though she wasn't in the mood for being tickled and was getting far too old for it. 'Take your uncle for a turn around the garden?' he suggested. 'While Mary works her wonders?'

'You've been neglecting us,' Isis complained as they went outside into the cold sunshine. 'Where have you been?' When he didn't answer, she added, 'George is dead; don't you know? We found him and it was simply frightful.'

'Evelyn mentioned it in her letter.'

Isis gaped at him. 'She wrote to *you*? She hasn't written to *us*.'

Her pleasure in Victor's visit was spoiled by a throb of crossness. '*Why* didn't she write to us? It's not fair. And then there's all this Tutankhamen business,' she added.

Victor smiled maddeningly and tapped the side of his nose. 'Of that, more later.'

'What Victor, what?'

But he would not be drawn. They walked through the tangled weedy orchard.

'Obviously we're going to need a new gardener,' Isis said.

Victor picked up a stick and reached up to hook down a last few stubborn apples.

'Look.' Isis pointed to the silvery wasps' nest. 'Isn't it perfect?'

Victor went as if to poke it with the stick.

'Leave it,' she said sharply. 'Or they'll come out in a swarm and do for you, Mary says. And what a bally awful way to go.'

'They'll be hibernating or whatever they do.'

He dropped the stick, took a cheroot out of a case in his pocket and made a great business of lighting it. The smoke came out of his mouth in a purple ripple and he leaned back against the wall, not far enough from the wasp's nest for Isis' liking, crossed his legs and closed his eyes. With his head tilted back like that, you could see the scar, thick and livid, emerging from his cravat.

The train went rumbling past and steam leaked through the branches. Since George had died, Isis rarely went right down the garden or anywhere near his shed, and so she hadn't watched the train for weeks. It seemed rather a childish occupation now.

'Come on.' She pulled him away from the nest. When they reached the icehouse steps, he stood meditatively breathing smoke and Isis guessed that he was thinking about Mimi – *she* was remembering, in any case.

'Where's Mimi?' she said.

'Oh, we went our separate ways.'

'Did you love her?' She searched his face for a sign of distress, but he had no particular expression. Did women find his scar and trembling leg repellent? After a war those are things you have to face, she supposed, you have to learn to love.

Though it was so damply mossy, Victor sat on the top step and patted the space next to him. Looking down at the dank entrance to the icehouse, Isis noticed that the padlock was askew. When she went down and rattled it, it came off in her hand. She stared at its rusty iron face. When she'd been searching for Dixie it had been locked, she was certain. Mary would never have let them open that door. 'You stay away from there,' she'd often warned, when they were smaller. 'You fall down that hole and you'll be in a right old pickle. No one would hear you from the house.'

Isis pulled open the door. Of course there was no ice left now. The pit hadn't been refilled since Grandpa died.

'Someone's been here,' she said.

Victor shrugged. Isis leaned in, breathing the chill earthy smell. It was too dark to see much, except for a few etiolated weeds rooting up from between the bricks. She let the door swing shut, pushed the padlock back into place and went up to sit beside Victor. Her hands stank of rust now, and she scrubbed them on her dress.

'*We've* only had one lousy postcard from them in months,' she said.

'What did it say?'

'*Darling Beasties*,' she parroted Evelyn's voice and then her own crept through, with a childish whine. 'Oh read it yourself. But it's not fair.'

'You wait,' Victor said.

'For what? I think we're going to be here for ever, Osi and me. We'll be old people with wooden legs and ear trumpets.'

Victor hooted. 'No you won't,' he said. 'Some lucky fellow will sweep you away.'

'Won't.'

'Beautiful girl like you.'

'What's beautiful about me then?'

He put his finger under her chin. 'Lovely eyes, lovely hair, pretty nose, peachy lips.' He kissed her on the end of her nose and she pulled back, flushing – partly from pleasure, partly from the shame of having fished for the compliment. You could always get one from Victor, so easily that it scarcely counted.

He took a last puff of his cheroot, ground it out with his toe, and then he put an arm round her. She leaned into him; it was nice in the chilliness to feel his warmth. His leg was only jumping a little and she put her hand on it and pressed to stop it.

'Poor Victor,' she said.

He gave a tight sort of sigh. 'Dear little Icy.' They sat quietly for a moment until something felt different to Isis, she didn't quite know what. Victor stroked her hand and then her knee, which gave her a tickly velvet feeling and felt queer and wrong.

She thought of Mimi and her bare white legs and jumped up and started back to the house.

'Come on, Mary'll go bally mad if we're late for lunch.'

Mary had managed to scrape together enough to make a decent table, though there'd be nothing left for supper. They sat in the dining room and ate broth, meat loaf – the end of the lamb padded out with carrot – with dates to follow as a pudding. There was no sherry so Victor drank brandy, his voice getting fat and slurry much quicker than Arthur's ever did. He was telling them about his car, and how it would do 65 miles an hour.

'Someone's been in the icehouse,' Isis announced and a flicker crossed Osi's face. Mary had stayed in the room, standing with her arms folded as they ate, asking Victor how she was supposed to run a house on nothing. And what about a replacement gardener who would actually *garden*?

'*You've* been in the icehouse,' Isis said to Osi.

'So? None of your business. It's not yours.'

'It's not yours either.'

'Now then!' said Mary.

'But it's not locked. It should be locked,' Isis insisted. 'It's dangerous, what if someone should fall down it?'

'Steer clear is my advice,' Victor said. 'You're neither of you babies.'

Mary heaved a long-suffering sigh and went out.

'What *was* in the letter then?' Isis asked. 'Are they coming back?'

'No.' Victor raised his eyebrows and grinned. 'But how would *you* like to go to *them*?'

Osi's mouth fell open as suddenly as if his jaw had snapped.

'Where?' said Isis.

'*Egypt*, you goose. How should you like to visit them there?'

'Yes!' Osi shouted so that a lump of half-chewed date was propelled from his mouth. 'You mean we can really go to *Egypt*?'

'They're getting close, they really are, and can't drag themselves away. Besides, they want you to share in it – the glory and whatnot.'

'*Want* us?' Isis said.

'Herihor!' Osi said. 'They're going to beat Mr Carter!'

'And they want jolly old me to take you over there.'

'Hoorah!' whooped Osi.

Isis put down her fork. 'I'm not sure that I care to go,' she said. The sour dusty taste of her imagined Egypt was in her mouth. 'Though it's nice they want us there,' she added, thinking, it's *unbelievable* that they want us there.

'Don't be a wet blanket, Icy.' Victor refilled his glass.

'We're going to Egypt!' Osi said. He got up and scurried from the room.

'Please may I leave the table?' Isis yelled after him.

'It'll be a lark, don't you think, Icy?' Victor said. 'Quite the adventure.'

'Do they really think they've found the tomb?' she said. 'Will they come back with us afterwards?'

They could hear Osi shouting, 'Mary! We're going to Egypt!'

Mary came hurrying back.

'It's perfectly true,' said Victor.

Mary blinked. 'That's all very well,' she said. 'But what am I supposed to do?'

'It'll be a break for you, Mary,' Victor said.

'I s'pose so,' she said, trying to conceal her pleasure.

'And when we come back we can be like a normal family,' Isis said and caught the face that Mary pulled. Well, all right, not quite normal.

After Victor had roared off down the lane, Isis went back to the garden with a paraffin lantern and a box of matches. It was late afternoon now. Clouds had covered the sky and a pesky wind got up. The dying grass swished coldly against her shins.

She went down the icehouse steps, lifted the padlock away and stepped inside for the shelter in which to light the paraffin lamp. The first bluish wisp of flame hardly illuminated anything, but as it grew and as her eyes adjusted, she began to see what she had feared, without knowing that she feared it. There were things down in the pit where the ice once was. There were colours. She must climb down to see.

She tried to secure the door open, but it was hung in such a way that it would swing closed. She took a last look outside at the blustery grey sky and the violent green moss on the steps, before letting the door clunk shut. The way the lantern flame fluttered made scary shadows but they were only shadows and shadows are nothing, a shadow could never hurt you.

She sat on the brink, the sharp, damp edges of the bricks digging into the backs of her thighs and taking deep steadying

breaths of the paraffin tinged air. And then she let herself drop
– it was just five feet or so, not enough to hurt her.

The interior of the ice pit was rounded like the inside of an
egg and painted like a tomb, though the paint had not taken
well. He had tried to whitewash it first, but the damp from
the bricks had come through, wetting the paint, blurring the
painstaking work. There were hieroglyphs and pictograms –
boats, Rameses, Horus, eyes, birds, scarabs – and on the floor
was a box, a painted cigar box, a miniature sarcophagus.

She crouched down. The paint glimmered gold and red and
blue. A brutal fur of silence prickled around her. She opened
the box and found a tiny mummy and some grave goods – a
ping-pong ball, the skeleton of a bird, and there was Bastet
too, glinting richly in the lamplight. There was a jam jar full
of dark wet, but it was not jam. This was her kitten, she knew
at once. Now a tight twist of cloth, thin and straight with a
shocking bulge of skull.

She put him back in the box and replaced the lid. There
were other mummies as well, less elaborate – one that almost
could have made her smile: thin and straight as a poker, ridiculous, a grass snake, she guessed, or slow worm. Her hands felt
grimy and so did the inside of her mouth and stomach and her
soul felt grimy too.

She put Bastet in her cardigan pocket, but she couldn't
climb out with the lamp; she needed both hands. It was so
thick and quiet she felt her breath go and her heart set up a
fierce thudding, and she didn't dare shut off the flame. It was
quite safe there, it would stay alight until the paraffin ran out
and then it would be dark again and dark forever more. The
wall decorations fluttered and she turned her back and struggled her way up, hard to climb, the bricks were slippery, the

sides almost sheer. When she finally got out she banged the door shut and stood panting in the grey and rust of autumn, in the cold freshness, feeling the first long spits of rain.

Her dress was stained with green and black, her knees were dirty, her hands unspeakable. And she was shaking as she walked towards the house. Mary caught sight of the state of her dress as she rushed through the kitchen and called her back, but she didn't stop. She went straight upstairs and through the door to the nursery where Osi was crouching in his tiny chair, a heavy book across his knees.

'I know what you did to Dixie,' she said.

He gaped and she was almost gratified to see him react with surprise, with shock, like a normal human being. Shuddering, she hugged herself as she waited, staring at him, until at last he spoke.

'I found him down by George's shed. I think his back was broken.'

She examined his peaky face, the pupils of his eyes stretched big and black. 'Is that true?'

'Yes, Icy, yes.' There was a childish pleading in his voice. 'Cats are sacred. I would never hurt a cat.'

She kept her eyes on his expression for a long moment, trying to divine the truth. It wasn't so hard to believe that George had done something to the kitten, after all.

'And I picked him up to bring him to you,' Osi continued miserably. 'But he shivered and went all stiff and died.'

'Why didn't you *tell* me then?'

Here he hung his head and shrugged his thin shoulders that were already hunched up around his ears.

'I was searching and searching,' she said. 'You know I was distraught for *weeks*. And all the time you knew!'

'Not at first and then I found him and I so wanted . . .'

'You wanted!'

He shrugged miserably, '. . . to get it right.'

He stopped. There were tight strings of sinew in his cheeks and greenish hollows beneath his eyes. 'I didn't hurt him,' he said. 'Honestly, Icy, I just made him ready for the Afterlife. It was better than burning him to nothing. Mary would have burnt him, then there's nothing for the ka to get back to, there has to be a way back you see or he'll roam forever. He would have been lost, *lost*. And I know how much you loved him.'

Isis continued to stare at him, so very much like Evelyn – and Victor – so unlike herself, although he was her twin. 'And I found this.' She took Bastet from her pocket.

'It was for him, for Dixie, to guard him in the Afterlife.'

She ran her finger over the bronze and gold, the lapis, the carnelian.

'I thought it had been stolen,' she said. 'You could have got someone into most awful trouble.'

He continued to look down at the floor so that she could see the chaotic swirl of hair that was his crown. It was the one physical feature they shared. She felt her anger shrivel into misery, almost to pity. 'Well I suppose that was kind,' she forced herself to say. She knew that he was sorry to have upset her, though not sorry for what he'd done. As far as he was concerned, he'd done the best thing for Dixie. The right thing. In a way. And true to his own beliefs.

Numbed, she turned from him.

THERE WAS NO time to hesitate or to procrastinate. Having finished his Bacardi Breezer, Spike was clearly eager to be off and would be if I wasn't careful. The drink would act as something of a stiffener, I thought, and finished mine, banging the empty bottle down on the table.

'Come on then, dear,' I said. 'Let's go and visit my brother.'

He looked longingly over his shoulder at the door before he followed me down the channel between the catalogues and packaging, which is quite a squeeze. He was very quiet. At the foot of the stairs we stood and looked up. Curious how you see things afresh when you have another person in the house. I hadn't taken in how much bird dirt there was from all the pigeons that live upstairs. The whiteness of their droppings all fluffed with down and spiked with feathers cascaded over the stairs like a frozen waterfall, strangely beautiful, though with a caustic reek that made your eyes water.

I saw Spike noticing the bucket and its contents, and I explained the system.

'We haven't seen each other or spoken for ten years,' I said, 'and it's worked well.' Aware of his uncertain expression, I added. 'Really, it suits us very well.'

'But what about . . .' He hesitated, groping with both hands in the air for something. 'What about *Christmas*?'

'I send up a mince pie and a card. But Osi really isn't bothered.'

'But what about you?'

It was as if stuck inside me was a weight of something, call it sorrow, call it what you like, a weight of something I haven't let myself acknowledge, creaking, straining against a door.

'They do a Christmas lunch in U-Save,' I said. 'I treat myself on Christmas Eve.' But my voice was strangled. I had to force out the words, aware that they might sound sad to anyone un-acquainted with the whys and wherefores of my life. Our lives.

As long as no one is sorry for me, I am quite all right.

Pity melts resolve.

'I've never been a great one for celebrations,' I added.

Spike turned his face away, a glint in his eye. 'Ma-am, I have to go,' he said.

Ma-am! No one has ever called me that. It must have been his American upbringing coming out, of course, and it sounded childish too; made him seem not much more than a child, and a scared one at that. I was able to pull myself together as I always am. Pulling myself together is something I have down to a fine art. Perfected over the years till it comes as naturally as breathing.

'Come on,' I said, attempting to buck him up and I clutched his damp and woolly arm. It was the missing tread of the third stair that worried me, that and my cronky knee. 'You help me up. There's rugs galore up there. There's all sorts.'

'But I don't see how . . .' He looked up the stairs. 'It's dangerous. It's a death trap.'

I suppressed a shudder. 'Well, we can help each other,' I said.

'Oh my God, this is *weird*,' he said, with a sudden laugh, shaking his head and reaching into his trouser pocket. 'Mind if I have a smoke?'

'When we get down,' I said. I could feel him stiffen. 'Please,' I added.

He flicked his head so the pale snakes writhed, and then he shrugged. 'I guess.'

'Thank you, dear.' I squeezed his arm. 'I warn you, Osi is not the easiest person. Don't expect a normal welcome.'

'Believe me, Ma-am, I don't.'

He had to lift me like a parcel over the missing step before we clambered up the rest. Our feet stirred up clouds of birdy-flavoured dust that made us choke, the both of us. Osi had certainly not been down, there was no sign of footfall apart from the damage to the crusty mess that we were wreaking. He had not been down and not been eating.

'And my brother might not be altogether in the pink,' I added, when we'd reached the top. 'This is something of a mission of mercy that we're on.'

'OK.' He coughed. 'Fuck,' he said, wiping his eyes on the cuff of his jumper.

'Yes, I do apologize for the . . . atmosphere,' I said. 'It all needs a damn good sweep.' A pigeon swooped close and he ducked, covering his head with his hands. 'Hate birds inside,' he said, with an audible shiver. 'Give me the fucking creeps.' The pigeon had perched on the bannister and was studying us coldly with the round bead of its eye.

'I quite agree,' I said, thinking uneasily of my spudgies. But there was no need for him to see those.

We crunched along to the bedroom and stood outside the door. My poor heart had slowed now to a small, cold throb and my eyes were streaming.

'This is like a dream,' Spike muttered, and though his face was greenish white, there was a twist of something like amusement in his voice, or the promise of amusement to come when he related this tale to his friends.

'Shall we?' I said.

'Sure.'

But we stood a few moments longer. Vainly I strained my ears for a sound of movement from behind the door, but there was nothing. My hand shook as I put it on the handle, and all those other times I'd stood on this landing came back to me; the years in layers pressing me in wafered versions. The house is full of moments, frozen. Oh pull it down, I thought, and welcome. Here's to a great reverberating crash! Bring in the bulldozers. Bring them in; raze Little Egypt to the ground.

PART TWO

9

To her own surprise, Isis loved being on the ship. It was a good place to be a child and she wagged like a puppy from group to group, pretending to be younger than she was, shamelessly begging to be petted, spoiled, and fed with tit-bits.

Victor left her to it, there was a lady on board he had his eye on, and Osi spent most of the time in their cabin, being sick, or reading and making notes. He was writing a diary in hieroglyphs – though since he did nothing but sleep and vomit, she could not imagine what he was putting.

Aboard the Hieronymus she loved the dipping of the deck beneath her feet, and felt proud not to feel even a whiff of nausea when the ship lunged and creaked and lumber crashed and rumbled in the hold. *The Hieronymus* was a cargo ship that took some passengers, just twelve or so, who had a portion of deck segregated from the crew.

She loved the smells of the ship: gravy seeping up from the galley, wood and oil and the smell of wind that has scoured the sea for hundreds of salty miles. Sometimes she'd go up on deck, even in the stormiest weather and pretend to be a figurehead, stand with her face in the gusts, eyes streaming, hair stiff and tangly from the salt.

Mrs Grievous – at least, that's how Isis understood the name – was the best bet for tit-bits. She and her husband (who had grey hair but a black moustache) had 'never been blessed to have such a pretty, clever, little girl.' They had one son, but he was a man now, and they were on their way to visit him. Mrs Grievous was plumply silky and smelled of talc, and though really too big to be so babyish, Isis liked to snuggle against her and accept pieces of Turkish Delight from her handbag. Evelyn would have snorted with derision if she could have seen. Mrs Grievous had colourless moles on her neck which hung like fleshy tears. When her husband was there, she stammered – making a pickle of saying Isis – *Sisisisis* would come out first – but the stammer went away when Mr Grievous did. Mrs Grievous taught Isis to play cribbage, something she vowed to take home to teach Mary as a change from whist and rummy.

Isis and Mrs Grievous were sitting in a cold, sunny part of the deck one day, starting a game. Mrs Grievous had a rug over her knees and she had just dealt the cards into her own tartan lap, when Victor strolled past, behind the trailing scarf of Melissa, an actress with yellow curls and circles of pink on her cheeks. Victor flicked Isis a look and a wink.

'My Uncle's a sex maniac,' she told Mrs Grievous, whose hand flew to her mouth.

'My goodness,' she said, 'that's not the sort of language little girls should use.'

'Sex or maniac?' Isis asked, though she knew perfectly well. She had heard the expression from Mary once in an eaves-dropped conversation with Mr Patey, and had been longing for a chance to use it.

'The 's' word, dear. Whoever did you hear say that?'

'Mother says it all the time.'

Mrs Grievous shook her head and rummaged in her handbag. The sea was choppy today and she had to suck barley sugar to stop her feeling queer. She handed one to Isis, who loved the comforting handbaggy taste. Mrs Grievous tucked a fold of blanket over Isis' knees and they sat contentedly, sucking and watching a sea gull on the rail of the boat. Its eye was flat and yellow and there was such a hard, grim set to its hooked beak that Isis had to look away.

Mrs Grievous took her hand and stroked it.

'I wish I had a mother like you,' gushed out of Isis, just from the loveliness of being kept warm, and fed sweet things, and stroked.

'Oh my!' Mrs Grievous took a hanky from her sleeve and dabbed at the dampness that had happened round her eyes. 'Oh, how I wish it too,' she said, a creamy throb coming into her voice. 'That's quite the nicest thing a person has ever said to me.'

Isis watched the sea gull lift itself heavily off the rail and with a smirking cry, swoop out of sight, leaving a big splattered dropping on the deck. She undid her hand from the grasp of Mrs Grievous and for the first time felt a queasy pang.

'I'd better go,' she said. 'I'd better go and see my brother.'

'Take a sweetie for him,' Mrs Grievous said. 'Take the bag, I've got a supply.'

Isis accepted the crumpled paper bag and went down into the gloomy, vomit-smelling cabin where Osi was busy straining his eyes over his diary. She put the barley sugars down and spat the taste into the basin. There was a bulge in her throat as if she needed to cry, but she spat some more and cleaned her teeth instead. In the cramped cabin she felt grotesquely huge, and the babyishness that Mrs Grievous brought out in her seemed shameful and absurd.

'Why not come up for some fresh air?' she said.

Osi frowned and sucked the bristles of his brush into a point, leaving his lips smeared blue.

'You can see gulls up there and the sea and Uncle Victor following a lady around – who's no better than she should be,' she added, wishing urgently for Mary.

Gazing at her blankly, Osi dipped his brush into the black. He had his tongue trapped between his teeth as he worked on a pictogram: an eye, delicate and elongated. She thought about him painting the inside of the icehouse. He must have spent hours down there, daubing on the walls, playing with his revolting dead things. It made her shudder. *He* did. She had not quite forgiven him for Dixie and the thought of that tightly-wrapped little skittle brought back her nausea.

Besides, it was too stuffy and annoying to stay in the cabin and she slammed the door as she went out and climbed back up onto the deck, legs weary on the stairs, the way she expected an old person's legs might feel. Victor had got Melissa sitting down now and was leaning into her, saying something in French. The scar was hidden by a tartan scarf, and his elbow was casually pressing down on the knee of his trembling leg.

'Will you play cards with me?' Isis took the pack from her pocket and waved it between them.

'Not now.' Victor plucked two cigarettes from his case and fitted one into Melissa's silvery holder.

'Quoits?'

'Run along.'

'Charades?' Though she knew this was ridiculous.

Melissa put the cigarette holder between her painted lips and dipped forwards as Victor clicked his lighter behind a cupped hand. She took a deep draw of her cigarette and smiled. 'Poor kid's bored,' she said. She pulled Isis close to her silky knees and petted her hair. She smelled of strong violets and smoke. 'I'll tell you what, dearie,' she said, and from her bag she pulled a book. 'This is a good one, a little racy . . .' She eyed Victor for his reaction, which was none.

'Thank you.' Isis gave up on them and took the book away. Out of the corner of her eye, as she walked on the sunny side of the deck, she saw Mrs Grievous beckoning, but she pretended not to see and went round to the port side where there was no sun and it was beastly cold. Mrs Grievous felt the cold, she always said, and only sat out in the sun for the sake of her health, so she was unlikely to follow Isis here. Someone had left a blanket on a seat and Isis snuggled into it and looked at the book. *Salamander Summer,* it was called, and there was a man with a black moustache and a lady with her dress coming off her pearly shoulder.

Isis read a page or two, but she wasn't it the mood for reading. She put down the book, rolled herself up like a sausage in the blanket and lay flat on her back on the bench, looking up at parts of the ship that she couldn't name and at the sky, pale blue like the sherry glasses at home, shading to lampshade white. She stared and stared at the blue, keeping her eyes wide open, not even allowing a blink, till they started to water and to close of their own accord. This she found a good method of getting to sleep – and after all, there was nothing else to do.

She let her eyes close and drifted back to the kitchen to teach Mary how to play cribbage – she could ask for a cribbage board for Christmas. Or perhaps Victor – or

Arthur – would buy her one in Cairo. If they have even games like that in Egypt. She'd enjoy explaining how you do the counting, the lovely orderly rows of holes that you jump the matchsticks over when you count, so you always know just where you are, and where your opponent is too.

If only Mary would still be there when they got back and not run off with Mr Patey.

She saw a darkening through her eyelids and opened them to see Mr Grievous looming above her, and she sat up quick, smart, almost banging her head against his, which had been far too close.

'You all right?' He eased down beside her and took out his pipe.

'Yes, thank you.'

He rapped his pipe on the edge of the bench till the sticky dottle came out.

She struggled out of the blanket and put her feet on the deck. He had shoes with a pattern of holes like in the cribbage board, only swirly, and all the holes were full of flour, or maybe Mrs Grievous' talcum powder.

'Rather nippy this side,' he said. 'Why not go and sit in the sun?'

'I just felt like . . .' It took her a moment to find the right word. 'Solitude.'

Mr Grievous hooted, then straightened his face. His moustache was so black it must be dyed, and his teeth were beastly yellow.

'Solitude,' he repeated. 'I like that. What's your age?'

'Nearly fifteen,' she lied.

'Don't look it,' he said, eyeing her.

She wrapped her arms around herself and looked away.

'You know we're saying toodle-oo at Marseilles?' he said. 'Tomorrow morning, that is.'

'Well, it's been a pleasure to meet you,' she said stiffly.

'Maisie has formed quite a soft spot for you,' he said, adding, 'poor old fool.'

'She's good at cribbage,' she said.

He snorted.

'Well, I must be going.' She stood to leave, but he grabbed her hand. His was hard and warm and squeezed her chilly bones until they nearly hurt.

'Did she tell you why we're going to Marseilles?'

'It's where your boy lives.' She stood as far away from him as possible, her arm stretched till it felt as if it would pull right out of her shoulder.

'She's going to say goodbye. She's dying, you know.'

'She's not!' Isis said. 'She's perfectly all right.'

'A few weeks, at most. We won't be going back to Blighty. Not together, at any rate.'

Isis stared at him, his moist eyes and moustache and the bundles of hair crammed in his nostrils that surely must made it hard to breathe.

'Won't you go and sit with her?' he said. 'She's taken such a shine.' He let her hand go and she staggered backwards.

'Of course,' she said, recovering her balance.

The sea was growing rougher as she made her way back to the sunny side, where Mrs Grievous was still seated, blanket-wrapped, eyes closed. Isis held her breath and crept close. The slack flesh either side of her face had drooped and the folds were caked in orange stuff. The eyelids were blurred with green, but you could still see the blood vessels. She thought of the crossness of dead George's face. Mrs Grievous had no expression, her face was merely slack. Sensing her presence, Mrs Grievous opened her eyes. At once her face stretched into a smile. 'It's my little angel,' she said.

'Shall we have a game?' said Isis.

'Of course! I thought you'd forgotten me.' Mrs Grievous reached into her bag for her cribbage board. As she did so she coughed and Isis heard a rumble deep in her chest, like thunder a long way away that you know is growing closer. Mrs Grievous dabbed her mouth with a hanky and pulled out a box of Turkish Delight, big squares of pink, dusted in icing sugar.

'Look what I've got, just for my favourite girl.'

Isis accepted a piece and the powder fluttered down the front of her coat. There was nowhere to put it but in her mouth. As Mrs Grievous dealt the cards on her lap, Isis' teeth dug into the squashy sweetness. She could not look at the fleshy pendulums on Mrs Grievous' neck, or the icing sugar on her lips, but stared instead at her hands, writhing with swollen veins, like a tangle of worms. She had to swallow hard to make the sweet goo slide down her throat.

Victor and Melissa came staggering by, her hand tucked in his arm, his face flushed with success.

'Hello!' Isis called.

'Windy enough for you?' Melissa pulled up the furry collar of her jacket. She shrieked and giggled as a gust of wind lifted the edge of her skirt.

'Weather's closing in,' Victor said, shading his eyes with his hand and looking out to sea as if he was an expert.

Melissa was studying Isis' face. 'Come and play quoits, dearie?' she said.

Victor looked at her with surprise.

'Mind if we steal the kiddie away?' Melissa asked Mrs Grievous.

Isis jumped up, too eagerly, scattering her cards. 'Would you mind awfully?' she said.

'No, you run along,' Mrs Grievous said.

'I'll come back later,' Isis promised and hurried across the tilting deck to take Melissa's outstretched hand. But it was really too rough for quoits; anyone could see that. Big clouds had boiled up out of nowhere and soon there was the spiteful, sideways spit of rain.

'This is hopeless,' Victor said, as his quoit was caught in a gust and almost blown overboard.

'Fancy a stiffener instead? Melissa asked, and she and Uncle Victor went below clutching each other and giggling. Isis wandered back to Mrs Grievous, but her seat was empty and the whole deck deserted now. Isis clung to the rail watching the struggle and surge of the waves until she was chilled to her bones.

In their cabin, she found Osi flat on his back, hieroglyphs abandoned, eyes shut tight, a bucket sliding to and fro on the floor beside his bunk. She climbed the ladder to the top bunk, got under the covers and strained her eyes over *Salamander Summer*. She could taste the lingering rosiness of the Turkish Delight and felt an uneasy squashiness in her stomach as the man and lady – whom she pictured as Victor and Melissa – kissed.

The storm had died down by the time the ship berthed in Marseilles in the early hours of the morning. Isis stayed in her bunk listening to the clanks and shouts, till she was certain that disembarkation was underway. She got up to the deck in time to see Mr and Mrs Grievous make their slow way down the gangplank. Mrs Grievous stopped and looked back, searching for Isis, and Isis waved her handkerchief. She waved till the couple disappeared amongst the crowds on the quayside – and then she stayed at the rail till the gangplank was pulled in, watching the wheeling of the gulls above the bilgy harbour water.

And then Uncle Victor was beside her, face raw from shaving, eyes red and glassy. 'That old duck was looking for you,' he told her, 'and she asked me to give you this.' He handed her the drum of Turkish Delight, thin wood with a picture of a veiled dancer on the lid.

Later, when they were out to sea again, Isis lifted the wooden lid and watched the breeze swirl an icing sugar ghost into the sky. And then she took the sweet and fleshy lumps and one by one she threw them to the gulls.

10

At Port Said, Osi came alive. The stink and roar of the harbour drew him, pale and blinking, into the daylight, and opened his mouth to a stream of facts. Victor snapped at him to pipe down and Isis was made sorry enough by his crestfallen expression to say, 'Tell me about the Ptolemaic Temples again,' and to pay attention for 5 minutes.

Once they were on solid ground and out of the ship-board breeze, the heat was glorious, like nothing Isis had known before – or like the lovely heat of the bath where every bit of you can move and relax and you feel as if you could grow an inch all round.

Melissa was going to work in Alexandria, and she and Victor kissed goodbye on the quayside where a taxi was waiting to carry her away. The kiss was the long sort on the mouth and Isis saw a man look daggers as he went past and spit on the ground, but Victor and Melissa didn't care. Uncle Victor emerged from the kiss with red smeared round his mouth, his whole face damp and swollen.

Victor took the children to the Hotel Cecil, where they were to meet the guides who would take them to Evelyn and Arthur.

They strolled through an avenue of towering palms to enter the hotel, and sat in a cool, mirrored lobby drinking crushed lemon with ice and sugar you could spoon in yourself, as much as you liked. In her greed, Isis made her own drink rather too sugary, even for her own sweet tooth. Victor drank beer and ordered a plate of sandwiches. It was quiet in the hotel after the noisy quay, and Isis shook her head as if to dislodge water in her ears. Osi was staring with his mouth agape at the frieze of hieroglyphs that ran round the walls.

'That doesn't make sense,' he said, pointing.

'I expect it's decoration,' said Victor.

'But it's not *proper*. It's not *right*. It should be *right*.'

'No matter.' Victor raised his eyebrows at Isis.

The sandwiches came stuck together with cocktail sticks. As Victor unspeared his sandwiches, Isis collected the sticks, which would do very well for her cribbage board.

'You've still got lipstick on you,' she told Victor. She pointed to the place and with a thick cotton napkin he wiped the last trace of Melissa away.

'Are you sad to say goodbye?' Isis said, examining him for signs of being love-lorn. 'When you write her a letter, can I add a line?'

Uncle Victor shook his head. 'She's not the type you write to,' he said.

'What type would you write to, then?'

His answer was a scowl and she saw his leg was jumping. Well, even if he didn't, *she* would to write to Melissa. When they'd said goodbye, Melissa had crushed Isis against her thin silky dress so that she could feel the complications of flesh and straps and smell violets, smoke and sweat. The pale fluff on her face had been clouded with perspiration and her feet squashed much too tight into high-heeled sandals. You could see the clefts between her chubby toes pressed tight together by the shiny leather. Isis was fascinated by the way her body was there, hidden by her clothes, but still shouting *here I am*, while most people's bodies were simply hidden and gave you no cause to think about them. Victor had certainly kissed Melissa in the dark of the cabin and perhaps been allowed to move aside the straps and silk to see and touch her pearly, naked skin.

Victor lit a cigarette and Isis left him alone and nibbled a sandwich, egg with cress, wondering if he was putting on a brave face. He'd certainly seemed extremely sweet on Melissa. When Isis had returned *Salamander Summer*, Melissa had given her another book: *Desert Longing*, and said that she could regard it as a parting gift.

'Eat your sandwich,' she said to Osi, and without taking his eyes off the wall, he reached out and she watched as the cocktail stick spiked him up the nostril. She sniggered and he swung his leg and caught her on the shin. It really hurt and mortifying tears jumped into her eyes.

'Don't kick me,' she yelled.

Osi stuck out his tongue, clotted with half-chewed sand-wich.

'For God's sake!' Uncle Victor snapped. Isis rubbed her shin and looked round, but there was no one taking any notice, only the brown man who had brought their food and drinks standing with his back to the door, a perfectly neutral expression on his face.

The sandwich had a funny taste, something was different, the kind of egg or butter or cress or something, and it wasn't quite nice. But still she finished one and reached for another.

Osi had discarded his cocktail stick, but she left it, not wanting one that had been up his nose.

Victor had had another beer and smoked two more cigarettes before the guides arrived. One of them was old, one young, both dressed in white jellabas over dark trousers.

'I'm Haru,' the younger man said, extending his hand to Victor, who was in the act of unfolding himself from a low chair. 'I apologise for our lateness. This,' he stood back and gestured to the older man, 'is my Uncle Akil, he's a cook and a very fine one too, though his English is not so good.' Haru's English was perfect and only faintly accented. Both men were bearded and wore skullcaps, and sandals that revealed their naked, dusty toes.

'Why should it be?' Isis said kindly. 'I don't speak a syllable of your language.'

Haru smiled. 'You must be Isis. And Osiris. Grand names! Welcome.' His teeth were startlingly white against his coffee-coloured lips and the thick black of his beard, and his eyes shone damson dark. His smile flashed on and off like the beacon of a lighthouse, and when it was off he looked rather frightening.

Victor and Haru moved towards the hotel doors to converse about the journey south, and Osi followed, rummaging through his satchel, to show Haru something. Isis remained at the table finishing the rest of the sandwiches and sipping Victor's abandoned beer. Akil had stayed just where he was, face to the floor and so it was safe to stare. It seemed queer to have a cook who was a man. She had a pang thinking of Mary all alone in Little Egypt where it would be so cold. How she would enjoy this warmth. One day they should bring her here, to this hotel where people would serve her with drinks and sandwiches and she wouldn't have to lift a blessed finger nor skivvy in any perishing kitchen while she was at it. Isis smiled. Though Mary liked to say *perishing kitchen*, it was really the warmest place in the house.

Akil's small black cap perched on hair like wire wool and there was a deep scar on one side of his face that dragged his eyebrow down over half his eye and pulled his mouth out of line. How did you do it? she longed to ask. It could have been a fight, or even an attack by a lion. Or maybe, like Victor, he'd been in the war. Was Egypt in the war? She didn't even know that. Akil's skin was thick leathery brown, so unlike the pearly stuff Melissa was covered in, or the flaking slackness of Mrs Grievous', who might be dead by now. A rosy taste filled her mouth at the thought of that poor old duck and she swallowed more of the sour, flat beer.

Their luggage had already been loaded onto the back of the lorry that Haru was to drive to Cairo, where they'd meet Evelyn and Arthur, transfer to a dhow and sail down the Nile, in style. 'In style upon the Nile,' Victor said, in an attempt at gaiety.

But the lorry part of the trip was far from stylish. Akil and Osi sat under canvas in the back with the trunk, and Victor and Isis in the cab, while Haru drove. Surely Victor should have let Osi be inside? Isis thought, since he was supposed to be looking after them, but she could feel a throb in her shin still and why should *she* care if Osi got covered in dust?

The heat didn't suit Victor one bit and he was shiny with grease and sweat, with a beer stain, already, on his pale trousers and his linen jacket shamefully crumpled. They had bottles of water and cut-up pineapple to quench their thirst on the long hot drive, much of it over bumpy, sunburnt land. Haru was a fast driver who swore in Egyptian, and swerved and tooted the horn, and the seats were rock hard. Before they'd been driving for half an hour, Isis could feel the bones in her own plump bottom, so goodness knows how Victor and Osi, neither of whom had any padding, were feeling.

The landscape was tedious and Isis shut her eyes, leant her head against Victor's arm, and managed to sleep, drooling and bouncing against his sleeve. Now and then he took out his cigarettes and offered one to Haru so that the cab was full of smoke, as well as blindingly hot and bright.

Later in the journey, Haru pointed out that they were following the Nile into Cairo, and the land had become green with palm trees and tall crops – sugar cane, Haru said. He stopped at a place with a WC that was actually just a filthy hole behind a screen, so that they could make themselves comfortable. Haru returned to the cab with pieces of sugar cane for the twins to chew on. Isis put hers between her lips and puffed as if it was a fat cigar, and Victor laughed and squeezed her leg.

'Soon be there,' he said.

Haru pressed his hooter as they overtook a man with a great net of melons balanced on the back of a poor sagging donkey. They were passing houses now with luxuriant gardens, oxen grazing on patches of roadside grass, cats and chickens and children. There were women in long frocks with scarves over their heads, which must be beastly hot, and every person they passed gawped and pointed at the lorry. Most of the vehicles they saw, as they came into the town, were horse- or ox-drawn, and there were bicycles too, piled with much more than they were meant for, whole families sometimes, wobbling along the rutted road.

They had to stop as a flock of grubby, runty-looking sheep

– or were they goats? – crossed the road, and when they set off again, a crowd of boys ran along beside them waving sticks and shouting. Isis didn't know whether to wave or to pretend she hadn't noticed. But soon they speeded up and left the boys and their shouts behind.

The plan, Victor had explained, was to meet Evelyn and Arthur at the house of the Hudsons, friends who lived in a suburb of Cairo, to stay the night, and early tomorrow embark on the sail to Luxor. Now that they were near, Isis was in a fidget of excitement about seeing Evelyn and Arthur after such an age. It would be interesting, after all, to see them in their natural habitat; in their element. She allowed herself to day-dream that they had already found the tomb of Herihor, so all they'd need to do would be to have a quick look and then return home all together. She could go to school, and maybe Osi, and the shut-up parts of the house would come alive with all the money they'd get from the grave goods. They would be famous, and Isis would be a little famous too, just by being their daughter. When it was over she would forgive them for being Egyptologists, she might even be proud.

'Oh yes, I was there,' she'd tell her new pals. Imagine *friends*, with houses you could visit, other girls to talk to and confide in. She could learn to dance and all the plumpness would fall away. She would grow her hair long and wear it pinned up with a silvery comb, and Osi, he would make friends too, perhaps, or just become an Egyptologist himself and spend his whole life grubbing happily in the desert. It seemed what he was born for – the only thing.

The lorry stopped in a leafy street where wide verges of shorn brown grass separated the road from the footpaths and, set back behind palms and clambering greenery, was a row of great mysteriously-shady houses. Haru jumped down from the cab to find the home of the Hudsons. Isis climbed out stiffly; her posterior and legs were bruised by all the jolting and her head ached. She ran her fingers through her stiff, tangled hair; it hadn't been washed since they'd left home and she must look a perfect fright. Uncle Victor didn't care about such things, but she didn't want the Hudsons to think she was a guttersnipe. Osi climbed out of the back of the lorry and she looked at him with despair, he was at his awkward worst and resembled nothing more than the bedraggled nestling of a bird of prey crammed into human clothes.

Victor lit up a cigarette and leaned his back against a tree. Looking up into the waving fronds, Isis saw branches of dates. Arthur always made a great to-do of presenting a crate of dates to Mary when they arrived home, as if she should be delighted and surprised. 'I suppose we can live on them when Mr Burgess strikes us off his books,' Mary had muttered last time, when Arthur had left the room. The dates on this tree were tight and green and the ground beneath was strewn with crunchy broken palm fronds. A bird screeched and screeched, though Isis couldn't see it, and a skeletal dog skulked along the pavement.

'Poor thing!' she said and went to pet it, but one of its eyes was missing and the socket weeping yellow pus and she shrank away disgusted.

Haru came back frowning, speaking rapidly to Akil, who shrugged his shoulders and spat.

'They are not at the address I have.' He waved a piece of paper at Victor who took and examined it as smoke leaked from his mouth.

'Perhaps we have the number wrong?' he said.

'I have tried, no one knows this address or the names of these people.'

'Maybe it's the wrong road?' Isis suggested.

Haru shook his head and puffed out angrily. 'Wrong road!' he said. 'What am I to do?' He snatched back the paper from Victor and stamped off across the road again.

'What if we can't ever find them?' Isis' voice rose into a childish wail.

Victor had no answer to that; he simply stood watching for Haru's return, a baffled expression on his face. They waited for an age while Haru tried the rest of the houses in the street. He found the right one at last, but it was shut up, and a servant told him the Hudsons had gone away.

'Gone away?' Isis felt a plummeting sensation in her belly. 'Gone where?'

'I say, that's the bally limit,' Victor said weakly.

'I'm sure it'll be all right,' Isis said. She took his hand. 'It's just a misunderstanding.'

He looked down at her with a dent between his eyes, and she noticed the flaring of his pupils.

'Let's not panic,' she said. He was a fragile man still and the only time he was all right, really, was when he was with a lady. Now that Melissa had gone she would have to manage to keep him calm somehow or other.

'Do you think you should take one of your pills?' she suggested.

He gave her a glazed look, but nodded and took a tablet from the little brown bottle in his pocket.

'We need refreshment,' she decided, 'while we think what to do.'

AFTER A LONG argument with Akil and much spitting on the ground, Haru took them to a quite different class of establishment from the Hotel Cecil. There was no cool marble in this place; it was a low dark room, packed with men sucking smoke through bubbling tubes, men who stared at them all, but mostly at Isis. Her dress was too tight round the chest and stained under the arms with sweat, and it was too hot for stockings so her legs were bare to the knee. Akil had gone off somewhere, and Haru and Victor stood at a counter drinking tiny cups of coffee, while Isis and Osi sat on cushions before a low table drinking something sticky sweet from bleary glasses.

There was an argument going on at the bar, and even though Victor had taken a pill, Isis could see that he was agitated, face twitching to one side, which she recognised as a danger sign, and what would she do if he lost control among all these strangers? There were flies buzzing around the sweet drink and she felt one tickling her upper lip and smacked it away so hard she hurt herself.

'Ow. Oh Lord preserve us,' she said, comforted by using a

Maryish expression. 'What *are* we going to do?'

There was a fly crawling on his lips too.

'Get that fly off you,' she said.

He looked at her and sipped his drink and another fly joined it, one at each corner of his mouth. 'I don't mind,' he said.

Isis looked hard at her drink. She didn't know the taste, it would be something tropical, she expected. 'Lost in Egypt,' she said.

'We're not lost with Victor here,' Osi said.

Isis widened her eyes at his faith in Victor.

'Is it how you imagined?' she asked him. 'Egypt?'

'We've seen enough photographs to have given me a good idea,' he said. His voice sounded like Arthur's, sensible and grown-up and measured, but his eyes darted about and she was gratified that he too seemed uneasy.

'I hope they're are all right,' she said, watching for his expression. 'What if . . .'

'They're right on the brink of discovery. Perhaps even –'

'But they can't not come! You can't send halfway across the world for your children then not bother to meet them!' Isis' voice rose and she sensed a prickling of interest amongst the men. 'If only Mary were here,' she added quietly.

'What could *she* do?' Osi was clenching and unclenching his fists and then pulling the lobes of his ears, a childish habit Isis had supposed him grown out of.

She breathed deeply to quell her rising panic and her airways filled with tarry scented smoke. 'It's rather thrilling, don't you think,' she said with a desperate smile, 'being somewhere you don't know and not knowing what's going to happen next?' The idea of Mary being here was a stupid one, anyway. Victor was a man of the world, after all; she should trust him. What would Mary know about being lost in Egypt?

Her hands felt dirty and she grew more and more uncomfortable and distracted by her need for the lavatory. Victor was drinking something from a small glass now, and refusing to catch her eye. Haru was slumped across the bar talking earnestly and laughing, she saw him punch someone on the arm and it was the kind of punch, done with the kind of laugh, that could have been a joke or a threat, you couldn't tell. Akil had come back and was crouched with the other men, sucking smoke through a bubbling pipe. There were no women in the bar, Isis noticed, which probably meant they didn't have a place for ladies to pay a visit, and in any case, she didn't feel she could walk about in here, better to stay as small and unobtrusive as possible in the shadows.

She began to play patience, dealing the cards out in seven columns. If it came out right by the fifth time, everything would all be all right, and by tonight they'd have met Evelyn and Arthur. It would all turn out to be a silly misunderstanding and then there they'd be with egg on their faces but none the worse. One day it might be a funny story, something she could tell her children: the time we were lost in Egypt! It'll all come out in the wash, Mary would say. No black queen, no red seven. She reshuffled for another try.

Osi took out a book and sat with his head over it, gnawing the joints of both thumbs; the spitty scraping of his teeth was maddening. Over and over she got stuck with the patience, kneeling with legs pressed tightly together as the pressure in her bladder grew. The cards picked up a stickiness from the table, the top of which was made of leather tooled with patterns, once gold, but now ingrained with blackish grease. Isis squirmed and dealt again, looking pleadingly over at Victor who ignored her.

Her stomach felt swollen with urine, it was as if a wire was twisting inside her and she felt as if something would break if she couldn't relieve herself soon. She had no choice but to get up, legs fizzing with pins and needles, and cross the room to pull on Victor's sleeve. He started and gawped around him as if he'd just woken up. She whispered her need and he shouted to the man behind the bar, 'My niece needs the toilet,' so the whole room could hear, and using that dreadful common word, too. Isis was so hot and uncomfortable already that she couldn't blush any more and she needed to press her fist between her legs, but she could not do that.

Haru grabbed her by the arm and took her through a curtain made of swinging chains and out into a yard where there was a wooden box, like a coffin on its end. 'There.' He shoved her towards it.

There was a sound like thunder coming from the place and such a stink she had to open her mouth to breathe and that meant she could taste the filthy air. It was dark except for streaks of light leaking through gaps in the wood, but she didn't want to see anyway. She pulled her underwear aside and let the urine out in a hot torrent, splashing down the insides of her legs and wetting her shoes as flies zizzed and needled around her face. For a moment there was the bliss of relief, but there was nowhere to wash her hands and she grew afraid of all the germs that there must surely be. Mary said foreign germs were worse and stronger than English ones and you could hear them in here vibrating like something about to boil right over. And now she had to go back and everyone would know where she'd been and the pale leather of her shoes was darkly splattered.

'We should leave here,' she told Haru. 'This is not the place for us.'

He looked down at her, his dark eyes seeming to suck up the light. She noticed how thick his lashes were, each one shiny and live like an insect's antennae. He considered for a moment before he said: 'And where would you have us go?'

'To the boat,' she said. 'If they won't come here, then something important must have held them up, and we'll simply have to go to them. It's what they would expect.' She wiped her hands on her dress and lifted her chin.

Haru kept his serious gaze on her for a moment longer, and then his head went back and he shouted a laugh. 'It's what they would expect,' he said. 'Well, maybe you're not so wrong.'

He led the way back into the café, which seemed darker now, and she kept her head high, ignoring the bright sparks of eyes and grinning teeth that flickered through the gloom. Haru and Akil issued the three of them out of the café and into the street, where the sudden brightness made Isis stagger.

Victor was staggering too, for different reasons, and Isis took one arm and Haru the other. 'So we will go to the boat,' Haru said. 'And I must spend my own money for this.'

'They'll be sure to pay you, the minute we see them,' Isis said.

'They *will* be sure to,' Haru said, and he was not smiling now. 'What can I do?' He turned to Akil and shrugged and talked Arabic, until Akil nodded and looked up, for the first time, looked properly first at Isis, then at Osi, then at Victor. And then his eyes came back to Isis, and again he nodded.

12

O SI CLAMBERED INTO the back of lorry, without complaint, and Akil climbed in after him. Isis and Victor resumed their positions in the cab, and Haru drove with one hand, smoking continuously till the air was filled with greyness, bad breath and temper. Victor lolled against Isis, making her hot and squashed and she was parched – but after that awful visit to the lavatory she resisted drinking from the bottle of scummy water.

The drive was long, with just a stop or two, one to buy fuel, one when Haru stood and relieved himself in clear sight, shocking Isis with the accidental glimpse of a yellow arc, and then Victor staggered out and did the same, not even bothering to go far from the lorry. Hearing the heavy splatter made Isis need to go again and she had no choice but to jump down and hide behind a wheel to squat.

They drove and drove on dry brown roads through the dry brown land. What would they do when night fell? Where would they sleep? And the night did *fall* – one moment there was a fiery balloon low in the saffron sky, the next it had burst into scarlet shreds – and swiftly the sky went dark. Victor woke up and smoked at some point, and then the lorry began making stuttering sounds and ground to a halt. Haru swore and jumped out, shouting something to Akil in the back.

Isis allowed herself a small sip of water and climbed stiffly out to check that Osi was all right. It was cold and the sky was crammed with stars, crushed together far too tightly so it was like a scrumple of silver foil.

'Osi?' she called, but he didn't answer and she couldn't see him. Akil was standing a little way away with Haru, who was talking in a fast, terse undertone. She clambered up, barking her shin on the rusty metal. 'Osi?' She made out the small hump that was he, put her hand out to reach him and caught hold of his shin, ice-cold and stiff and prickled with hairs. She let out a cry.

'What is it, Icy?' called Victor.

Her breath had caught like something thick, like wadding in her throat. He was stone cold dead and she opened her mouth to scream but no scream came, and then she felt him move.

'What is it?' Osi said and she sat down with a thump beside him. 'I was *asleep*,' he said crossly, but she didn't care how cross he was, she hugged him, so cold he was like a statue of a boy. He needed to wear more clothes if he was to continue in the back of the lorry. He would freeze to death and if Victor wasn't going to look after him then she bally well would.

'We need to open the trunk and get some clothes out,' she called. 'We're perishing cold.'

'I'm all right,' Osi said. He never felt the cold, but Isis was shivering now. Where did all that heat go? In summer at home it never got so hot, but on scorching days it stayed warm in the evening. This heat was like bathwater, all run away in the dark, as if down a plug hole.

'Why have we stopped?' Osi's voice was cross and scratchy with sleep.

'We've broken down,' Victor said. 'Here, Icy, you open up the trunk – I could do with a pullover myself.'

Isis reached over and took the key. The trunk that contained clothes for all three of them was behind a partition; she'd seen Akil and Haru load it.

'Help me,' she said to Osi. She was thinking of putting on a cleaner dress, stockings and a cardigan. There were cakes of soap in there, the ivory sort that Evelyn liked best. They could pour water from the bottles over their hands and wash them properly at least.

But behind the partition there was nothing. It was too dark to know for sure at first, and horrible to put your hands into a space you could not see, but she had to make herself feel and she felt and felt and came across nameless bits and pieces but nothing the size or shape of the trunk. She would not believe it but kept feeling about, measuring the space with her hands until she was certain she'd covered every nook and cranny.

'It's gone!' she wailed at last.

'Don't be such a clot,' Victor said.

'You find it then.'

Osi was on his knees now, feeling about. 'Not here,' he confirmed.

Victor got up onto the back of the lorry and stumbled towards them. Isis' eyes were growing used to the dark now and she could see the absence of the trunk, she could see how Victor was holding out his hands like a sleepwalker.

'Here,' she said, guiding him. 'It was just here. I saw them put it in.'

She caught Victor's hand to put it into the absence and felt that it was trembling.

'It must be here,' he said. 'Perhaps they moved it.'

'Haru!' Isis called and her voice came out querulous and panicky, and when he came to see what she wanted, she smoothed it down. 'We can't seem to locate the trunk. We need some warmer clothes.'

'It's there,' he said, 'pull away the . . .' and then he clucked his tongue and jumped up to show them. And he did seem surprised that it wasn't there. As far as Isis could tell in the darkness, he really didn't seem to know.

'It's *all* our things.' Her teeth were chattering now and her voice wobbled. Mary had spent ages washing and ironing and folding, and Isis happened to know there were some treats hidden amongst the clothes – she had seen the humbugs and aniseed balls. Uncle Victor's things were in there too – though they had made a fearful squash – as it had been decided at the last minute that travelling with one trunk only would be cheaper and easier. There was silence in the back of the lorry, and for the first time it struck Isis how very, very quiet it was out there, a different kind of quiet from that at home. All you could hear was the hissing of the stars as if the sky had a million punctures.

'Akil!' Haru leapt off the back of the lorry into the darkness and they heard shouting.

'What shall we do?' Isis asked Victor. 'I want my cardigan.' Her voice wobbled on this last, homesick kind of word.

'Buggered if I know.' Victor slumped down and put one arm round Isis, and one round Osi. At least there was some warmth that way. They sat stunned for a long time, listening to the silence of the desert, punctuated at first by quarrelling and the thwack of someone being hit, and later sounds of the engine being tinkered with, and at last the stuttering roar of success.

Haru shouted over the back. 'We'll stay here till dawn.'

'Can you offer an explanation for the trunk?' Victor called, but there was no answer, only the slam of one cab door, and then the other. Isis gave him the key back, though there was no point in it now. Through the removed partition they could hear the rumble of Haru's and Akil's voices. They all listened but could make out nothing, of course, but their tempers.

'It'll all come out right in the morning, you'll see,' Isis said. 'We can all keep warm together.'

'That's the spirit,' Victor gloomed.

'See the dog star?' Osi said, and his pale forefinger pointed upwards. 'That's Sopdet. I can't see . . .' He got up and stumbled and stood head back, muttering away about Sah and Soped and other soapy-sounding names. 'In one story, let me see, 5th century I believe, Isis calls herself Sopdet and states that she will follow Osiris to heaven.'

'So Sopdet is my star?' Unexpectedly, Isis felt her interest snagged. 'Which one?'

He pointed and tried to describe, and she strained to follow, but it was impossible and the prickling of the brimming sky caused her eyes to smart.

'Between the First Intermediate Period and the Late Middle Kingdom, coffin lids were commonly decorated with star clocks or calendars . . .' Osi's voice had changed from that of a boy to a machine with Arthur's intonation which could, and probably would, go on and on for the rest of the night. 'Flawed by their failure to take account that their measured year was six hours short . . .'

'At least someone's happy,' Victor whispered, his breath a hot tickle in her ear.

Isis let her eyes close. Secretly, she let tears leak between her lashes for all Mary's wasted ironing and smoothing, for the ivory soap and the humbugs and the fresh clean dress and stockings. But there was no value in dwelling on it, as Mary herself would say.

Osi's voice droned on and on until eventually Victor was snoring. She rested her head against his arm and may, despite everything, have managed to sleep till dawn – except that she was suddenly hurled from sleep by the flail and scream of Victor, who stood and staggered about, hands over his head as if to protect himself from gunfire. He was like an animal and Isis, who hardly knew where *she* was, caught at his arm and shouted to try and wake him, but he was dangerous to be close to.

She and Osi crammed tight into the compartment where the trunk was not, their bodies going into their twin shape, her softness against his hard edges, and together they heard Victor vomit and maybe jump, maybe fall off the lorry, and the opening of the door and the voice of Haru, and a sound like a slap to the face, maybe, and terrible sobbing that seemed to come from somewhere deep, not something as insubstantial as a person, but more like a cave, or a crack in the ground and then, eventually, it was quiet again though Victor didn't return.

Crammed in their compartment, Isis could feel Osi's heart, slower than her own, beating so closely it seemed to be pumping her blood, and as they fell asleep she went into the wet squirm of her pre-birth dream where she was half of one whole with two heartbeats once again.

13

THE MORNING AIR was cool and clear and there was quite a breeze. Osi was already sitting up squinting at a book. Isis uncramped herself and stood stretching and yawning, watching the sway and struggle of palms fronds on some distant trees.

'Morning.' Victor's voice made her jump. He grinned up at her over the side of the lorry. His eyes were squinty pink and his chin peppered with grey and gingery bristles.

'You had a nightmare,' she said. Victor acknowledged the truth of this with a nod. 'All better in the light of day,' she said and ran her tongue round her teeth, furry from lack of a toothbrush. She picked the sharp grit of sleep from the corner of her eyes. Osi's hair was standing up on end where he had rubbed his hands through it and the seat of his trousers was filthy, but so was her own dress filthy, her hair stiff with sweat and sand.

'We must look like a gang of bally tinkers,' she said, and almost gaily, for they must keep their spirits up. 'Oh for a good old wash and brush up!'

Haru appeared beside Victor looking miraculously fresh, the whites of his eyes clear between his glossy lashes.

'We must apologise for the theft of your trunk,' Haru said, bowing his head a fraction. 'We can only suppose it happened when we were in the café yesterday.'

'That's all right,' Isis said in a small voice.

'And I offer apologies for my bad temper of yesterday. You see Mr and Mrs Spurling promised me payment and now I must borrow money to get you there.'

'Victor's got money,' Isis said.

'I'm hardly rolling in it, Icy,' Victor said. 'But my funds will cover hotels and whatnot. You get us there safely, Haru, and I guarantee that Mrs Spurling will pay you double.'

'But the lorry is no good for a big drive, I think.'

'Then you must hire another.'

'That will cost too much.'

'The train?'

'Too much and we are far from the station now.'

Akil's disembodied voice rattled round from the front of the truck.

'My uncle suggests we take a boat,' said Haru.

'That would be fun!' Isis said. 'After all, it's what was planned. Would you like that, Osi?'

But Osi was staring into the distance. Looking in the direction of his gaze she saw that he was absorbed with watching a big ragged bird, a vulture or an eagle, tearing at something with its bloody beak.

The lorry coughed clouds of black exhaust as Haru cranked the engine, but it did start. Isis took a sip of the remaining water and passed the bottle to Osi, watching the bulge in his thin, grubby throat as he swallowed it down. They all resumed their positions for the drive, and in only an hour or so, Haru had delivered them to a small, bustling place on the banks of the Nile. Immediately they stepped out of the lorry and their white faces were seen; pedlars and beggars surrounded Victor and the children in a frightening jostle, but Haru and Akil sent them packing with waving arms and a fierce volley of invective.

Victor was keen to do business with an English speaker, rather than get himself fleeced, and the only suitable available person was an elderly American lady, quite miniature, wearing trousers and a striped boy's shirt. Her hair was cropped grey and her face shrunken, crinkled like a monkey's. Her name was Miss Rhoda Vandercamp, she told them, and her dhow was called *Marguerite*, after her dear, dead friend.

Haru's plan had been for them to hire the boat from her and for him to sail it, but that she would not allow.

'I'm the Captain of this tub,' she said, 'and I don't let her out of my sight.' Haru gave up, muttering something that sounded very rude and spitting in the dirt. Rhoda caught Isis' eye and smiled and Isis moved towards her.

'I'm Isis,' she said, 'and this is Osi, and this is Uncle Victor.'

Rhoda choked. 'Isis? And Osi – don't tell me – *Osiris*?!'

There was silence for a moment and Isis caught a smile flicker across Haru's face before he turned away.

'We can't help it,' she said hotly.

'Poor kids,' Rhoda said.

'If you're going to be so rude –' Isis began, but Victor cut across her.

'Do you know the Spurlings, by any chance?' he asked.

'Oh yeah, I know the Spurlings,' Rhoda said. She was eyeing the twins with an amused twist to her face. 'That adds up. And isn't the little guy the goddam image of the mom?'

Osi stared at her blankly.

'Are you friends then?' Isis asked.

Rhoda's face was asymmetrical, so that the wry expression was permanent. Perhaps she'd had an accident? Her small eyes were like currants pressed into a leathery bun.

'I know *of* them,' she repeated. 'Known of them for years. They're quite a *legend,* your folks.' The way she said it was not entirely nice, Isis was afraid, but perhaps the peculiarly squinty face just made it seem so.

For the journey, Haru bought flat discs of bread, white cheese and dates. Sitting with the sun glinting off the river and the breeze lifting her hair, Isis rolled dates and cheese in the bread and crammed her mouth and it was the most heavenly breakfast she had ever had. These dates had not the withered, dusty texture of the pantry ones, but a crisp, fresh sugaryness. There was clean water to drink, and if you are thirsty, that's the best thing, as Mary always maintained.

By now the sun was high in the sky and the thin sharp air of morning had turned thick and hot so that it was refreshing to be out on the river, where there was breeze enough for the *Marguerite* to skim.

Isis silently forgave Rhoda for her scorn, after all they *were* stupid names for English children, and it was a relief and a comfort to be in female company. Rhoda seemed all made up of strings and gristle, but was strong and agile, not like an old person at all, nothing like Mrs Grievous, and it cheered Isis to know that there were other women who wore trousers and no lipstick and who talked and acted and smoked like men. Perhaps Evelyn wasn't such an oddity as she had supposed; perhaps in Egypt that was *de rigueur*? She took a surreptitious sniff of Rhoda's arm when it was near her nose and the female smokiness caused a fierce dart of longing for her mother.

Marguerite was an elegant dhow, the tall sail scarlet as a runner-bean flower. There were places to sit at both ends and a covered section in the middle with canvas screens you could pull across. As soon as they cast off, Victor went under the cover and slumped down as if he'd been shot, while Osi hung over the side gawping. Haru and Akil didn't help at all, but sat and smoked and spat, grumbling and eyeing Rhoda coldly, but she clearly didn't give a fig and looked back at them with an equal measure of contempt. Isis stayed at the back of the boat with Rhoda who was navigating deftly between other boats – dhows, fellucas, rafts and the small crowded steamers run by the Cooks' holiday people. Rhoda said there was a craze for Egypt since the war and raised an eyebrow comically as if that was stupid.

It was cool on the river, the smooth green glide so much nearer and more intimate than the sea had been. The water bucked and writhed beneath the boards at first, but as they progressed they settled into an even slide. The rising smell of the water reminded Isis of ink, when you put your nose to the neck of the bottle – a dark, swilling breath of unborn words.

'In what way are they a legend?' she asked Rhoda.

'Huh?'

'Our parents.'

Rhoda was smoking a thin black cigarette, and she let smoke plume from her mouth before she spoke, in the very manner Evelyn did, as if the smoke was part of the process of the thought itself.

'I only meant that they're well known.'

'For what?' Isis said.

'For their *enthusiasm.*'

Isis frowned, not quite liking the way she said the word, as if there was something wrong with enthusiasm.

'Once they've found Herihor–' Isis began, but Rhoda choked on her smoke.

Politely, Isis turned away to let her recover herself. 'They really *will* be a legend then,' she said.

Rhoda threw the end of her cigarette into the water. 'There are all types of folks scrabbling to dig up the tombs these days. There's crooks and looters and treasure hunters, there's scholars, there's millionaires with nothing better to do with their money.' She paused, lifted her hand to shade her eyes. 'And then there's fools.'

Isis frowned at the glitter of the river. A pink flower floated past, and then a playing card and then a sandal. Perhaps someone's boat had gone belly up.

'And which are they?' she asked quietly.

Rhoda lit another cigarette, her thin lips crinkling into a starburst. 'It's all changed,' she said, 'since Independence, it's not so easy for amateurs and,' she lowered her voice, 'they resent the British coming in and taking all the loot, their *heritage,*' she corrected herself. 'And if you want my opinion, they've got a point.'

Isis blinked. It had never occurred to her that it might be *wrong* to take treasure out of the tombs and out of Egypt.

'It's more dangerous lately,' Rhoda continued. 'People like your folks, well, tell the truth, they're out of their depth.

Carter has the right idea,' she added. 'Bona fide foreman for his workers, funding from some nob – but even then there's –'

'*Mummy*,' Isis surprised herself with the word, 'is funding it all herself, from her estate.' More playing cards, a ribbon and what might have been a glove swept by. 'Look at all the things,' she added.

Rhoda nodded.

'Which are they?' Isis said again.

'Well,' Rhoda thought for a moment. 'They're not the greatest scholars, but they sure do make up for it in enthusiasm.'

'You said that. What's wrong with that? Mr Carter must be enthusiastic too.'

Rhoda lifted her hand to greet a white robed man on the bank. He shouted something in Arabic and she replied, her voice harsh and rattly and they both laughed.

'And they do nothing but study and read and search – they must be quite good scholars,' Isis said hotly. 'I should say they're very good scholars indeed. I shouldn't like to call them amateurs. '

A Chinese fan went past, flapping on the ripples like the wing of a bird.

'Well, like I say, there are some unscrupulous folks about,' Rhoda said. 'Folks that might take advantage of *enthusiasm*.' She steered the dhow past an island lush with trees and flowers, lit another cigarette and seemed disinclined to say any more.

Crossly, Isis moved away to where Osi was pestering Haru with unwanted information about the Temple at Abydos, which they had recently passed. He'd wanted to stop and look, but Rhoda said she wasn't in the business of doing a guided tour; she simply wanted to get there and back.

Isis put her head against the wooden side of the boat and

gazed at the banks of the Nile as they slid past like a biblical frieze: palm trees, long horned oxen tilling the soil, figures in robes with baskets on their heads, goats and sheep and corn, ibis, and sometimes a bird that looked like an eagle, swooping low. She watched a group of women kneeling by the banks wringing out clothes and spreading them on rocks to dry as their children played at the river's edge. Isis waved and one of the women lifted her hand and her child jumped and squealed and splashed excitedly.

She was still smarting with Rhoda's implication. Or perhaps it was more than an implication? But no, she surely couldn't mean that Evelyn and Arthur were fools? It was only the odd twist of her face that carried through into her voice that made it seem so. Rhoda was scornful of everyone, after all: the Cooks' tour people, Haru and Akil, probably Osi and Isis too. It was just her way. But she was right about one thing. It did seem wrong that foreigners could come into a country and take away its treasure. It was a fresh idea.

The worrying began to make her head ache and to distract herself she listened to Haru trying to tell Osi about Queen Hatshepsut, and Osi spoiling the story by interrupting and contradicting in an infuriatingly superior voice: 'I think you'll find . . .' until Haru grew quite sick of him and moved off to smoke and spit and mutter with Akil.

Everything will turn out in the wash, she told herself. *Look on the bright side*. It was lovely to watch the wake unfurling like watery ferns behind them, and the other craft sailing past. Sometimes a small boat would come close, trying to sell fish or trinkets, but Haru would send them off with a shout and a threatening jerk of his hand. And once there was a legless child hand-paddling a tiny raft and begging for baksheesh. Isis' heart hurt to see him, but all she could do was look away, just like the others.

As the day wore on, the heat pressed down and Osi's nose turned a nasty crimson. They should have sun hats. Victor should have thought of it. He wasn't really looking after them at all. He had his own Panama that he kept in a tube like a fat cigar, which popped into shape when he released it, and Isis had been looking forward to receiving one the same. Now the sun beat down and she could feel her skin burning, her hair seeming to sizzle in its own grease. When she talked and smiled, she could feel the skin of her cheeks pull tight. The sun reflected off the water like daggers in her eyes. She did not feel quite well, she realised – perhaps a touch of sunstroke.

She lay down on one of the wooden benches with her handkerchief over her face. She could see dots of light coming through the weave and it made her think of the neat rows of holes in the Cribbage board and of Mrs Grievous saying goodbye to her son, and fancy a mother going all that way for that reason, while Evelyn and Arthur had not even bothered coming to meet them at all.

The voyage took three days. At night Rhoda slept aboard the *Marguerite*, Akil and Haru went goodness knows where and Victor found rooms for himself and the children, poor rooms that scuttled with scorpions and black beetles, where bed was a shelf and a sheet, sometimes not even a pillow. They grew used to kneeling on the floor to wash their hands and faces with cold water from a bowl and eating in darkened rooms or sitting outside in the cool of the evening when bats and great moths swooped and looped in the air around them. In the garden of one such place, Isis was entranced to see a swarm of fireflies rise from a shrub, so that it seemed the bush itself was rising and flickering, and settling back elsewhere.

As they neared Luxor, they stopped at a place run by American friends of Rhoda's, who sold ice-cream which was heavenly, though as she ate her dish of creamy yellow, Isis was made uncomfortable by the dark eyes of the other customers watching her in the too-tight frock where her chest itched and grew, looking at her legs where the skirt was rather too short. She felt grubby and cramped and childish, but not in a pretty, pettable way any more. It was as if the hot sun and the fertility that oozed out into the desert from the Nile was forcing her, like a hothouse flower, to swell till she did not fit herself.

14

'GOOD LUCK, KIDS,' Rhoda said when they had disembarked at Luxor. 'You're sure gonna need it.' She pinched her cigarette between her lips as she reached forward to tie a rope around a stanchion. Isis watched her clever monkey fingers tighten and secure the knot.

'Why don't you come and have a cup of tea with us?' she said, finding herself unwilling to say goodbye. 'My folks will certainly want to thank you.'

Rhoda's face twisted into its wonky smile and she patted her pocket. 'I've all the thanks I need.' She jerked her head over her shoulder. 'You need eyes in the back of your head in these parts. Be careful.' She came close to Isis and whispered, 'Most of the Arab fellas you could trust with your life. But till you know them, best trust no one.' And then she lifted her hand and stalked off. Her gait was as skewed as her face. Isis watched until she was lost amongst the crowd of men in jellabas, the porters and traders, the dogs and donkeys and camels, the mothers holding the hands of tiny dark-haired children.

'Nearly there,' Victor said. Isis smoothed down her smutty

dress. She felt a perfect fright. Victor's bristles practically constituted a beard now, glinting an unexpected gingery colour under his pale flop of hair. Osi simply didn't bear looking at.

Haru bade them wait while he and Akil went to find some transport. Isis sat on a low wall, Osi and Victor on either side, and hugged her knees, watching the traffic of horses and camels and a few motors. A Cooks' steamer went past, the faces of its passengers startling pink and white, like a row of marshmallows under shady hats. She could see a lady sipping something long and cool through a straw and felt she would explode with longing. Now that they were near, her pent up anger with Evelyn and Arthur caused her nails to dig sharply into her palms, nails that needed cutting, palms that needed, as always, to be washed.

A man with one white, blind eye bowed and knelt, laying out his wares on a cloth in front of them – beads, scarabs, cats, ankhs and pyramids. There was a tiny turquoise cat that Isis coveted, but before she could reach for it, Victor had sent him packing, shaking his fist and shouting in nervy English that they wanted none of his tat. Hawking a long brown stream of spittle, the man gathered up his merchandise, muttering curses. As he left, he twisted his head over his shoulder and fixed on Isis with his sightless eye and though she knew it couldn't see her, she was filled with a strange sick shame.

'We could have bought *something* from the poor blighter,' she said.

'They weren't genuine artefacts, Isis,' Osi said, in Arthur's voice. 'It's only tourist tat.'

The man had gone now, but he'd left a speck of white in Isis' vision that she couldn't quite blink away. Victor said nothing, only scratched his neck where the beard was growing round the edges of his scar, the ginger horrible against the livid shiny red.

Another fellow approached them with straw hats, a column of them nested into each other, balanced on his head.

'We do need hats!' Isis said. She jumped up and the man smiled and clowned, moving his head in such a way that the tower of hats swayed and almost toppled.

'We'll take two.' Victor held up two fingers. And as soon as he had bought them, other men and boys came crowding round, with toys and drinks and food wrapped in banana leaves, offering bags of spices, sweets and taxi rides and boat trips, ignoring Victor's pleas for them to go away. It was with great relief that Isis spotted Haru and Akil returning with a donkey and cart.

For hours they all sat on the cart in the lumpy, sweltering heat. It was dangerous for there was nothing to stop them falling off, and Isis kept a tight hold of Osi's ankle though he tried to wrench it from her sweaty hand. Whenever the donkey slowed or stumbled, Haru jeered and whipped it with bamboo.

'Poor donkey,' she whispered to Victor. 'Can't you tell him not to hit it?'

'Leave him to it,' Victor said. 'It'll be the only language it understands.'

She thought she would get off and walk to save the donkey that extra weight, but in truth she was too stunned by heat to shift herself. They would probably have died without the hats, she thought, grateful for the speckled shade across her eyes.

When the cart stopped, at last, the sun was already slumping towards the horizon, a swollen, feverish red. The place they were in looked like no place at all, except that a camp had been set up there, with a stove built of sand-coloured stones, one large khaki tent and several smaller. They were far enough away from the river that the surrounding trees appeared as nothing but a green stain shimmering in the distance.

Here, Haru had expected that they would meet Evelyn and Arthur – though there was no sign of them and no message.

'Where are they?' Isis shouted at the only person there, a tall youth, too young to have a proper beard yet.

The boy opened his hands and looked helplessly at Haru.

'Aren't we even going to a proper *house*?' she said, looking at Victor, who only gave a miserable shrug.

'Selim.' Haru embraced the boy in such a way that Isis guessed he was his son or nephew, and skidded her eyes away from this show of familial affection. After their greeting, Haru and Selim fell into a rapid, furious conversation, and she sensed a horrid twinge of wrongness in the air. The anger she had pent up ready for Evelyn and Arthur had no choice but to drain uselessly away.

'Where is their house?' she said, 'Where do they live?' But no one answered and she went to pet the donkey, who had at least been given a bucket of water, but at her touch he jerked his head and went for her with his great yellow pegs of teeth.

'Leave him,' Haru called peremptorily and muttered something disparaging in Arabic before he showed them where to wash and relieve themselves – in a structure like a khaki sentry box – and pointed out the tents in which they were to sleep. Isis crawled inside hers and sat within the mosquito net on the thin sleeping mat, hugging her knees, glad for some moments on her own. But it was stuffy in the tent and there were ants in the seams. She spent some time trying to flick them away but gave up, crawled out and wandered off.

The flat, dry smell of the sand was like the smell of old books, which she had always known would be the scent of Egypt, a breath of something dry and sour and ancient that coated her tongue, a taste impossible to rinse away.

In her wandering she came upon some ruins, a sort of rubbish dump of broken columns, and bits of statue – the toes of an enormous foot protruding from the ground as if a stone giant had plummeted into the earth. Many of the fragments were etched with sand-scoured hieroglyphs – which Osi was already copying urgently into his diary as if they wouldn't still be there tomorrow.

She wandered about exploring, though in truth there was nothing much to explore, and any moment the sun would fall away. She found a few fragments of shell and stooped to pick them up. How could there be shells so far – she had no idea how far – from the sea? Already there were dark red shadows on the gritty ground and the air was heavy with the buzz of flying things. She was unnerved by the sideways slithering of a little snake and shrieked as she caught the movement of a larger animal, but it was only a dog – in fact, there was a small pack of dogs prowling near – one of them a tufty black pup. She moved towards it, clicking her fingers and clucking encouragement, but Haru came roaring over and hacked the pup in the ribs so that it yelped and slunk away.

'How dare you!' Isis shouted, angry enough to kick Haru and see how he liked it, but he turned and scowled so darkly into her face that she quailed. And he told her that these were scavengers and scroungers, not soppy British pets. You had to keep them scared or they'd steal food and bring in fleas. And there was also every chance, he added, that they were rabid.

15

AT FIRST LIGHT, Haru sent Selim off with the donkey to locate Evelyn and Arthur, and it was left to Osi and Isis to amuse themselves. With no spare clothes or books there was little to arrange and, for Isis, absolutely nothing to do.

Victor was sitting on a canvas chair outside his tent, smoking. 'Do you suppose they're all right?' she asked him, and thinking of what Rhoda had said. 'Do you think we can trust Haru and Akil?'

'You can't trust your Arab further than you can throw him,' Victor said. 'But what choice do we have?'

'Selim seems nice,' she said.

'*Nice*!' he laughed. 'Christ almighty. Don't go making eyes at Arabs.'

'I didn't mean it like that.' Blood surged to her cheeks.

He tilted his head back to observe her from under the brim of his Panama. 'Any of them touch you and they'd be stoned to death,' he said. 'That or have their hands chopped off. Now leave a chap in peace, there's a good girl.'

Isis stamped away, shocked and scowling. *Hands chopped off?* She avoided Victor for a while and mooched about collecting cusps of shell that were shaped liked smiles or frowns depending on how you looked at them.

When her hands were full she went to show Osi, who was sitting cross-legged in his tent, reading. She knelt and put her head inside; it smelled awfully strongly of dirty boy. He took a piece of shell, fingered it and held it up to the light. 'From the Great Flood, I suppose,' he said, 'three thousand years ago.'

'What, *Noah's* flood?'

His face sharpened. 'Ah, interesting question –' he began and cleared his throat, preparing for a lecture.

'It's all right,' she said, and scrambled up, hurrying towards the WC tent in a pantomime of urgency.

Later, she lay in her tent scratching a new set of bites on her leg and watching the sun sparkle through the weave, noticing how it showed up like shadow puppets the flies and other creatures crawling on the exterior. She fell into a trance watching the patterns of their separate journeys. It was perfectly true what Victor said. There was no option but to trust.

She arranged the bits of shell inside her tent to make flowery patterns. Shells that were 3,000 years old – or even older, and they did have a tiredness about them, worn smooth of detail by time and scouring sand.

All she had to read was *Desert Longing*, which at least was appropriate in terms of landscape, though the story desert was far more picturesque than the real one, with not a single mention of the flies that landed on traces of damp at the corners of your mouth and tried to crawl inside your eyes. Not a mention of the grit that got everywhere, between your fingers and toes, into your belly button and the backs of your knees, into the roots of your hair and between your teeth, crunching in everything you ate.

The story desert was full of shifting silken sands and sweetly scented breezes, of full moons and plangent birdsong in cool, leafy oases. She already knew her favourite sections of the book off by heart and would murmur them when bored and baking and alone in her tent.

Nobly silhouetted by the full moon, the Arab Prince stood motionless but for the stirring of his robes. Lady Fleur approached with trepidation, velvet-clad feet treading as silently and delicately as the paws of a cat. She thought him unaware of her presence, of her very existence, so transported by his reverie was he. In consequence she took courage and crept near enough to see the moonlight glisten on the ebony of his hair and his fine stately profile. And then with one sudden movement he turned and reached for her, his breath cool on her burning face, and she could not prevent a cry and a shudder as he grasped her so strongly. With midnight eyes he gazed down into her face, those cheeks so pale with shock, her curls dishevelled in the desert breeze.

'I did not see you there,' she said, ashamed to have been discovered in her stealth. 'I will leave you to your thoughts.'

'My thoughts were but of you,' he said, lips held so close to hers that she could feel their warmth and smell the sweet aniseed of his breath.

Sweet aniseed. She would like to smell that on someone's breath. Neither Haru's nor Akil's could possibly smell of anything but tobacco and dirty teeth, and as for the reek of Uncle Victor's . . . She cupped her hands round her own mouth and breathed and sniffed and sighed, longing for a toothbrush.

When Selim returned it was with news that Evelyn and Arthur would follow, so that the atmosphere became freshly taut with expectation. Haru cuffed Selim round his ears for returning without them, which Isis thought tremendously unfair.

'Why don't we go and see *them*?' she said. 'They can't be that far away.'

'Unsuitable conditions, Icy,' Victor said.

'But if it's unsuitable for us, it must be for them,' she pointed out. 'Anyway, surely *these* are unsuitable conditions?'

Victor only shrugged. Isis stamped away from him, but it was too hot for temper. Mutinously, she imagined the horse and hound in their unsuitable conditions – eating from nose-bags and dishes on the floor, no doubt, and bedding down in straw. Unsuitable conditions! From a little distance she looked back at the shabby khaki encampment. If you half closed your eyes and squinted through your lashes the tents dissolved against the brown desert as if there was nothing there at all.

At least Selim was back. That cheered her. She watched from a distance as he stood with Haru, talking and laughing. He was friendly, and at least when no one else was looking, would return her smiles. He seemed to be about her age, or maybe a little older? If only he spoke English she would ask him – she didn't dare ask Haru who was in a permanently bad humour. Though he was tall, Selim was slight, with thick, shadowy lashes and his nose was as absolutely, fascinatingly straight as if someone had drawn it using a ruler.

A fine stately profile.

Behind the pile of ruins, the dogs slept and Isis went there each day, to visit the pup. The other dogs, three of them, were bigger and yellow-haired and after an initial sniff took no notice of her, but the pup, whom she called Sweep, began to run up to her and lick her fingers when she fed him scraps of food. He had a way of tilting his head and looking up at her with his ears forward and his brown eyes fixed intently on her face that made her heart contract. No one had ever paid her quite so much attention.

He did have fleas, it was true, that often jumped from their camouflage in his coat to visibility on her arm, and now she had flea bites along with the marks of ants and mosquitos all over her.

It was a sort of torture to be tense with expectation, yet at the same time bored, as hour followed hour followed tedious hour. Victor was no company, Osi was busy with his 'work' and Haru only spoke to any of them when it was necessary; Selim didn't have more than a word of two of English and besides Isis had the sense that Victor was watching, ready to preclude any friendship which might grow between them. And Akil rarely spoke at all, only to Haru in rapid tetchy volleys of Arabic.

Isis gave up on the lot of them and spoke to herself instead, muttering the words of *Desert Longing*, or rehearsing the scolding she would give her parents when they arrived, and when Haru wasn't looking she crept away to train the pup.

Akil washed their clothes each night and they all – even Victor – wore robes while their own garments dried. Everything was too long for the twins, but Victor rather fancied himself in Arab dress, Isis thought, since he kept his blue robe on long after his own clothes were dried to a crisp in the sun.

After a few days, the camp began to seem an ordinary

place to be. In the mornings Haru would take the donkey to a nearby village, and sometimes Selim went with him. Isis would be filled with envy as she watched them shrink and shimmer away towards the vague green haze of the river valley. Why could not the camp be there, instead? Why could they not be in the village? Or in Luxor? Evelyn and Arthur *must* have a house, after all. Why could they not wait there? Or in an hotel?

Oh for some waving green and cool shade. But at least she knew Haru would return with water, vegetables and lemons, coconuts and pineapples, fish and sticky pastries, coffee and tobacco. Sometimes he'd bring an English newspaper and Isis would devour every word of it. The weather in England had been unseasonably warm – a proper Indian summer – which Isis hoped Mary had enjoyed; something awful was happening in Ireland and George Cadbury, the chocolate man, had died. She hoped that didn't mean an end of Cadbury's Chocolate Flakes, of which she intended, one day, to eat a lot.

She was relieved there was nothing about Mr Carter or King Tut. If anyone *were* to make a big find it might as well be Evelyn and Arthur. The paper left newsprint on Isis' sweaty hands and she transferred smutty fingerprints onto the pages of her book, making deliberate patterns like daisies on the flyleaf.

Now that he had achieved his purpose and delivered his charges as far as he could, Victor had gone meek and flaccid. And he was having nightmares again, screaming and vomiting in the deep of the night, dreaming, she must suppose, of Gallipoli. Whatever Haru, Selim and Akil must think of him, she could not imagine. If white chaps were supposed to be superior, then he wasn't a very good example. When such thoughts occurred to her, she would look at Selim, going so gracefully about his tasks, at his delicacy and beauty – somehow he looked fresher than everyone else, fresh and vivid – and then her eyes would return to the disgraceful, reeking slump of Victor and she would be ashamed of her own kind.

Early in the mornings, the air would be cool and carry wisps of green scent from the Nile, which soon became blurred with the smell of cigarettes and coffee. Each morning, Victor would drink cup after cup of it, as he emerged from his nightmares to settle into his daytime idleness. She should try and distract him, she thought. He had run out of pills, not expecting to be away so long, and probably he needed more than pills. Perhaps he would need to go back to hospital for more electric shock treatment when they got back to Blighty.

She went and squatted down beside him. His glass cup was half full of coffee grounds, thick as tar.

'How can you drink that stuff?' she said, and when he didn't answer: 'Will you play cribbage with me?'

He peered at her with bleary, sore-looking eyes and shook his head.

'If Mary was here, she'd play,' she said.

He snorted. 'Can you imagine Mary here?'

'I can't actually imagine *me* here,' she said, and Victor harrumphed.

'Dear little Icy.'

Noticing a fond sort of thickening in his voice, and too hot for any petting, she moved an arm's length away. He was missing the company of women, of course, perhaps secretly pining for Melissa, but when she asked him he only shrugged as if Melissa was gone from his mind. Whenever she read *Desert Longing*, the pages darkening under her sweaty hands, she was troubled by the memory of Melissa, the smoky violet scent, the way her body was there, hidden by her clothes, but still shouting *here I am*. Uncle Victor had probably kissed her in the dark of the cabin, kissed her and done more, hot and naked secret things. Her stomach felt dark and tight when she thought like that, and she stood and stamped and swung her arms to drive away the feeling, which was surely wrong.

'We should take a present back for Mary,' she decided. 'What shall it be?'

Victor only lit himself another cigarette.

'Do you think she'd like a dog?' she said.

'A dog!' he scoffed, and added startlingly: 'Hot stuff, Mary.'

Isis gaped. 'Do you mean to say *you* like Mary?'

'How could anyone not like Mary? She's a peach.'

'But in a romantic way?'

He sighed out feathers of smoke.

'Victor?' Isis looked at him with fascination, as a new notion occurred to her. 'Have you ever kissed Mary?'

'Not for want of trying,' he said with a shame-faced grin.

Isis was careful only to go behind the ruins when Haru was away from the camp. With some success she was training the pup to sit, and she planned for him also to learn to play dead and to walk on his hind legs. Once Evelyn and Arthur saw him at his tricks, how could they resist him? On the day she first got him to sit on command, she looked round, bursting with pride and wishing someone could witness her success – and discovered that Selim was watching.

If she had not already been so hotly red she would have

blushed. He was leaning against a broken pillar, arms folded, definitely watching her from beneath the sweep of his lashes. She lifted a hand and he smiled, teeth dazzling in his brown face, and her own mouth stretched into a grin.

'Hello,' she called softly.

He only continued to watch and smile. She ordered Sweep to sit again, but perhaps there was less conviction in her voice now and he only jumped up at her legs, yapping for a treat and when she looked back over her shoulder, Selim had gone.

16

Flopped on his side in the shadow, Sweep was fast asleep. Isis longed to poke him awake, but it wouldn't be fair. His paws were twitching as if he was running in his dream. She sat on the giant toes that projected from the sand, it was quite comfortable if you wiggled your bottom into the cleft between the big toe and the next one, and hugged her knees. With her ears full of the hum of flies, she was on the brink of dozing off, when she sensed movement. She turned her head and found that Selim was standing close beside her, his robe almost brushing her shoulder.

He said something, pointed to the pup and smiled. She loved that smile, she thought, and was shot through with fright. Love? Such smooth lips, the colour of milky cocoa, such white teeth, eyes deeper black than ink. How could anything so black be so bright and sparkling? His eyes held hers and she flushed and looked away. No, not *love*, just a beautiful smile in the midst of all the boredom.

Still smiling, he crouched beside her, pointed to the pup and said a word, tilted his head on one side.

'Dog,' she said.

'Dog,' he repeated.

'That's right! Dog!'

'Dog,' he said again, and they both laughed with the pleasure of this communication.

She put her hand on her own chest. 'Isis,' she said, although he probably already knew her name, but it was lovely to hear him say it in his heavily-accented, slightly gruff, boy's voice. It was probably the proper Egyptian way of pronouncing it and she repeated it back, like him. He was close enough for her to smell – not aniseed, just a healthy scent of skin and hair. The pup twitched and whimpered in his sleep and they smiled at each other.

'Hair,' Isis said, pointing to her own, then wishing she hadn't drawn attention to it, such a dirty mess.

'Hair,' he said, pointing to his own.

'Mouth.' She touched her lips.

'Mouth.'

His face was very close to hers and as if someone else was lifting her hand, she reached out and with her index finger touched his exquisitely straight nose. 'Nose,' she said.

His eyes flickered, but smiling steadily he touched the tip of her nose and a bolt of electricity shot through her.

'Nose,' she said, her voice faltering.

Akil called and he stood abruptly.

'Nose,' he said and grinned before he walked away.

She sat blinking, hardly able to believe that she had dared to touch his nose and that he had touched hers. There was a feeling as if a firework was trying to go off in a cramped space inside her as she went over it again and again, the surprisingly cool, firm feeling of his nose, his finger pressing on hers. That flicker in his eyes. And then she looked down at her thick, red, bare knees and groaned. What must he see when he looked at her but a girl with dirty hair and bitten legs, bursting out of her too-small dress? What ever must he think?

She waited till she was sure he had gone before she trailed back where Victor was sitting under an awning on his canvas chair, smoking.

'They better bally well arrive soon or he'll slit our throats,' Victor said nodding across at Haru, who chose that moment to eye them fiercely.

'Don't be such a chump,' she said. 'What a perfectly ridiculous thing to say.' She tore her eyes away from Selim, who was telling Haru something. They both laughed, looking at her, she was sure. Her face burned. Haru was saying something and moving his hands in the air, making rounded shapes like bosoms. No, he couldn't be, he wouldn't be, she must stop imagining things to do with bodies, she was driving herself demented.

'Oh, I dare say they'll arrive soon,' Victor said. 'Perhaps today, you never know.'

'Or we could insist on being taken to them?' Isis said.

'No, best stay put. They know best.'

Isis unfolded a little canvas stool, and though she guessed he'd rather be left alone, seated herself beside him. 'Victor. I don't feel at all myself,' she said.

Victor smoked silently for a moment. His beard was thick round his mouth now, flecks like iron filings amongst the messy gingery thatch.

'No more do I,' he said, at last.

His fingers were dark yellow from all the smoking, and his teeth too, and with his red and staring eyes he looked really frightful, as if he were metamorphosing into something from his own nightmare. She recalled the terrible sounds he'd made in the night, the deep terrified bellowing, followed by the retching.

'You had another of your dreams,' she said. He grunted. 'What's in them?' she dared to ask and watched as his leg began to jump. He sucked in smoke and held it down.

'Mine are frightful at the moment too,' she said, encouragingly. 'I keep dreaming about being lost, or hearing bad news.' She stopped and frowned; she'd forgotten until that moment how last night she'd seen Evelyn and Arthur, tiny as dolls, dead and floating on a tea tray down the Nile.

'Rats,' said Victor. Roughly, he grasped her hand and held it against the jumping leg. 'The rats were bloody enormous in the trenches,' he said. 'You know how they got so big?'

Isis shook her head.

'By eating flesh. They were like this.' He let her go and jerked his hands a couple of feet apart. 'And their heads were white from eating all that man-meat. They were like fucking great luminous ghosts. But they were real. And they weren't scared. They'd look up at you and go right on gnawing at a fellow's face.'

'Oh,' whispered Isis, squeezing and rubbing her eyes to try and rid them of the image. It was stupid of her to have asked, and now his leg was jumping as if it wanted to be free of him and hop off on its own. 'Oh, fuck, fuck,' he was saying and trying with his fists to press it still. He shouldn't be saying that awful word, but he couldn't help it, she could see that, he was *beside* himself. What could she say? She looked for help to Haru, who was with Akil and Selim on the far side of the stove, but when she met his eyes he crossed his arms and turned away.

'Remember, you're a hero,' she said in a small voice.

He hacked up a rotten bit of laugh.

'They'll be here soon,' she said. 'And then everything will be all right. You see, Victor, it'll turn out all right.'

He laughed again, but it was more like vomit than anything joyful. Selim was staring at her, as if to see what she would do.

'I'm going to lie down,' she said, and slunk off to her tent.

Late the following morning, she lay propped on her elbows in her tent, draped in mosquito net, scratching at a swollen bite – flea, mosquito or some other desert creature. Her mind was in another desert, more picturesque than this, and her mind was filled with Lady Fleur and Lord Greatorix, and the love affair they conducted, even as they fled the handsome Arab Prince who, now that they had kissed, wanted Lady Fleur for his harem.

The Prince had a hooked and noble nose, eyes of liquid black, long, hard limbs; Selim, she thought, but older, and she changed the hooked nose to one that was beautifully straight, and she added thick shadowy lashes. Although he was bad in the book, the Prince made Isis' heart beat faster than Lord Greatorix did, especially when he tried to force his way into Lady Fleur's tent.

Lady Fleur had a tiny waist and tumbling, unruly curls and whenever she read that description, Isis' hand would go to the flat and dusty greasiness of her grown-out pudding-basin cut and it almost hurt to think what a fright Selim must think her. She thought about Victor, about the mewing sounds of Mimi and of Melissa's flagrant fleshiness, but always her thoughts returned to the darling straightness, the firm coolness, of Selim's nose. She rolled over on her back and mouthed the words on the final page.

And at last Lady Fleur was enfolded in the safe masculine strength of his embrace. 'Forever,' he murmured into the rosy shell of her ear.

'Truly? ' she questioned, exquisite lips aquiver.

'Forever,' he repeated, stilling her mouth with his fervent kiss.

She turned over to stare at the sun-bleached canvas above her. '*Forever*,' she whispered, '*forever and everandeverandever.*'

17

IT WAS CHOKING hot in the tent within the mosquito net; her underarms itched and there was a real pain in her belly now. 'I don't feel quite well,' she said aloud. 'I really don't feel myself.' But that is ridiculous, how can you not feel yourself? Though you can be beside yourself, or beyond yourself. When Victor had his nightmares that is exactly what he was: *beyond* himself.

She realised that there were new voices out there – longed-for voices. She sat up, struggled with the mosquito net, fought her way out of the tent and flung herself at Evelyn, who embraced her, though rather crossly, then pushed her away and stood looking at both twins.

'Look what a state they're in!'

Evelyn herself was darkly burned and, peering out from beneath a pith helmet, looked horsier than ever.

'It's not our fault!' Isis said. 'Where *were* you? Why didn't you meet us?'

'Well, evidently we were unable to come immediately.'

'But –' Isis' mouth hung open. All the worry and the waiting and the disappointment, even the fear, shrivelled in the scorching light to nothing but silly childish temper.

'And we're here now, aren't we? And you – you're here safely. What's the matter then?'

Isis' bottom lip begin to curl down as it used to when she was small, and then it would pull cords in her neck and make her sob. But not now, she was too grown-up now for that, and besides, Selim might be watching.

'Icy!' Arthur came striding across. His beard was a ridiculously whiskery fuzz reaching halfway down his chest, he was wearing a dirty pith helmet too and his pipe dangled from the corner of his mouth.

'Are we going to the excavation?' Osi said. 'Today? Now?'

Arthur cleared his throat. 'We've had, um, a bit of a . . . hiatus.'

'Another wild goose chase?' Isis said.

'Truth is,' Arthur continued, 'most of our labourers have gone off to work on Lord Carnarvon's dig. That bastard Carter seems to be getting warm.'

'Warmer than you?' Osi said. 'No! Let's go.'

'While we, um, regroup and so on, we thought we'd take you for an outing.'

Isis looked out at the hopeless desert.

'Children like outings,' Evelyn told her.

'Hello, there.' Victor had crawled out his tent. Isis saw how Evelyn recoiled when she saw him – bearded, red-eyed, shambling, the borrowed robe streaked filthily with food and coffee. 'You took your bally time.'

'Well, we're here now. I say, you do look a sight, Victor. Are you all right?'

'He's dreaming every night, of rats,' Isis told them. 'He needs more treatment, electric shock, I shouldn't wonder.'

Arthur eyed him dubiously and exchanged glances with Evelyn. 'Come here, Icy.' He gave her a hard hug amongst the smoky tickle of his beard and turned to Osi. 'How's my boy? As predicted, Haru's making a fuss about the funds,' he remarked to Evelyn over the children's heads.

'I've had devil of a job keeping him sweet,' said Victor.

Arthur grunted. 'Sweet's hardly the epithet I'd choose!'

'What's the matter with the fellow?' Evelyn said.

'We were stuck with no money and no nothing and not even a *toothbrush!*' Isis could not prevent her voice from rising to a shout.

'Aren't children supposed to be pleased to see their folks?' Evelyn said. 'Aren't they supposed to smile?'

Osi did make some sort of boat shape with his mouth, but Isis was too furious and her lips pinched tight against her teeth. Victor stood swaying, seeming not to know what to do. Arthur went back to Haru, who was in a huddle with Akil and Selim. Selim lifted his lashes and his eyes met Isis' and held for a second and there was the stupid flush again, boiling up like red ink under her burning skin.

Osi trotted after Arthur and stood beside him as an argument began. It was almost comical how son mimicked father's stance and his gesticulations, but Isis didn't feel the least bit like laughing. She went back into the tent, tied the fastenings and pulled down the mosquito net, though none of these soft fumblings were as satisfying as the slamming of a door would have been. She lay face down on her flat, grubby pillow and no, she didn't cry, not quite, but ground her face against the fabric, feeling idiotic. After all, they were safe and sound and none the worse, except . . . She jumped up and fought her way out of the tent again.

'The trunk's gone,' she yelled, 'with all and everything and even your soap too.'

'Victor told me,' Evelyn called back. She was sitting on a stool beside him, emptying grit out of her boots. 'How very careless of Haru.'

'Wasn't his fault,' Isis called back, though it must have been, she thought, at least in part.

She went back into the tent and reached for *Desert Longing*, but really she was bored with it. In the trunk there had been a few more books, and what she wouldn't give for something new to read, a story set anywhere but the desert.

Evelyn and Arthur were here, but they were just their disappointing selves, and what a terrible, ungrateful thought that was. There was an empty slump inside her, and she wondered if she had a fever. Her hands felt big and stiff and there were dazzling after-images in her eyes, specks of white; greasy blurs like the faces of Victor's rats. She bit her the inside of her arm as hard as she could and watched the colourless oval of tooth marks turning pink. Her head hurt and there was a weary feeling in her legs, a dirty sort of nagging in her belly.

'Come on, Icy,' Arthur called. 'Do buck up.'

'Do I have to come?' She could see the shadow of him looming over the canvas.

'We can't leave you here all alone, can we?'

You could, Isis thought, *and if it suited you, you would.* But she crawled out of the tent and straightened her dress.

'She's grown,' Evelyn said, eyeing the tightness of the dress across Isis' chest and the plump knees showing under the hem of her frock. 'Looks like someone's been at her with a bicycle pump!' and she hooted with laughter.

'Yes, she's growing up all right,' Arthur said, more kindly, and gave her a queer and curious look.

Isis flinched and looked towards Selim, but he had his back turned. 'Why have you come back now?' she hissed. 'Why not just leave us here for ever?'

'Icy!'

'And why did we have to come at all?'

'We thought you'd like it,' Arthur said.

'I like it,' came Osi's voice from somewhere. 'Are we going to the Valley of the Kings?'

'That place is over-run,' Evelyn said drily.

'But can't we go and see?' begged Osi.

'And join that throng of opportunists?' Arthur said.

'What about *your* king?' Isis asked.

'He's not a king, he's a general,' corrected Osi.

'Oh shut up,' Isis said.

Evelyn and Arthur exchanged dreary looks.

'And what about the map?' she said. 'You said it was definitely genuine. You said –'

'Well, that turned out to be bogus,' Arthur interrupted, ignoring Evelyn's scowl. 'But we do have new information,' he said. 'It turns out some scoundrel pulled the wool over our eyes, but Abdullah's sorted him out and now we have another lead.'

'But how do you know *Abdullah's* not a scoundrel?' demanded Isis.

'*You* don't know anything about it, Isis,' Osi said. 'You're not even interested. Please can we go and see Mr Carter's excavation?'

'No!' It was rare for Arthur to raise his voice and they all looked at him.

'There are the fools and those that prey on them,' Isis said into the silence and the rush of her heart caused a crackle of stars at the edges of her vision.

'What did you say?' Evelyn stared.

'You need eyes in the back of your head.' Isis heard Rhoda's voice in her own. And she remembered the blind white eye of the pedlar in Luxor. They should have bought something from him, that little turquoise cat, or a scarab for luck. Luck is what they needed. From the corner of her eye she could see the pup and looked away, afraid he'd come trotting across to greet her and earn himself a kicking.

There was the sound of an engine and a cloud of sand became visible in the distance.

'Ah ha, here's the transport. Punctual, eh? There you are, that's Abdullah for you, not your average Arab,' Arthur said.

Isis darted a look at Haru and Selim, who were surely near enough to hear.

The ball of dust came closer and out of it emerged a truck. The man who climbed out was fat, heavily stubbled and hatless. His hair was thick and grey and he wore European dress: dusty white trousers and a sweat-stained linen jacket. 'This is our excellent Abdullah,' Evelyn said. 'And here's Osiris, and this is Isis.'

Abdullah nodded and greeted the children with handshakes. 'I've heard so much,' he said.

'Really?' Isis said stiffly. She wiped the sweat of his palm onto her dress.

Osi began to bombard Abdullah with questions, and he held his hands up as if in defence and laughed. 'Steady on!'

'By the time he was twelve he'd mastered the three written

forms of ancient Egyptian,' Arthur boasted. 'Something of a prodigy, aren't you, son? Give him a few years and he'll be out here himself.' He clapped Osi, who seemed likely to burst with pride, on the back and Isis wandered away to watch Haru, who was angrily slinging food into the back of the truck. Selim lugged a sack of flour across and swung it high, but it hit the side and some of the pale powder spilled onto the sand. Haru shouted and clipped him on the ear. Selim flushed and slunk away.

'That's not fair,' Isis said. 'He didn't mean to.'

Haru made a noise in the back of his throat as if he'd like to spit.

'Why did we have to stay here?' Isis demanded of Evelyn who was tapping her foot and smoking a cigarette as she watched the scene through narrowed eyes. 'What about your house in Luxor? I thought we were going to stay in a proper house.'

'We no longer have a house,' Evelyn said shortly.

Isis stared as her mother sighed and sucked on her cigarette. She looked almost defeated and Isis felt a little stir of hope. 'Things have gone rather . . . pear-shaped, you might say.' And in a flat and uncharacteristic tone, Evelyn explained that there was a problem with money and that they seemed to have got themselves on the wrong side of the authorities, made some enemies, so to speak.

'*Enemies?*' Isis' voice came out in a screech. 'Why? What do you mean?'

Evelyn lifted her chin and sent out a stream of smoke.

'Why don't you give up then?' Isis said. 'Just for a while. Why don't you come home with us?'

'Impossible. Too much to sort out here.'

'Why?' Isis tried to catch her arm, but Evelyn flinched away and raised her eyes to heaven as if it was obvious.

'*Why* is it impossible?' Isis insisted.

'Don't be tedious, Isis. It's getting more and more difficult to get a concession – a license to dig. They've got so many ridiculous rules and regulations now! They're getting quite officious. Quite above themselves, if you ask me.'

Isis noticed Abdullah glancing over as she said that.

'But Abdullah's our man.' Evelyn continued in her loud embarrassing voice. 'Abdullah will pull strings and wangle one if anyone can.'

'But why should he?' Isis whispered.

Evelyn gave her a mystified look.

'Why would he want to help you find the treasure? Why doesn't he just get it for himself?'

'That's not how it works,' Evelyn snapped.

'After all, it is *Egyptian* treasure, not English.'

Isis caught Abdullah's smirk, before he turned his face away.

The lines between Evelyn's eyes were dark and gritty, grains were caught in her sparse eyebrows and her almost lashless eyes were rimmed with red; she looked as if she were going mad.

'Who've you been talking to?' she snapped.

'Oh, loads of people,' Isis said, gesturing towards the desert. 'All my throng of friends.'

'Sarcasm is the lowest form of wit.' Evelyn took out her cigarette box and lit herself another.

'But what if he's tricking you?' Isis said quietly, looking across at the man who appeared to be absorbed now in securing the picnic equipment to the back of the lorry.

'Why should he? We're the ones with the . . .' She frisked her fingers together to indicate money. 'Now, surely we must be ready. *Abdullah*!' she called imperiously as she stalked towards him.

18

EVELYN AND ARTHUR were travelling on their motor-bike and sidecar. To Isis' mortification, Evelyn, in pith helmet and monstrous goggles drove, while Arthur crammed himself into the sidecar, knees up round his ears as they roared away. Abdullah was to drive the lorry, with Victor and the children up front, which was a squash, with Haru, Akil and Selim balancing amongst the picnic equipment on the back.

Jammed beside her in the hot, fly-ridden cab, Osi spent the whole drive yakking and yakking about the 19th dynasty until Isis' jaw ached from the gritting of her teeth. Fortunately she had the window to her other side and was able to let her head hang out and ride along with the breeze in her hair and her eyes shut tight. Her head was heavy now and too big for her, like a melon lolling on its stalk. She felt bloated all over, but not with air as from a pump, it was more like a heavy fluid, weightier than water, like mercury, and she thought of the thin line of it in the thermometer at home and how once she'd broken one and Mary had let her keep the mercury in a match-box, like a slippery, silver pet. The thought of Mary sent a jag of homesickness through her and she snapped open her eyes.

A refreshing breeze overlaid the sour desert smell with a tinge of green, and loose sand blew in hazy patterns over the sunburnt earth. She tingled with the sensation of movement after being in one place for too long, and felt a small and unexpected spurt of gaiety. She was all right. Everything was, after all, all right. It had been an adventure getting here, but here they were, and on a family outing with a picnic promised, and perhaps she'd find the tomb interesting after all, if only Osi would shut his trap.

The truck caught up with Evelyn and Arthur, in the one place within the barren wilderness where there was actually a scrap of shade under a cluster of sickly palms. This, it seemed, was the picnic site. Isis climbed out and helped unfold the canvas picnic furniture, and then Evelyn, like a proper mother, took her to a place behind a boulder where she could relieve herself.

As they walked back to the others, Isis dared to take her hand, and Evelyn gave only the slightest flinch and did not pull away.

'Tell me, how has Victor been?' she asked, throwing a doubtful glance at her brother who was lolling against a rock, staring into the distance.

'All right. He's having nightmares though. Worse than ever.'

Evelyn compressed her lips. 'He did manage to get you here,' she said. 'I'm sure he'll be all right.' She let go of Isis' hand and strode across to talk to him.

Akil was making dough for the flat breads and Isis stole a piece and stowed it in her pocket. Selim was helping Akil by putting together the camping stove and Isis stood and watched, admiring the dexterity of his fingers. He did not look at her, of course, not with the others all around, but she thought she sensed a gathering of attention in his shoulders and neck and the back of his head.

The breeze flickered feathery shadows through the palms, and a flock of bright little birds chittered, almost like English birds. The smell of frying fish and fresh bread was delicious, and both Evelyn and Arthur were in fairly good humour. Even Victor seemed to have pulled himself together, though he made it clear that he was disappointed in the lack of anything but mint tea or water in the way of drinks.

As they settled to eat, Arthur put his hand jokily over Osi's mouth. 'Let your sister get a word in! How is it at home then, Icy? Tell all.'

'Nothing to tell,' Isis said. 'Oh, except the budgies have got out and set up home in the ballroom, on the chandelier.'

Arthur laughed and slapped his forehead so hard he dislodged his helmet. 'We must clear them out,' he said.

'What's the matter with Cleo?' Evelyn said. 'Don't we keep a cat to do for vermin and so on?'

'Budgies aren't vermin,' Isis said. 'And anyrate, how would a cat reach the chandelier?'

'*Anyrate*,' Evelyn said. 'Listen to her!'

'How about a dog?' Isis dared.

'That still wouldn't reach. You could send in a hawk,' Osi suggested.

'We could look into it,' Arthur said, through a squashed-down smile.

'Mary says *anyrate*,' Isis said, vexed. She looked to Victor for support, but he wasn't listening.

'Precisely,' Evelyn retorted.

But they were all smiling now and the smile spread to Isis.

Even Osi was acting like a normal happy boy, well almost. He was managing to resist the mention of Tutankhamen, which was unusually sensitive for him, enough to give Isis a flicker of hope that he might grow up to be normal after all. And there was a proper family feeling, and this was a *proper* family occasion, a picnic like other, normal, people had.

'Victor met a floozie on the boat,' she said, and got the desired effect from her parents: hoots of laughter, though Victor gave her a dented look and she felt a stir of disloyalty.

Abdullah, who had been standing and shading his eyes, turned and lifted his finger. 'Ah ha!' said Arthur. 'Now, for our surprise. Shut your eyes, until I say so.'

Isis almost shut her eyes, but could still see through her lashes if she tilted her head back, and with sinking heart she watched the arrival of a pair of camels, led by two tall men with utterly black skins and red turbans.

'You can look now,' Evelyn said.

The camels towered ridiculously, blinking down at Isis as they chewed the cud with their vast brown teeth. Their hair was full of grit and their eyes with spite, and she didn't want to go anywhere near them. Arthur's plan had had been that she would ride with Evelyn and he with Osi, but she did not want to be up there, so high, her own height today was questionable.

'These fellows are Nubians,' Evelyn said in her loud, confident voice. 'Rather handsome in their way, don't you think?'

'They *can* hear you,' Isis muttered, edging away from the camels.

'She's scared,' Osi said. 'Isis is scared!' Usually that taunt alone would have been enough to make her do anything, just to show them.

'So what?' she said. 'I can walk.'

'Where *does* she get it from?' Evelyn complained.

Isis felt Selim's eyes on her and the blood rose to her cheeks.

'It's supposed to be a treat, Icy,' said Arthur.

'Spoilsport.'

'If she doesn't want to, she doesn't want to,' put in Victor.

'I don't feel quite myself,' Isis said.

Though their face held no particular expression, she sensed that the Nubians were jeering too, but it didn't matter, the more they jeered the more she'd dig her heels in – no, don't think that – she lurched at the thought of sinking heels. The nearest man stared down at her from his elegant height until she looked away, and then he spoke rapidly to Haru.

'Will you ride the donkey?' Haru asked.

'He doesn't like me,' she said.

Haru hacked out a laugh and, in Arabic, repeated what she'd said to Akil and the camel men who all looked from Isis to the donkey and hooted and slapped their sides.

'Come on, Missy,' coaxed Abdullah.

Selim was stroking one of the camels. Isis met his eyes and read encouragement there. She must seem really pathetic to him, to be so afraid of what to him would be a normal, every-day event.

'Oh, very well then, if I must,' she said. 'But I don't see why I shouldn't walk.'

'It's easy once you're up,' Arthur told her. 'And the camel will kneel, see.' He barked something at one of the men and he made the smaller creature, the paler of the two, get awkwardly down on its knobbled knees and prostrate its long neck on the ground.

'There, see how friendly.' Abdullah smiled and as she stared at his face, the bland and insincere shine of it, she knew with a pang of clarity that he would never lead Evelyn and Arthur to the tomb. That he had taken them for fools. That he was fleecing them and they were like children in their eagerness to believe in him. Unable to bear it, she looked away.

She managed to clamber onto the camel, and Evelyn sat behind her and at a word from the camel man, the creature unfolded itself like an ironing board and they rose upwards. Isis and Evelyn set off first, Osi and Arthur behind them, and Victor was roared away in the truck with Abdullah, Selim and Haru.

The gait of the creature was uneven and swaying and at first she felt the need to cling to the ridge of her saddle. But soon her body grew used to the rhythm, and although she was sore and chafed with sand and sweat, pressing down on the saddle gave her an oddly exhilarating sensation, a kind of pleasant ache, and though her head felt huge and full of wadding, she enjoyed the rocking movement and wished they could go faster and faster and gallop between the high sandy cliffs.

Osi and Arthur's camel came up beside theirs and the two creatures twisted their snaky necks to hiss and spit at one another and she found herself laughing, they were so preposterous with their giant liquid eyes and glamorous lashes and she enjoyed the sun-baked tang and rough, dull texture of camel hair.

'Fun, Beastie?' said Evelyn from behind her, and Isis gave a nod and smiled.

19

AFTER AN HOUR or so they approached the cliffs and the men commanded the camels to kneel. Isis' legs were rubbery as she clambered off and sparks flew in her eyes. It was the sun, only the sun, but it pressed down on her with heavy hands, and the ground was so gritty bright it made her squint. Sweat trickled from beneath her hat, stinging her eyes with sharp salt. The lorry had already arrived, and Victor and Haru were leaning back against it, smoking as they waited. Selim shot her a quick bright look and turned his head.

Abdullah paid the camel men and they mounted and rode swiftly away, the soft splayed feet that had plodded so soggily, taking off into a hectic lollop, fast and thrilling, as if it was a race.

Since the Great Place – the Valley of the Kings – was swarming with tourists and journalists, they were to visit a tomb belonging to one of the tomb-makers, Arthur explained, rather than to a pharaoh. Here was quieter, more suitable for a family visit and – though, of course, the mummy and all the grave goods were long gone – there were particularly fine and interesting decorations to be seen.

Before they set out on their trudge, they ate slices of orange and drank warm, goaty-tasting water from a skin bag. First of all, Arthur and Evelyn took them part of the way up the cliff for a good view of Deir El Medina. This had been a village populated by the builders who made the tombs for the pharaohs. They would begin the work, Arthur told them, the moment a new pharaoh was crowned, so that the monarch was able to travel from Thebes and see the progress of his own resting place.

'Imagine standing in your own tomb!' Isis said, staring down at the pattern of sand-coloured ruins. You could clearly see the outline of houses and streets.

'I wouldn't mind,' said Osi, and pointing: 'Is that the Temple of Hathor?'

'Quite right.' Arthur patted his head. 'The tomb-makers were an uppity lot, don't you know,' he said, 'a lot of artistic temperaments and so on – and not above going on strike if they weren't satisfied with their rations – and they ate like lords. And of course they made their own tombs beautifully. We've got some superb examples of 19th an 20th dynasty – you wait and see . . .' His voice skipped with supressed excitement.

The entrance was nothing but a heap of rubble that you might pass without noticing, but at Abdullah's instruction, Selim and Haru hauled stones out of the way to reveal a rough panel of planking. At the shifting of the wood, a mouth yawned open in the rock. Though she was hot, goose-pimples riffled over Isis' skin, and her stomach clenched at the thought of being swallowed down there.

Abdullah issued them all with torches and began to explain about entrances and antechambers while Osi interrupted and contradicted. Before her irritation could overtake her, Isis took the dough from her pocket, dampened it with the sweat from her palms and stuffed it in her ears. The warm dough swelled, blocking Osi's voice, everyone's voice, in lovely bready silence. It was a strange effect – the soundless wagging of everyone's chin – and she became aware of a rushing sound coming from inside herself, that must have been the passage of her own blood, the secret sound of self.

Osi went in first with Abdullah, Haru, Selim and Victor. Evelyn followed and then, reluctantly, shoved along by Arthur, Isis entered the cracked lips of rock and stumbled down the throat, floored roughly with splintery planks. Stuck on ledges in the lumpy rock were candles and beneath them complex gnarly veins of trickled wax. A dry, knowing kind of smell caught in her nostrils and she caught up with Evelyn and clung to her arm; *it'll only be a minute, it'll only be a minute*, she told herself. Evelyn frowned down at her, said something silent and pulled her arm away.

Selim had grazed his knuckle on a rock or the rough wood; she saw him wipe away a trickle of blood and then suck at the wound. His eyes were deeply shadowed by his lashes but he looked up and met hers in a long, unsmiling gaze. She looked away. Abdullah was showing them the three chambers of the tomb, teeth flashing as he pointed out details in the decoration. She stood apart from the group, seeing them as fish in an aquarium with their silently opening and closing mouths.

She turned to stare at the skin of pigment on the walls that in the wavering torchlight appeared so freshly painted as to be still wet. The air was stiff and stale, like the air trapped in a dead person's lungs, and she felt a flutter of panic. The images made the blood beat harder, like birds trapped in her ears, and she lifted her hands to try and remove or loosen the dough, but it had cooked tight in her ear canals and her fingers were disconnected and clumsy as if she were trying to operate the vast, numb hands of a puppet.

Osi's mouth flapped open and shut as if his jaw was coming unhinged and Abdullah, Haru, Victor, Arthur and Evelyn all of them were talking excitedly, sliding their torch beams about and pointing at images – here was the richness of lapis and gold, here was a star chart, and images of fish and ducks and cows and suns and sheaves of wheat and here was Anubis and Horus and Bastet and boats and scales and everywhere tiny working figures with their sideways faces and their forward facing eyes and on the ceiling, the Goddess Nut, wings stretched open, swallowing the sun.

Victor caught her eye and winked, but he appeared so ghastly, with his brown teeth emerging through the beard, half lit by wobbling torchlight, that she tore her eyes away, swallowing down a surge of panic. Selim was standing near her, sucking at his damaged knuckle, separate from the crowd of them.

Her eyes snagged on an awful creature – part crocodile, part hippo, part lion – that seemed to quiver into movement. She might have made a noise of fright, Selim was gazing at her steadily, eyes too dark to see but for a flash of white. Evelyn tapped her on the shoulder to point something out, and Isis' mouth filled up with the taste of dirt.

Time went as stiff and sluggish as the air and she could no longer tell if she were hot or cold, only that her temperature was wrong. The lines were so precise and clear and clean, and stuffed up in her skull she could hear the artist licking the end of his brush, hear his breath, the wet of his tongue, and his brush strokes, feel them on her skin, and there was an incantation or a drum, not her own heart, it was words, ancient words travelling up her through the floor and the mocking grin of a crocodile.

And after some time, she did not know how long, they must have started to move, to leave; Evelyn first, was it? The hole of her mouth opening on darkness to say something, someone shook her, did they? And then she was alone, she thought alone; this was where any clearness ended.

Was there someone behind her, breathing on her neck? Selim? Her hand hauled up to her mouth and her head went back till she saw the Goddess Nut, on the ceiling, a great winged figure with a flat pudding-basin cut and long black eyes. And as she saw Nut she also saw her own face looking up and with a sucking sensation was flattened onto the ceiling, thin as paint and motionless, fingers stiffened into quills, while a commotion went on below: a girl falling – a silly pastel pink amongst the lapiz, azure, gold and dark – and a beast, bird was it? struggling with her. She was nothing but a skin of pigment, an ancient glitter – and then she was plummeting hot and solid, a thud against the floor, and one of the earplugs was dislodged and time, which must have stopped, resumed with an eager hum and there were footsteps thudding away, unless it was her heart.

And after a gap Evelyn was pulling Isis to her feet, then stopping and staring, putting out a finger to touch some wet on Isis' face, and straightening her frock and frowning at the dirt and shouting for Arthur as she dragged her into the sting of the blinding sun. And they were all round her then, hand to her forehead: 'She's burning up,' someone said, but no, she was slippery ice, and there were handkerchiefs and water bottles and a dabbing and a cleaning of her face, a worrying at a rip in her dress, at a smudge of blood on her chest, but not at the dark shame of wet between her legs.

Evelyn bundled her in the sidecar and roared back to the camp. Eyes screwed tightly shut, Isis felt the desert wind scouring her face. And then for days she lay alone in her tent, prickling in the light and shivering in the dark, watching the flies on the outside, the ants running along the thick, gritty seams and listening to how the humans went on out there. When her eyelids closed, as they would of their own accord however much she struggled, there was the beast and the pudding-basined Goddess, stiff fingered, painted eyes stretched dry and blind, and there was a coldly grinning crocodile. Sometimes she shivered; sometimes she sweated.

Evelyn told her the sluggish leak of blood between her legs was the curse. 'Trust you to choose here and now.' Awkwardly she instructed Isis how to deal with it. Though it was gruesome it was a normal thing, Evelyn told her, but never in her life would Isis bleed without the memory of the tomb and a smothered confusing sensation, a wet filament deep inside her, like a shooting streak of gold.

As well as the onset of the curse, she had a touch of malaria, it was decided, and for days lay swaddled in mosquito nets, watching shadows, listening to life going on outside the tent.

She lost all sense of time as she lay feeling her heart thump on and on as if bored with its own repetition. At first she couldn't make sense of anything anyone said to her. It was as if she had a fever in her brain. She could eat nothing, but drank gallons of water, queerly tinged with quinine. Sometimes Osi came into her tent, and he didn't talk, just sat turning the pages of a book, and there was comfort in the silent presence of her twin.

20

It was past dawn when Evelyn woke Isis by crawling into the tent. The space was too small, and when she was crammed, crouching, knees cricking, beside Isis, her head made the canvas bulge and the light filtering through cast her skin in a greenish hue.

'I've got some fresh water for you here. Hungry yet?'

'Maybe.'

Evelyn put her hand on Isis' brow. 'Cooler, thank Heaven.'

'I want to go home and see Mary,' Isis said

'As soon as you're well enough to travel.'

'I am well enough.'

'Sure?' Evelyn scrunched down so that her face was too close to Isis' and peered at her as if she were a curious specimen. 'So, you're feeling more like it?'

Isis stretched her toes and fingers and moved her head, which felt like the right-sized head. 'I do,' she said. 'More like myself,' she added, but that was not quite right. What was herself? She could hardly remember. She propped herself up on her elbow to sip the water.

'Then it's about time you told me exactly what happened,' Evelyn said. She sounded oddly nervous.

'Don't remember.' Isis tried to shrink away from the stale tobacco on her mother's breath. 'I suppose I fainted or something.'

Evelyn was silent for a time, and there was a dry click as she swallowed.

'Don't be silly. You must remember. You can tell me the truth. I won't be angry. No one is angry with *you*.' She stopped between each sentence as if she was reading from a script, but her eyes were focussed hard on Isis' face. 'I do wish I'd taken more notice when we came out. . . So. Who was it?'

'What?'

'Who attacked you?'

'No one.'

'You were on the floor, your collar was ripped, there was blood on your frock. Which one was it?'

Isis stared up at the wiry hairs on the tip of her mother's chin, and the dark caverns of her nostrils. Her muddy eyes, whites smeared pink, were like proper caring mother's eyes, searching her own. Isis felt she must say something to fulfil her expectation.

'Was it Haru?' Evelyn's voice was brusque. 'Tell the truth. No one will be angry. Not with you. We've sent the cad packing, in any case,' she added.

'And Selim?'

'And Akil. It's only us – and Abdullah now. Abdullah at least can be trusted.'

'Did you pay them?' Isis said.

Evelyn hacked out a laugh of incredulity, flecks of spit flying from her mouth and sticking to the canvas.

Isis watched them glitter and fade. 'It's not fair if you didn't pay them,' she muttered.

'Well?' said Evelyn. 'Haru? Or was it that boy – Selim, was it? Whichever it was, he shall be punished, don't you worry. He'll be sorry.'

Isis pictured Selim's hands, those slim, delicate fingers. She would not have them chopped off. She would not have him stoned. She wasn't even sure; he'd been close but . . . she'd wanted him to be close, hadn't she? She'd wanted . . . oh *what?* There had been the blood on her dress . . . she thought of him sucking his knuckle, eyes so dark beneath the sweep of lashes. But he couldn't have made her see what she saw, he could not have turned her into pigment on the ceiling or made her fall and forget herself or start the curse or have a fever.

'*Nothing* happened. I was only ill,' she said.

Was he helping her when she fell, or was there more, some sort of touching that she had willed?

'Your frock was torn,' Evelyn said. Her voice rose. 'It was one of them, Isis. Which one?'

'None, neither!' Isis scrunched her eyes and shook her head against the slippery, sickly memory, which was all of a piece with the bloated, dirty ache and the eyes everywhere of rats and boys and gods and the white eye of the pedlar, all of a piece with the heat and taste of dirt. 'I just fainted.'

'Come *on*.' Evelyn's voice was beginning to crisp with irritation.

'I don't know.'

'That's not good enough.'

Isis turned her face towards the canvas. Oh, it was so hot, so beastly hot.

'Wasn't Selim; wasn't Haru,' she said.

Evelyn struggled to say the next thing. 'If it was neither . . .' she began. 'Oh, I wish I'd bally well taken more notice of who'd come out in what order. I got so absorbed with what Abdullah was saying, I just followed him out, didn't even miss you till . . .' There was a long ache of silence before she spoke again. 'I should have been looking after you.' Her voice cracked and Isis was startled.

'It's not your fault,' she mumbled.

Evelyn swallowed, 'Please tell me it wasn't Victor?'

'No.'

'And of *course* not Osi.'

'No.'

'Then it *must* have been Haru or that boy.' Evelyn sounded relieved.

Isis shut her eyes against the intensity of her stare.

'Which one? Tell me, Isis, speak. We'll get the blighter.'

Isis pressed her fists against her eyes and saw a fuzz of floating colour, bright as if still wet.

'Tell me.'

'It *wasn't* Haru or Selim.'

'But you said . . .' Evelyn sighed. 'Who then?'

Isis' mind was scrambling. At least Victor would not be punished like them, no chopping off of hands or stoning. He was a hero, after all.

'You have to say.' Evelyn's stomach made a loud, hard gurgle. 'Look at me, Isis.'

Isis did so and was skewered like a creature on a pin. If she had to keep thinking about it, the feverishness would come back; she could feel it lurking like a bad smell at the fringes of her mind. She just wanted to be left alone and to forget. But Evelyn would not leave her alone, not till she said a name. *Someone* had been behind her when she'd thought she was alone. Selim? Her memory wavered like torchlight skidding over hieroglyphs. What if it had been Victor, after all? It came back to her how he'd looked in the tomb, the dark yellow of his teeth, like rat's teeth, and she shuddered.

'*Isis*,' Evelyn insisted.

And so, with great reluctance, she mouthed her uncle's name.

There was a long silence in which she could hear the drumming of Evelyn's heart. 'Are you *certain?*' she said at last. Her nostrils gaped as if panicking for air.

Isis nodded once.

'It's vital to be certain.'

'I know.' Isis shut her eyes, retreating to saffron fuzz.

More silence, not silence, a creaking of bone and sinew, a clicking and swallowing, a scurry of heartbeat, until at last Evelyn crawled out of the tent and it was possible to breathe again. Isis lay looking at an ant walking upside down quite gaily, waving its feelers, and she felt envious of that ant with nothing, nothing, absolutely nothing on its mind.

She turned miserably onto her side, drew her knees up to her chest. Victor would not get into serious trouble, not in the way an Arab would. And she would put it right, as soon as they got home, she would set the story straight. She sipped a little water and let her eyelids close.

Later there was shouting and she lay with her hands over her ears. Apart from staggering out to the WC tent, she lay in a trance all day and no one came to see her until Osi brought her a biscuit and she found some appetite for it – though Mary's food was what she craved: cheese pudding, perhaps, followed by pink blancmange.

And later still, when sunset flushed the fabric of the tent, she crawled out and blinked. Half the tents had gone by now, and Victor too, of course, and she quailed to think how angry with her he would be, how *disappointed*. They had always been such chums, such allies. But it would be all right. Once they were back at home she would make it be all right.

'I am overjoyed to see you so recovered.' Abdullah bent towards her. Despite the fatness of his lips, his smile was thin and slippery and she shrank from it.

Arthur blustered over and gave her a hard hug. 'Come on, Icy, let's get you something to eat.' His voice was overly hearty, and he avoided meeting her eyes. She embarrassed him, she realised. What they thought had happened, had changed her in his view, perhaps in all their views.

They ate bread and white cheese and apricots – now that Akil had gone there was no more cooking, just the boiling of the tea can for tea and coffee.

'Where did Victor go?' Isis dared to ask.

'Away. Obviously.' Evelyn was abrupt.

'After what you said,' Osi told her.

'It wasn't *my* fault.' Isis bit and chewed angrily. The bread was leathery. Akil's breads only tasted good when they were warm and fresh with pockety bubbles of fragrant air. Her throat closed up so it was impossible to swallow, and she leant away from the others and let the gob of half chewed bread fall from her mouth.

'Nothing is your fault, Icy,' Arthur said.

'Back to England?'

'You won't see Victor again, don't you worry.'

'But –'

'No buts.'

'But nothing bad will happen to him?' Isis pleaded.

'You have to understand, he's not been the same since the war.'

'I know that. He can only forget himself with the ladies.'

Arthur choked. 'I beg your pardon?'

'It's only what Mary said.'

'Let's drop the subject.' Evelyn's voice was flat and Arthur looked chastened.

'Of course,' he said. 'Rightio. Subject dropped.'

Victor was Evelyn's twin, just as Osi was hers. Of course she would be most terribly upset. Isis would take it back, somehow, soon, she would take it back so they could all be reconciled. She could hardly *now* say she didn't mean it – not now he'd been sent away. And it wouldn't make any difference to him at this moment. Perhaps he'd be on his way home, patrolling the ship for a new lady; perhaps he'd gone in search of Melissa. He would be all right, after all he had survived the war.

She got up and wandered away from the table.

'Where are you going?' Evelyn said.

'Nowhere.' She stopped. Evelyn never cared where she went. 'Thank you for asking,' she added awkwardly, feeling an odd sensation under her breast bone at this crumb of maternal care.

She approached the pile of broken pillars, looking for her pup. She had pocketed a piece of bread for him. It was very nearly dark now, the sky violet, the first stars prickling and, low on the horizon, a sneer of moon. She wandered around but there was no sign of any dogs. Away from the glow of the lamp-lit table, the darkness clotted around her and she looked back at her family lit by the kerosene lamps like a group of silly actors on a stage.

'There were some dogs,' she said, when she returned, standing just outside their circle. 'A nice pup.'

'Haru did for them,' Osi said.

Isis stared at him

'The little one came begging for food. He did away with them.'

'It's not true?' Isis pleaded, looking from Evelyn, to Arthur to Abdullah.

'They were only strays, Icy,' Arthur said.

'But one of them was *mine*,' Isis said. 'I'd trained him to sit.'

Abdullah cleared his throat. 'You must understand, we don't share the sentimental British approach to animals.' He was making himself sound sympathetic, but Isis detected a cloaked triumph in his voice, and in the gleam of his heavy-lidded eyes.

Since her arrival in Egypt, Isis had hardly cried: not when Evelyn and Arthur failed to meet them; not at any of the discomforts, fears and disappointments of the journey; not during or after her ordeal in the tomb, but now she ran back to her tent, hurled herself down and cried hard into her pillow, sobs racking and hacking out of her till her neck and ribs hurt.

After a time, she felt the tent shake as Evelyn crawled in, but she couldn't and wouldn't stop or even turn over and look at her, thinking all the time of the sweet cocked head of her pup and how he'd trusted her. Maybe she'd made him trust Haru too and Haru had killed him and it was her fault.

'Delayed shock,' she heard Evelyn pronounce.

'Let her have a good old cry,' Arthur agreed from between the flaps. 'Better out than in.'

It was her fault the pup was dead and that Victor had been sent away. Misery rolled over her in waves and there was nothing for it but to give in and weep some more and moan and groan. Awful sounds they were but she didn't care how she must sound or what anyone would think. It reminded her of the way Victor went on in his nightmares. Tangled in her mosquito net, she ground her face into the salty swamp of her pillow and groaned some more.

Eventually, worn out, she rolled onto her back. It was dark now except for the stars, so bright they were, like the points of tiny thorns pricking through the canvas. Her throat was sore and she was shaken by intermittent spasms. It was like the end of a storm and she felt oddly peaceful, weathering detachedly the last few squalls.

When everyone else had gone to bed, Isis crawled from her tent. The moon had swelled as it had risen, big and brazen as a slice of tropical fruit spilling juice, bright enough to cast sharp shadows. She wandered round the site. The flattened places where the missing tents had been appeared so much tinier than the lives lived in them, and already the sand was skimming across and blurring the traces of Selim and Victor, Akil and Haru. And soon their own tents would be taken down and all trace of their presence erased. Except for the shells. Tomorrow she would throw them out and soon they'd become buried by the sand again, to be collected, perhaps, by another bored child in another three thousand years.

She went behind the broken heap where her pup had been and there was no trace of anything alive there, just the breezy movement of grit in the moonlight, which had no purpose and meant nothing at all. She could never have taken the pup home, she knew that really. It had been the silly fancy of a silly child, and that child had died.

PART THREE

Spike and I stood for a long time on that landing outside Osi's door. Rain dripped through a hole in the ceiling above us and pigeons crooned, a sound incongruously summery. If he's dead he's dead, I told myself, the sort of sensible remark that sounds as if it helps. Oh sometimes my poor old mind thinks it can't take any more shocks, but then it gets another and seems to go on working – working after a fashion.

'Ma-am?' Spike said eventually, he was casting nervous looks up at the rafters and shivering, not surprising in his wetly woollen jumper. I should have had him take it off and dry himself.

'Here goes,' I said, with an attempt at jauntiness, and stretched my face into a smile before I turned the handle.

Cold brightness met us, windows open, curtains on the floor. The pigeon smell was not so powerful in here; there was something else. And then I saw Osi. He was alive, naked, crouching on the bed, back pressed against the wall, knees drawn up to his chest, eyes huge, beard like a doormat, string of grey gristle slumped between his legs.

'Cover up, for pity's sake,' I said, when I could speak. 'We have a guest.'

Though Spike had backed out of the door.

I picked a blanket from the floor and draped it over my brother's knees. His skin was cold, surely could not be colder if he *had* been dead. 'What a state you're in,' I scolded. 'Really, Osi!'

He'd gone bald since last I'd seen him and his nose, always so long and beaky, seemed hardened now; it *was* a beak, the mouth shrunken away beneath the copious dinge of beard. His eyes were two dark tunnels leading to . . . I shudder to think.

'Osi!' Now that he was decent I shook him and he squawked. I jumped back at the raucous sound, bird sound, and all at once understood that that is what he thought he was. He was crouching as if perched, long horny toenails splayed like claws.

'Osi, it's Sisi . . . Isis,' I cranked out that old name and how awkwardly it issued from my mouth. '*Isis*. It's me.'

I watched but nothing was occurring in his eyes.

'What have you been eating?' I said. 'You haven't pulled the bucket up for days.' Of course the floor was strewn with balls of gold and silver from his Dairylee and chocolate bars, and there were stacks of cardboard wheels reaching to the ceiling like his blessed temple columns. Everything was scrawled with hieroglyphs, all the walls, overlapping, blurring each other, and some of them were done in blood, I think, and some in something thick and brown I cannot even bear to name and once I'd noticed that, I caught the smell too, that filthy human smell. His fingernails, those awful horny twists, were caked with dirt and stuck with hairs, enough to make you sick.

This was Osi. This was my twin. I thought my heart would break.

I heard a cough behind me and almost left my skin behind. I had forgotten Spike was there. I turned and tried again for the reassuring smile but my face felt tight and false.

He had a hand clamped over his mouth and spoke through his fingers. 'I reckon I'll go now, Ma-am?'

'First, be a dear and fetch the food from the bucket,' I said. 'And some water? Please, dear. I could do with a hand. He's really not himself.'

Spike went out and I heard him struggling and slithering on the stairs and a yell as his foot went through the third. He was swearing continuously and who could blame him? I stood and listened. *Oh my fucking God, Jesus fucking Christ, fuck fuck fucking fuck* and so on in a sort of dirge, punctuated by gasps and sneezes and retching sounds. To do him credit, he didn't run away.

'Come on, Osi,' I said and at last he seemed to register that I was there and cocked his head to focus on me.

'It's me, *Isis*,' I said. The name was dangerous, likely to haul me back. 'Sisi, your sister,' I said. 'You haven't pulled the bucket up for days. Remember the system? I've come to see how you are.'

As I talked I found another blanket to drape around his shoulders. I tried to shut the windows, but the frame had broken and, in any case, the glass was gone. The curtains were in a squelchy heap from all the blown in rain; part of the ceiling was down, the rest of it intricately mapped with stains.

I continued to talk to him, just soothing nonsense, soothing to myself at least, though my mind was scrabbling for what on earth I was going to do with him like this. He squawked again, a dreadfully chilling sound.

'Speak properly,' I scolded.

As I watched, his jaw began to move, stirring the beard and a hole opened underneath the nose, and then he spoke a word, although I couldn't catch it. His voice was so unused to speaking that it would hardly work.

'Again,' I said. 'Try again.'

And he tried several times, with effort in his eyes, an expression come into them now, a pleading for me to understand, and then, with a plummeting of my heart, I understood him. He was saying 'Horus'.

Spike came back in, bless him, with the Dairylee and Jacobs cream crackers.

'Thank you, dear. Just the ticket.'

He put his offerings on the bed and stretched one of the sleeves of his jumper across his nose and mouth like a sort of mask, eyes widened above it.

'Could you fetch some water?' I asked. He went off again and I listened to him on the stairs again. This time I was afraid that he might really leave, but no, he came back with one of the Bacardi Breezer bottles filled with water.

'Why not look around the bedrooms?' I suggested. 'You might find a rug – or take anything. Have a good old poke around.'

When he'd gone I tore the Jacob's wrapper open with my teeth, peeled the foil off a cheesy triangle, mashed it onto a cracker, and held it close to Osi's mouth.

'You're not *Horus*, you're *Osiris*,' I said and when his

mouth opened, popped a bit of cracker in. 'Remember?' His hunger woke once we'd begun and he ate five crackers, most of the cheese and glugged the water. The feelings of love, relief and revulsion as the lipless hole churned at the food were so strong I could barely contain myself, but I went on feeding him until he would take no more.

And the sensation of another person upstairs in Little Egypt, wandering the rooms alone, was strange to me and I thought of the fox with the feathers between his teeth, I thought of the bird hearts beating their blood all through the house, tangles of red and blue, veins of life, wet and warm and red amongst the rotting timbers.

I sat with Osi, and I listened so hard I could hear the old nails niggle in the floorboards and the soreness of the gaps between them whistling with draughts like tooth decay. I could feel the grumble and belch of the crusted pipes and the roof beams aching with the slope and shoulder of the remaining slates. I sat listening to Little Egypt properly and wholly for the last time until Osi's eyes were closed. As he fell asleep he became gradually unperched and slid along the bed so that I could tuck him warmly up before I left.

I'd forgotten Spike and was alarmed by the sound of him in the Blue Room. I hadn't been in there since Victor. It was in comparatively good condition, just a corner of the ceiling gone, and in that corner the wallpaper with its repeating bluebirds peeled right off the wall, but otherwise it was fine and dry, the window properly closed, and even the curtains intact. Spike had rolled a rug up and had it under his arm.

'You sure?' he said.

I went and put my hand on the bed. 'This is where my

Uncle Victor used to stay,' I said. 'A hero of the war. The Great War.'

'The first World War?'

I nodded.

'*For sure?* Did European history at High School,' he said. 'That's cool.'

'I'll tell you all about him,' I said. 'One day.'

We went out onto the landing and I shut the Blue Room door, the firm click of it stirring up a turmoil in my belly. Osi would be all right for tonight. He was warm and fed. But how to manage him from now on I could not even begin to think. And all at once it was too much for me. My head was reeling with too much feeling and I had to be alone. I felt an urgent need to get downstairs away from all the memories that hung like sheets, invisible, to snag and tangle me.

Spike helped me down the stairs and then I sent him away.

I sat in Mary's chair beside the stove, hunched around my broken heart. Nine tried to jump on my lap but there was no room for her, what with all the grief. Osi still alive. His life continuing like this was almost worse than his death would have been.

I simply did not know how to carry on.

21

Being out in the world had changed me. On our return, I saw Little Egypt through new and disappointed eyes. I had become more *worldly*. I had so looked forward to being home, to seeing Mary, to returning to my own skin – but my skin was different now, coloured by the sun and with a stain that went deeper, that soaked right through to my bones. The house, though rattling huge and empty, seemed *littler* in some important way.

It was mid-January and the very air froze and crackled in our lungs. Icicles fanged the gutter and dangled perilously above the door, and all the bedroom windows were thickly frosted with ferns. It was as if the house had fallen under a frozen spell, and to my own surprise, I missed the sun and the desert heat most dreadfully, and found it hard to believe that I had ever complained of being too hot.

'You'd never credit the heat,' I remarked to Mary one morning, a few days after we'd returned home. She had come upstairs where Osi and I were still in our beds, to call us down for breakfast.

'You never stop flaming mentioning it,' Mary muttered.

Osi was tightly sealed in sleep and I had my blankets pulled right up to my chin, loath to get out into the cold – and besides, I'd gone to bed in my clothes and didn't want Mary to know. She was standing by the window, silhouetted by the fuzzy light, hair standing out in a glistening cloud. As I watched, she put her palm against the frosty glass to melt a space and stooped to peer through it.

'What are you looking for?' I asked, knowing the answer. Of course it would be Mr Patey.

'Your porridge is ready,' is all she said, and as she went out, slammed the door hard enough to make icicles crack and tinkle from the gutter.

The day before, I'd heard the rattle of Mr Patey's pony and cart and looked down from here. As I'd watched, Mary had appeared outside and they'd stood a little distance from each other, oddly formal. Mr Patey had been muffled in coat, hat and scarf so that I could barely see his face. Mary must have been freezing, hugging her arms, dressed only in her frock and cardigan. Though I could hear nothing, I saw the clouds of their words rise between them before he stepped forward and held her. She seemed to sag against him. But by the time I arrived in the kitchen to say hello, Mary was alone.

'I thought I heard Mr Patey,' I said.

Her lashes were wet and there was a finger streak of coal dust on her cheek. 'He's delivered the coal and that's that,' she snapped and turned away to hide her face. My heart hurt for her. I understood love now, having seen the world, having read about it, and for Mary I wanted a happy ending.

The kitchen was the warmest place in the house, but in this deep wintry weather, even it wasn't all that warm, and despite layers of clothing, I was shivering as I sat down at the table. Mary banged a bowl of porridge in front of me. The worse Mary's mood, the lumpier the porridge; as I stirred milk and sugar into it, I saw that her mood must be very bad indeed.

I chewed my way through the clumps as Mary stood with her back to me scraping burnt toast into the sink. I believe the smell of burnt toast is one of the most dispiriting in the world. I tried to think of something to cheer her up, but could feel the gloom settling on me as well.

Here we were again, just as before: Evelyn and Arthur away – Arthur had delivered us home and gone haring straight back to Egypt – and us stuck here waiting. Not even waiting any more, not me. I knew they were on a wild goose chase; that they had been taken for fools. There in my mind was the twist of Rhoda's face when she'd said as much; there was the blind white flash of the pedlar's eye.

But now at least I was older and I could see that the end was in sight. That was a comfort. I must be patient for just a few years more, and then I would up and leave. I'd work if I had to, make my own living. Perhaps I could teach something – but what? Or work in a shop. Of course, the horse would bridle at the idea – I laughed at that and wished there was someone to whom I could repeat the pun.

Mary kept a pile of the unsold papers that Mr Burgess brought her, and they were full of King Tut and all the treasures from his tomb. There was a craze for Egyptian fashion. I saw Cleopatra dresses in printed silk; there were Egyptian moving picture shows and dances and cocktails and there was even an advertisement for Palmolive Soap with a lady emerging from a sarcophagus.

Mary buttered her toast and sat down at the table. She had

lost her rosy cheeks and the skin around her eyes was puffy. She crunched her toast, put it down and squeezed the heels of her hands against her temples.

'Not your head again?'

She winced and nodded.

'You should put your feet up.'

'I reckon I'll soldier on.'

'Why don't we play cards when we've cleared away? I could teach you cribbage.'

She stood up, grating back her chair. 'The blinking washing don't do itself. The broom don't get out of the cupboard and sweep the floor, the scuttle don't march in full of coal . . .'

'Shall I pour the tea?' I broke in, trying to stop her going through *all* the chores and working herself into a frenzy. I poured a cup for each of us, though I didn't much like tea then. It would be friendly, I thought, if we sat and drank tea, two women – because I was a woman now – two women drinking tea together. Soon Mary would realise how much I'd grown up and begin to treat me differently. We could become friends and confide in each other, be a comfort to each other till the end of the waiting. I tried to think of something womanly to say. I did not dare to ask about Mr Patey, though the question was on the tip of my tongue.

The tea was awful, both weak and stewed and only with three spoonsful of sugar could I bring myself to drink it.

'Go easy on the sugar,' she grouched. 'It don't grow on trees.'

'Well, it nearly does,' I pointed out. 'On canes, at least.'

The ghost of a dimple hovered on her cheek.

'We had some to chew,' I said, and remembering the sensation of those sweet and stringy fibres in my mouth brought back the lorry ride, and with it a sharp memory of Victor beside me in the cab. He'd been tired and drunk that day, stinking and drooping heavily against me. I put my tea down. I didn't know what, if anything, Mary knew about Victor. Possibly nothing at all. Nobody had mentioned him since we'd been back.

'I'll help you today,' I said.

'You could help me by writing a letter to your pa telling him I can't take much more of this. If anyone ever was taken for granted –'

'I will, but –'

But Mary was getting in a proper paddy now. 'And what about the help I've been promised? And he needs to pay me up to date and settle up for the coal. We'll be running out before too long and if this weather keeps on we'll perish.'

'I'm sure *Mr Patey* wouldn't let you perish,' I said.

She glared.

'What?' I said.

'Mind your business.'

'I'll go and feed the birds,' I said.

'You'll catch your death,' she remarked, but didn't try and stop me.

She was chopping onions now and, skirting round her angry elbows, I collected a dish of breadcrumbs and some chop bones for the birds to peck at. In the scullery the water in the WC was frozen. I crammed my slippered feet into a pair of galoshes and put on the thickest coat I could find – an army greatcoat of Victor's. Cleo had been sleeping on it and it was coated in tabby hairs that flew off when I shook it and made me sneeze. The smell of cat battled with the smell of war in the stiff serge coat, which was wildly too big for me so that it trailed the ground.

Outside everything creaked and glistened. No breeze, no bird song; old snow in frozen heaps beside the door, puddles like plates of iron, hoar frost sugaring every twig and blade of grass. The weight of the icicles, long as walking sticks, had pulled part of the gutter away from the roof. What would Selim make of it, I wondered, but could not picture him here, all muffled up and wearing boots and socks instead of sandals.

I held out my hands and soon there were chaffinches and coal tits and a busy fluster of sparrows, their icy claws skittering on my icy fingers.

My footprints were clearly printed on the frost, despite the scuffing coat hem – and other footprints too. Mary's, and a man's big boots – Mr Burgess' – and the footprints of another man wearing narrower shoes that must be Mr Patey's. It had snowed since I'd seen him, so perhaps he'd been back and Mary was keeping his visits secret. I was sorry I'd said anything about the dead wives now. It was Mr Burgess' fault – I realised now that he was only jealous and wanting Mary for himself.

I wandered back through the kitchen. Mary had burnt the onions, and I didn't dare speak to her. I went into the ballroom to feed the inside birds – the two budgies had been joined by a little flock of sparrows, which had got in through the broken windows. Later they were to breed and I called them spudgies – sparrows with blue and yellow feathers flecked through the brown.

The tall windows were so thickly frosted that the light was white and solid in the room and there were even faint frost ferns growing on the mirrors. The birds were perched on the chandelier, fluffed and huddled for warmth. Beneath the chandelier was a miniature mountain range of droppings and feathers. I caught my reflection between the ferns, red-cheeked and ridiculous in the floor-length coat, my head tiny between the military shoulders. I was disappointed by what a child I still looked, and what a sight my hair – grown out of shape and stringy with grease. I was itchy under my arms but couldn't get to them to scratch inside the heavy coat.

Mary had long since given up cleaning the ballroom and the piano was thick with dust and droppings. After I'd fed the birds, I lifted the lid and pressed my finger on a high C sharp, and the note hung and shimmered on as if it didn't want to die. I dropped the lid with an echoing bang and caught a shiver of movement in one of the mirrors, like the hem of a dress sweeping past. It brought back a party there, when the ballroom was warm and full, alive with music and voices and dancing feet. Osi and I had been small enough to hide under the piano with our plate of iced fancies and watch the stockings and trousers swishing past, and feel the fuzzy thumping of the music through our skulls.

I hurried from the ballroom before I could catch myself – or anything – in the frosty mirrors.

22

Mary was in the pantry. 'Can we have a bath today?' I called.

She came out scowling.

'You've been at the Cheddar,' she said.

'Have not!'

'Well it wasn't Jack Sir flaming Frost.'

'Honestly, I haven't.'

'Well, most of it's gone and I was planning on doing a colly cheese for your lunch.'

I pushed past her and went into the dim smelly space, where the wax-papered shelves held crocks of flour and salt, slabs of butter and lard, wire baskets of vegetables, jars of jam, currants and honey. I hadn't been in at all since we'd been home. The wire cheese-cover was off and there was only a small wonky wedge left – and Mary always sliced things with beautiful precision.

'Osi?' I said, doubtfully.

'You know as well as me he only eats what's put in front of him.'

'Well it honestly wasn't me,' I said.

Mary sighed. 'I'll do a soup. That's not like you. And get that filthy old coat off. Whatever do you look like!'

'That's because it wasn't me. And who cares what I look like?'

'Well it wasn't a blooming mouse.'

I was tempted to shout, or to flounce away and slam the door, but I didn't want to make her headache worse, or her temper, and besides I liked to think I'd grown beyond such behaviour. Instead I went into the scullery and hung up the coat. Back in the kitchen, despite a discouraging look from Mary, I sat down beside the stove.

She stood with her back to me scrubbing the burnt pan with a fistful of wire wool. The scratch of it put my teeth on edge, but I made my voice sound warm and friendly.

'I've got a book you'd like,' I said. 'It's called *Desert Longing*.'

She sniffed and turned on the tap.

'It's frightfully romantic,' I said.

'I reckon I'll give it a go.'

'It's about a love affair between a Lord and Lady and there's this handsome Arab Prince and –'

'Don't spoil it, then.' She turned off the tap.

'I'll get it for you.' I stood up. 'And later on you can have a lovely read beside the stove.'

Mary put the scrubbed pan on the draining board and wiped her hands on her apron.

'We haven't had a bath since we got home,' I pointed out. 'I feel quite putrid – and as for Osi . . .'

She scritched her fingers through her hair and sighed. 'Oh, reckon I could do with a spruce up myself.' And to my relief she gave a weary smile.

I ran upstairs to fetch the book. Seeing the garish cover, battered and stained from its travels, brought back the inside of my tent, the heat and dirt and tedium of the desert, which hardly seemed part of this same world at all. In my dreams there was the wet of paint, breath on my neck, a plummeting sensation from which I would wake with a startled jolt. But when I was awake I was able not to think about the tomb, or rather to remember it as something from a story. No more real than *Desert Longing*. I flicked through the pages and saw my dirty fingerprints, smudgy daisy patterns on the flyleaf. Compared with Victor's nightmares my dreams were nothing. Poor Victor. My belly twanged with guilt.

I noticed that the place where Mary had melted a space on the window had frozen thinly over. And then I saw that another space in the frost had been scratched away, higher up and more recent. Only Osi was here and why would he want to look out? There was nothing to look at, only whiteness through a fence of icicles.

I went into the nursery where he was lying on his stomach reading.

'Did you make a hole in the frost?' I said.

He had to crick his neck to scowl up at me. 'What?' He clearly had no idea what I was talking about.

'Did you pinch some cheese?'

The end of his beaky nose was red, and he was sniffling. If he had a cold it was no surprise, he didn't bother about trying to keep warm at all.

'Did you?'

'No.' He resumed reading his blasted hieroglyphics.

'Well, someone did.'

He shrugged one shoulder as if it was no concern of his.

I felt like kicking him. I took *Desert Longing* downstairs for Mary, but I was thinking. What if someone else was in the house? A man with narrow feet. I could only guess that it was Mr Patey. And that's why Mary wouldn't talk about him – because she'd hidden him here. And that must be where the cheese had gone – I was surprised she couldn't work that out for herself. Wasn't she feeding him?

She was chopping another lot of onions for the soup. She was still pale, but smiled when I returned to the kitchen and put the book on the table. Once she'd read it she'd realise that I knew about love affairs now and perhaps she would confide in me.

'That looks good,' she said. 'I'll see if I can get that bathroom stove lit this afternoon. See if we can't work up a bit of a fug.' There were tears in her eyes, but they were only onion tears. *You don't need to keep him secret*, is what I wanted to say, but didn't dare. Instead I went upstairs to search.

There were seven bedrooms, two bathrooms and the nursery on the first floor, and in the attic a maze of cramped servants' quarters, including Mary's room. In Grandpa's heyday there had been a full staff, but by the time he was old there was only one manservant, a housekeeper, a cook and a tweenie – Mary. And now there was only Mary.

Most of the first floor bedrooms and one of the bathrooms had been locked for years. I had been walking past them without a thought all that time, but now, suddenly, it seemed dreadful to imagine all that stale and boxed-in air, all that dead space. All those mirrors with nothing to reflect.

But Mary would be keeping him in the attic, of course, perhaps even in her room. Perhaps they were keeping each other warm at night. I went up the attic stairs calling, softly,

'Mr Patey?' And I thought I heard a movement. I hesitated half way up, straining my ears. At the top I called, 'It's all right, Mr Patey, I know you're there.' Cautiously, I pushed open the door. But there was no one. Mary's bed was messy and unmade and her clothes piled untidily on a chair, papers from her headache powders were scattered about, which was not like her. I looked round – the wardrobe would be too small for a man to hide in – the only place he could be was under the bed, but there was only a suitcase and a box, a chamber-pot and a pair of shoes.

And then I heard footsteps on the stairs and Mary came storming in. 'What the flaming hell are you up to? Can't I have one room in this blasted mad house to call my own?'

'I was looking for Mr Patey.'

Her mouth opened and closed and opened again, the vapour of her breath fogging the air between us. 'You *what?*'

'I know he's here.'

'Stop this nonsense. Mr Patey indeed! Have you lost your wits!'

'I've seen his footprints,' I said doubtfully.

She was shaking her head at me. 'That foreign sun must have addled you brains good and proper. If you must know, Mr Patey's marrying a milliner from town what he got in trouble and apart from dropping off the coal I haven't seen him for weeks.'

I stared at her. 'A milliner?'

She shut her eyes and squeezed her hands against her temples. 'What with everything else and what with my bloody head,' she said. 'How am I supposed to cope? Now get downstairs.'

I left the room, closing the door behind me and heard the squeal of bedsprings as she flung herself down – not to cry, I hoped.

23

AFTER LUNCHEON, MARY went up to light the bath-room stove, but it took hours to take the chill off the room and by the time the frost on the window had melted the daylight was fading. The iron of the gigantic tub was so cold it cooled the rusty water that chugged from the taps, so we had to fill it twice – as with a teapot – once to warm it so that the next lot of water would stay hot.

When the bath was drawn, I threw in three fistfuls of Eve-lyn's Gardenia Bath Salts. I collected all the candles I could find and stood them along the edge of the bath and the candlelight mixed with the scented steam into a thick, sweet mist. Mary stood for a moment staring as if at nothing; she seemed insub-stantial, wavering in the steam. She had come down to make lunch without referring to my trespass. As well as a temper she also had a forgiving soul. She was distant though, vague with headache, and had spent most of the afternoon squinting at *Desert Longing* beside the stove. Now she sucked in a sudden breath and frowned, pressing the heel of her hand against her temple.

'Oooh, that's really sharp,' she said. 'That's like a fork. Call me when you're both done and I'll see if I'm up to getting in myself.'

'We won't let the water go cold,' I promised.

When we were small, Mary used to sit on the lid of the WC and chat while Osi and I wallowed in the tub. We used always to get in together, it was such a big bath, one each end and plenty of room to move our legs, but since we'd got older Mary thought bathing together wasn't quite decent anymore. She thought that we should have separate bedrooms too. Perhaps we may have done, if things had turned out differently.

It would take too long, I thought, if Mary had to wait for us to bathe separately. The water would be cold. It wasn't practical.

I found Osi in the nursery hunched in his tiny armchair copying something from a book. I felt a surge of fondness for him and bent over to see with what beautiful neatness he had filled his page.

'What does it mean, though?' I asked.

'This is an informal hieratic script, probably 19th dynasty,' he explained, and began to read: *'The scribe salutes his Lord, the Fan bearer on the right side of the King, re Chief of the gangs in the Place of Truth, Seal Bearer, Chief Priest of the –'*

'All right, all right.' I pulled back hastily. 'The bath's ready. Come on.'

I didn't want there to be anything Egyptian about the bath. It was an English bathroom on an English January afternoon and nothing could be further away from Egypt. It was amazing to think that this was the same planet and that all those miles away the Nile was flowing greenly between its banks and the sun beating, glittering down. And the horse and the whiskery dog? Oh I snatched my mind from them.

Osi picked up a fine brush and slicked it with his tongue, leaving a groove of black down the centre of his lower lip.

I pulled him up by the hand. 'Let's get in together; it'll be quicker. Mary needn't know.'

The bathroom was warm and the particles of steam gleamed in the candlelight. Condensation streamed from the walls and plopped from the ceiling in long drips. I felt rather self-conscious as I took off my layers of woollies, dresses, stockings, liberty bodice and drawers. But the light was dim and in any case, unless it was Egyptian, Osi hardly noticed anything past the end of his nose.

The bath was high and there was a wooden box you had to climb up onto in order to hoist a leg over and step in. I gasped as I sank into the water that was just too hot, a shocking luxury, and I forced my body down into it, gooseflesh riffling up my body till I got my shoulders under and equalised the temperature. As soon as they were warm my chilblains began to throb. Mary's cure was a raw potato rubbed on, which did help though it stung. I'd ask her to do it for me later. Osi undressed. He had a dark face, neck and hands, though his torso where the sun hadn't reached was maggot-white – and my skin was marked in the same way. I shut my eyes against the detail of his nakedness as he stepped in.

Once we were both submerged, our legs slid against each other and I caught hold of a foot and lifted it from the water. 'Your toe nails are a scandal!' I examined the way they curled under the ends of his toes. Between them the creases were dark with caught-up squirms of dirt. I soaped my finger and began to push it between his toes, but he yelled and splashed at the tickliness and I gave up. I held my breath to submerge my head and then I sat up and scrubbed my hair with soap, splashing one of the candles so that it expired with a smoky hiss. I tried to wash Osi's hair, but he struggled and snorted and I let him go.

Spits of rain against the window emphasised our cosiness. The water and the gardenia steam lulled us, slid us together, rocked and cradled us as they had through all our childhood bath-times; and my poor itchily throbbing toes buried themselves in the loose scrumple of skin between his legs, the softest gentlest place for toes. For a short time we lay there, comfortable and comforted, just for that moment of twinny peace and closeness, not waiting, not lonely, just *being*.

Then I heard footsteps on the landing, and sat up straight. Mary would be cross that we were in the tub together. I watched the door, waiting for it to open, but the footsteps went away. They didn't sound quite like Mary's feet – the tread was heavier.

'Did you hear that?' I said to Osi.

'What?'

'We should get out,' I said. 'Before Mary comes.'

We did not speak as we dried ourselves with stove-warmed towels, or as we dressed, backs to one other. Cold rivulets trickled from my hair down my back and I shivered and coughed. If Osi heard nothing, maybe there was nothing to hear. I must stop imagining things before I drove myself mad.

I was so glad that Osi was there. After a bath, especially in winter, we always used to sit by the stove in the kitchen brushing our hair as it dried, while Mary would make cocoa for us. I coughed again. The air was becoming choky with smoke leaking from a crack in the stove pipe. I would have to tell Mary about the smoke and hang the expense; we would simply have to have the chimney man in if we were ever to bathe in wintertime again.

'That was nice,' I said to Osi and he smiled before he went out – back to his studies, I supposed, though how could he bear to be alone? How could be bear to return to that freezing nursery with his hair all wet? It would turn to icicles. I was encouraged by that crumb though, that smile, just a small proof that he'd enjoyed the closeness too; crumbs were all you ever got from Osi.

Time to call Mary before the water was quite cold. And I would surprise her with cocoa when she came down, that would cheer her up.

'We're out,' I called from the landing, but there was no reply. 'Your turn, Mary. It's still warm.' I waited to hear her coming, but she didn't and I heard the creaking of a board in one of the rooms, I swear I did, like a cautious footfall and the click of a carefully shutting door. I went shooting down the stairs to the kitchen. I'd never been afraid in the house before, never noticed how much darkness there was, how many places a stranger could hide. *Don't be silly.* Mr Patey would be with his milliner and why would anyone else be there?

I wished that I could stay put in the warm kitchen and make my cocoa and dry my hair, but Mary – who must be up in her room – should have the bath before it got too cold. Reluctantly I crept up the stairs, skin bristling, ears on stalks. I called up to the attic, but there was no rely. I forced my feet to climb those dark, narrow stairs and my heart was punching.

I tapped on her door. At first there was no reply, then I thought I heard a groan. I called again, but there was nothing. My feet were squeaking the floorboards. I hesitated, teeth chattering, as my eyes adjusted to the scanty moonlight slanting through the skylight.

'Mary,' I called and my voice was thin and strange. If someone came up the attic stairs behind me there was nowhere I could run. 'Mary!'

This time I heard a high-pitched whimper. What if someone was in there with her? Someone could have crept up, perhaps Mr Patey after all, perhaps a stranger. When she moaned again I gritted my teeth and flung open the door.

She was lying on her back with one hand across her eyes, illuminated by a drizzle of moonlight, her hair lit up like choppy water. She was still wearing her clothes, even her shoes. I could smell sickness and saw that she had been ill in the chamberpot. Although it was horrible to see her so, I felt a flicker of relief that she was alone.

'The bath is waiting,' I told her.

'No. My blasted head,' she whispered in a papery voice. I knelt and stroked her hair, put my hand on her clammy brow, but she winced at my touch and feebly turned her head away.

'Can I get you something?' I asked. 'Cocoa? A cup of tea?'

She groaned at the thought.

'Have you taken your powders?'

'Can't keep anything down.'

'Do you want a candle? I could fetch you a lamp.'

'No light,' she said. When her head was bad, light was like daggers in her eyes.

'Poor Mary.' I stood up. 'You should get properly into bed, at least. Shall I cover you?' She was on top of the blankets, but I knew her Sunday coat was in the wardrobe. I took it out and spread it over her. 'Shall I take off your shoes?'

'Just leave me be.'

'I'll empty this.'

I carried the chamberpot away and emptied it and brought her a glass of water in case she should need it in the night.

'Bless you,' she whispered, without opening her eyes.

Bᴜᴛ ʏᴏᴜ ᴅᴏ carry on.
A broken heart can hold together.
Or am I simply hard?

Some time after Spike had left, I don't know how long, I stoked
the stove and made a cup of tea. I couldn't stomach food. The
stirred up silt was filthing up my head. I put the radio on, loud,
to try and sink it down, but the adverts for taxis, pop songs, a
phone-in quiz all set my teeth on edge. The batteries were old,
and Radio 4, where they're more civilized, would only hiss
and buzz.

That Osi could no longer fend for himself was clear. And it
was equally clear that I couldn't cope with going up and down
those stairs all day and night, nor could I bring him down and
even if I could, he wouldn't settle. And truth to tell, I didn't
want him in the kitchen: Horus in the kitchen in all his naked
glory, squawking like an idiot? No, it simply would not do.

I looked round at the chaos that I live in. I never meant
it to be like this; it just crept up. I was ashamed, mortified,
now that Spike had seen it – and even *he*, the *anarchist,* was

shocked! How had it come to this? I didn't know what to do with myself. What now? What next? There were the cards stuck in their game of patience for donkey's years. I can't remember why I stopped and left it there.

I took a knife and pried it under the cards to loosen them. Those in the pile were all right, if sticky. I lost the backing of some of them, the card fused to the wood. It had been an Egyptian pack with pictures of the Great Sphinx on the backs. The faces of those laid out (most of the hearts) were so splattered with food drips you could hardly read them. But still I played a game of patience. I did not let myself cheat. I played for an answer: if it came out then I'd sell and we would go. I don't know how long I played for until I won. Fair and square. Some of the cards were missing so I had to make allowances, and some you could not read and had to guess, but still I played and played and fate or luck was with me. The cards decided it. I'd have to sell; we'd have to go. The time had come. In Sunset Lodge it's home from home and every need is catered for. (Although I fancied Osi might prove something of a challenge.)

So, I would go and see Stephen and tell him yes indeed I'd sell. As soon as that decision was made I was in a lather of anticipation. I could hardly imagine his expression! To give someone what they long for – a gift for the giver, I'd say. If Spike were correct that U-Save would not let anything hold up its progress, then nothing awful would come out. Of course I'd check that Stephen was of the same opinion.

Oh, what a comfort it was to think that soon a bright place, all shiny new, a modern megastore, would lie on top of here, like a sort of temple. All glass and steel and gleam and normal people with their trollies and their wallets, picking out their sofas and their curtains, their beds and scatter cushions right where I sat. Oh yes, I thought, that was the way to go.

The next day was Tuesday, one of Stephen's days. His routine was to meet me in the U-Save café, first thing in the morning, to see if I was *ready yet*, was how he put it, if I'd *come round*. Oddly, I'd taken to Stephen, though he's a developer. He said seeing me of a morning was the highlight of his week. (Of course he exaggerated – still, what a charming thing to say.) It makes me smile to think how different from Spike he is, surely as different as it's possible for two young men to be. In Spike's parlance, Stephen is an *archetypal sucker*. Curious that I like them both, they're my best friends. I like young men, I do.

I pushed the trolley onto my bridge and watched the traffic flow beneath me. It was a glittery early morning, sun after rain, sharp enough to cause the eyes to stream. Three police cars, sirens screaming; the lumbering hulks of lorries, snarl of speeders, all moving, rushing somewhere with such purpose. I stood above inert, eyes wet, heart punching; in each of those cars one heart, at least, beating to its destination, all that rush of blood, the road an artery, petrol and oil and blood pumping along it, roaring, always, always, whatever the time of day or night.

A few cigarette butts – someone had been on the bridge. I nudged them with my toe and watched them fly to join the rush. There were two dead things smeared on the road, a crow, one wing flapping in the traffic's draught, and a poor hedgehog. People could get on the bridge but my gate, with its metal bars, its serrated top, was locked in three places. The postman left my letters in a box, a system that worked, and no one else had any call to mount the bridge but still they did, sight see-ers and council people, developers, vandals with their spray cans and their bikes and so on. But I have my portcullis and I let no one in. True until Spike. Why should I?

No sign of Spike in the service area and I didn't hang around to wait. I went round the front of U-Save and through the doors that open of their own accord and suck you into warmth and light and wonderful aromas. Always it made my heart lift to enter U-Save, so orderly, so full of goodness and availability. There's no dark corners, nothing that stinks or crawls. Nothing is there that shouldn't be there. Really it is like heaven.

In the Ladies I washed my face and hands. No one was there so I took off my cardigan, blouse and vest and had a go under my arms with worms of soap from the dispenser and, with the blower, roared myself hot and dry. I have been caught at my ablutions, but simply stared the culprit out and nobody has ever said a word about it. After all, what harm?

Once I was fresh I went to the café – but it felt different and wrong. *I'm Doreen how may I help you?* was not there. Why I'd depended so on seeing her, I don't know, but I felt a dip in my spirits. Someone had spilled a drink on the floor by the counter; there was a fizzy orange puddle and a danger sign. A boy I'd never seen before, a youth with stippled skin, brought my cappuccino over without a murmur of complaint. Not so much kindness as a lack of interest. They were short of pastries, no croissants or pains au chocolat, so I choose a muffin – overblown fairy cake with a hard lid of so-called icing on the top.

'Where's Doreen?' I asked him.

'Ooo?' is all he said.

'The usual assistant?'

He merely shrugged, jaw working like a camel's at his chewing gum. I let him go without a ticking off, without pointing out who I am. I was preoccupied with looking for Stephen, of whom there was no sign, though it was his day. I'd counted on Stephen coming, hadn't even considered that he might not. What would I do if he did not? The coffee wasn't its usual cheering self, but cool with scarcely any foam. The muffin was a dry catastrophe. The clock clicked round and Stephen failed to come.

I waved the boy – I'm Brian etc. – over from where he was mopping the floor. He dripped a trail across to me.

'You need to wring it out,' I said.

'Uh?' His mouth hung open to reveal his wad of gum.

'The mop. Has a young man with a briefcase, touch of the tar brush about him, been here looking for me?' I asked.

He chomped blankly before deciding, 'Nah.'

'It is Tuesday, isn't it?' I checked.

'Nah,' he said again. 'It's Monday innit?'

'Is it?'

'Summink else?' He regarded the coffee, hardly touched and the crumbled ruins of the cake.

I opened my mouth to complain about the quality of my breakfast, to complain about his shoddy service, and the orange drips, but only, 'No,' came out. 'Thank you,' I added, as an example to him.

I stared out of the window from which you could see the roof of Little Egypt and get a sense of how grand it must once have looked. Now it was cramped between two roads and a railway line, as if on an island, a triangle, trapped in a pell-mell of ceaseless movement. The look of it, the thought of being back inside that house, sickened me.

For once, the brightness of the aisles, the moving floor, the warmth, the ranks of flickering screens in Electrical, the plastic toys, the food, oh all that food, all those cleaning products, the buckets, mops and brooms, the brush-and-dust pans, so neatly, brightly, snugly packaged, held no allure, promised no comfort. I bought painkillers from the Pharmacy, lovely ones, that send you off to sleep, and swallowed some before I set off back.

Outside I looked again for Spike, but still no sign of him. How did I get the day wrong? I never get the day wrong. There was a smell of rotting cabbage and a scrabbling in the skip, not Spike, but vermin. With heavy legs, and oh my knee, I pushed the trolley back, unlocked the gate, entered the house. How dim and filthy and what a din of flies. I got a sudden flash of warmth, of Mary dimpling as she rolled out pastry, but it was only the flutter of a page of memory.

I'd have to go up those stairs again, alone this time.

I took some liver pate for him, had a Breezer as a stiffener, and scrambled up, hauled myself by the banister rails, though some of them were loose, some missing, but I managed, inelegantly, clawing and clutching, and who cares about blasted elegance, and who ever cared? Hands white with bird muck, eyes astream, knee ascream, I got there and scrambled to my feet. In the bathroom I washed my hands – the sink that once was white and garlanded with roses was grey and black, with the verdant green around the overflow of something thriving.

Before entering the bedroom I allowed myself to procrastinate and had a look inside the nursery, where I had not set foot for many years. Procrastination is the thief of time – well time's the thief of me.

You couldn't see much, the window so dirty, but sunshine came through a crack, illuminating the toy box, a shrouded cube of grey. Books were towered and scattered like the ruins of an ancient civilization. Osi's armchair, a child-sized piece that he hunched his lanky form in, used to be red velvet but had turned to black, springs struggling through a rip, a blurt of horsehair stuffing. Under the dust I knew how deeply stained the rug was; I could not allow myself to think of that. I stepped out and shut the door.

And once more I found myself hesitating on the landing outside a door, trapped between the layers of my own life, thick and airless as the pages of a book.

When I'd gathered myself sufficiently to step into the bedroom with a soothing greeting on my lips, there was no sign of Osi. Not on the bed, not on the floor. He could have left the room, of course, he could have been wandering in the house, but I knew he wasn't and my feet were drawn towards the gaping window. Standing on the wet squelch of curtain, I looked out and there, below me, on a raft of broken shrubbery he lay, wings spread out, quite still.

Half slithering, knee blasting like a trumpet, feathers rising as if there'd been a massacre of angels, I got downstairs and outside to fight through the undergrowth and get to him. No need to touch to know he'd gone, but still I did, fingers on his stiffened hand, the nails, that shocking tangle, snapped and scattered. Below the beak, amongst the fuzz, there was a shrunken smile. And I knew enough Egyptian claptrap to guess what had happened – Osiris had been transmuted into Horus, and Horus had flown away. I stroked his cold cheek bone. 'Goodbye, my dearest dear,' I said. There was a wrenching inside me as if something was being broken off.

My twin was gone.

24

I WAS SHIVERY FROM the bath and my hair was still wet, but at least the kitchen was warm. In fact the stove was roaring, sounding dangerous, *eating coal*, Mary would say, and I closed it down a bit. I went into the pantry for the milk to make cocoa. There was an odd grimy smell in there as if something was going off, and I couldn't see.

I'd turned to go and fetch a candle, when the door slammed shut. I went for the handle but there was someone there, the scratch of tweed, an off smell and I screamed and screamed until a hand clamped over my mouth.

'Shut up,' said a voice, not Mr Patey's, but Victor's.

I gasped for breath, my legs gone watery. He let me go. 'Now shut up,' he said again.

'What are you doing?' I blurted into the pitchy blackness. 'I nearly died of fright.' It was as if my heart would fling itself right out of my chest. His breath rasped hotly by my ear.

'I knew there was someone here,' I said.

I heard him swallow. The stench of him was overpowering.

'Uncle Victor, can we open the door?'

'*Uncle* ,' he mocked, but he did open it. I stepped out into the kitchen, never so grateful for a bit of light in my life.

'You little cunt,' he said.

I staggered back against the table. I'd never heard the word, and didn't know the meaning of it, but I understood that it was a terrible thing to say.

'How could you have told them that?' he said. 'You fucking little liar.' He was snarling at me, lips pulled back from dirty teeth. He was filthy, bearded, hair wild and stiff, eyes far too wide, far too red.

I couldn't speak. I backed away, stumbling on Cleo who shot off with a yowl. I pushed myself back against the burning heat of the stove. He stank of strong drink as well as sweat, tobacco, grime and I don't like to think what else.

'It was you,' was all that I could say, 'who took the cheese . . .'

'Cheese!' Spit flew from his mouth, hitting me on the lip but I didn't dare wipe it away. 'Do you know what you've done?' he said.

My throat had closed up now and I had to try again before I could make any words come out. 'I didn't mean it,' I said. The ball of spit seemed to burn and I had to scrub it off if it was the last thing I did.

He grabbed the top of my arms. 'Because of your fucking lies I have to stay away. If I come anywhere near you, she says, my sister's husband, my own twin sister's husband, will set the police on me. The *Police*, Isis. After all I've done for this country.' More spit was coming from his mouth and I shrank back into the corner beside the stove, feet sliding on the messy pile of newspapers. 'And all because of a stupid lying little bitch.' His sour breath was getting in my nose and

I could see red veins standing out in the yellow-white of his eyes. His fingers dug painfully into my flesh.

I kicked his shin as hard as I could and he yelped and let me go and I scrubbed the spit away and made sure to get the table between us before I said, 'I'm sorry, I'm sorry. I'll tell them I was wrong. Honestly Victor, I'm sorry, I'm so sorry.'

'*Why* did you say it?' He was bellowing so loudly that I thought surely Osi would hear and come down. Sometimes he would react to things, and I prayed that now would be the time.

'I was *confused*,' I said. 'Honestly Victor.'

'Confused!'

His head was jerking now, spasms that tore it back and sideways on his neck, as bad as it had ever been, and it was my fault.

'I'm sorry,' I said again. 'I will tell them. I'll write. Tonight, you can watch me. I'll tell them I was wrong. I didn't mean it.'

He was leaning against the table now, watching me with eyes like dying fires.

'You didn't mean it,' he repeated flatly. 'Oh that's all right, then.'

'Don't hate me, Victor,' I said. 'I was confused.'

'Confused!' he mocked, but he was losing energy. He staggered and steadied himself with a hand on the table. 'So what did happen to you exactly?'

'I don't know, I honestly don't know. I don't even know if it was anything at all.'

'*What?*'

'Evelyn kept on and on at me. I had to say something. If I'd said it was Selim or any of the Arabs he would have had his hands chopped off. You told me.'

We stood staring at each until I tore my gaze away.

'Victor.' I struggled to quell the tremble in my voice. 'Shall I make you a cup of tea?'

'Something stronger,' he said, and slumped down at the table.

Though I was scared to go back in there, I went into the dark of the pantry and stood on a stool to reach the bottles of strong drink, fumbling in the cobwebby space till my fingertips encountered the brandy. I brought it out and before I could fetch a glass he'd snatched it, wrenched the top off and was swigging it back.

I edged around him, quiet as could be, slicing bread, grating the remains of the cheese. Mary made Welsh rarebit properly with a white sauce and Lea and Perrins, but I was too trembly to do it properly, too aware that Victor might shout at, grab at, me again. But for now he seemed to have forgotten I was there and sat with one hand round the bottle, the other loose on the table, staring at something that I couldn't see.

As soon as the toast was ready, I called Osi down and waited in the hall for him.

'Victor's here,' I whispered, 'and he's angry, he's really angry with me, and drunk.'

'I'm not surprised,' he said and pushed past me into the kitchen. 'Hello, Victor.' He wiped his nose on the sleeve of his jumper.

'Use a handkerchief,' I snapped, keeping behind him.

Victor's mouth stretched into something like a smile. He was halfway through the bottle now.

'Where's Mary?' Osi glanced at the miserably scanty toasted cheese. He looked quite dreadful in the kitchen light, hair much too long and dried into messy tails, nose red and chapped.

'In bed with her head,' I said.

'Fortunate head,' Victor slurred and gave an ugly laugh.

Osi munched his food, but Victor pushed his away.

Now that Osi was there I felt a mite braver and sat down and took a bite of toast. 'How long have you been here?' I asked Victor. 'I *knew* someone else was in the house, I told you Osi, didn't I?'

'I've got every right,' Victor slurred. His face sagged and dragged against his supporting hand. It was as if all his bones had melted and his face, apart from the shock of the eyes, had gone into a stubbly blur.

'But where have you been?'

'Blue Room.'

'But I tried the door.'

'I know!' Again the ghastly attempt at a smile.

Osi was looking at Victor's plate.

'Go on.' Victor pushed it towards him.

'Are you sure? Surely you should eat?' I said.

But he only shrugged and so I shared his rarebit between myself and Osi. If it wasn't delicious, it was at least filling and still warmish.

Victor's arm gave way and he let his head down on the table and before we'd finished eating, he was asleep, drool spilling from his slackened lips. How shocked Mary would be to find him in the morning, and how cross. But I didn't dare disturb him.

Once Osi had finished eating and gone back to the nursery, I took out a pen and some paper and wrote the letter to my parents at their *post restante* address in Luxor so that Victor would see it as soon as he woke. He could take and post it tomorrow. I wrote that I'd been wrong and absolutely certain that Victor hadn't gone near me in the tomb, and that in all my life he had never been less than a jolly good- and kind-hearted uncle to me and Osi. And I begged them to forgive me, and to forget the awful muddle, and please, please, *please,* to come home soon.

I left the letter open on the table and cleared up quietly round Victor who was snoring now, in and out as regularly as someone sawing wood. And then I went to bed, wishing I could secure the bedroom door – but Osi would want to come to bed eventually, and I could hardly lock him out.

25

In the morning, for the first time since we'd been home, there was no frost on our bedroom window. I was cheered by this, though it was still hideously chilly and damp. I jumped out of bed, and, leaving Osi asleep, put on another layer of clothes and hurried down to the kitchen. It was dull and cold; the stove gone out. My letter had vanished and there was no sign of Victor except for the empty bottle on the floor.

Today he would post the letter and all would be well. And what relief there was in that. Mary was still not down, so I decided to try and light the stove myself, to save her the trouble and to take her up a cup of tea. The day after one of her heads, she was always peaky and sluggish. Today she could sleep in for as long as she liked. I would insist; in fact, I would take charge. And later, she could come down and sit beside the stove. She could sit there all day if she wanted to, she could finish *Desert Longing*, or simply doze, just as she liked, and I would make a fuss of her. I prayed Victor would not return today, since that would aggravate her, but if he did come, I would say she needn't worry about laying up the table in the dining room, she needn't take any notice of him at all.

I fetched coal and kindling from the outhouse and struggled with the stove. Mary had the trick of lighting it, and the trick of coaxing it to stay alight. It took me ages to get it going, but in the end I did manage. I put the kettle and the porridge pan on the stove-top, and went upstairs to see how she was.

On my way up, I knocked on the Blue Room door just to check whether Victor was still there. The Blue Room was the room farthest from Osi's and mine, at the other end of the gallery. It was a pretty, spacious room papered with bluebirds, with windows on two sides, and pale blue velvet curtains.

The door wasn't locked and the room was empty, though the pillow was dented and the eiderdown trailed on the floor to show that he had gone up to bed at some time in the night, but there was nothing to indicate whether he planned to return. The view from the back window carried the eye right down the garden past the orchard, the vegetable patch, the obscured icehouse and over to the railway line. I pressed my face against the damp glass – everything out there was still caked in white, but there was a glimmer of pallid sunshine.

It was as if, since we'd been home, we had all been frozen solid, but now the sky was streaked with lemon and pale blue and it seemed possible that things could change, that spring could come. I felt a surge of optimism, borne out of the relief of having faced Uncle Victor, of having had it out with him, as Mary would say, and of telling the truth in my letter. I could make it all right again for him with Evelyn again, and I would.

So it was in a state of precarious cheerfulness that I went up the attic stairs to Mary's room. I tapped at the door and, as I waited, heard from the roof the welcome whoosh of thawing snow. I tapped again. I would leave her if she were asleep. When I opened the door, very quietly, just to take a peep, I saw that she hadn't moved since I'd left her. The room was very still and the sudden hard hammering of my heart echoed as if in a cave.

'Mary,' I murmured, but I knew already. 'Mary?' Her eyes were half open showing little slits of shine and her lips were blue. Thin sunlight shone on the whiteness of her cheek. I put my finger down to touch her, and she was icy cold. 'Mary!' I said. 'Mary!' and stupidly and uselessly I shook her, as if I could wake her from this, and her mouth started to open and just for a second I thought . . . but it was only the shaking that caused it, and I recoiled from a glimpse of teeth.

'Wait there,' I whispered, crept out of the room and fled down the stairs. I could not get down fast enough and stood on the landing staring at our bedroom door. I looked along the corridor towards the Blue Room, wishing that Victor were still here. What to do? What to do?

Osi was sleeping on his back, snoring through his blocked nose and I shook and thumped him. He always took ages to wake up properly – his eyes would open blankly, only gradually tuning in. I stood and shivered, waiting for him to become fully conscious, and then: 'Mary's dead,' I said through chattering teeth.

He lay staring up at me, still blank.

'Mary's dead,' I shouted and the shout rang on and on.

As he sat up my legs went weak and I rested down on the

edge of his bed. A gust of wind rattled the window, strange after the frozen stillness we'd grown so used to.

'And Victor's gone away again. I don't know what to do.'

Osi wiped his nose on his pyjama sleeve. '*M*,' he said. 'The owl means *M*. *M* for Mary.'

'*Don't!*' I screamed, shocking myself with the sound. I jumped up. 'None of your Egyptian rubbish now, *please*.'

He sniffed, seeming to consider.

'Look,' I said. 'She might not be. I need you to come and see.' I snatched his hand and dragged him out of bed. I made him put on his slippers and dressing gown, and we went out into the corridor. The house seemed to stretch, to yawn hugely round us as we made our way up the attic stairs.

Mary lay in exactly the same position, her face, possibly, a little bluer and her lips drawn further back. Osi poked her cheek with his forefinger. 'She's dead, all right,' he said.

I was shocked by the heat of the tear that was rolling down my cheek. 'Don't poke her like that,' I said, because he was jabbing her harder and harder with his long-nailed finger: neck, chest, stomach. There was a fascinated glitter in his eyes. I grabbed his arm, pulled him out of the room and shook him. 'Osi! *Please*. Be *normal*. I need you to be normal now.'

The light in his eyes dimmed and he looked properly at me. 'Poor Mary,' he said, and sneezed horribly against the wall.

The stove had stayed alight and the kitchen was warm, the kettle coming to the boil and the porridge pan bubbling. On the dresser was Mary's list for Mr Burgess: onions, carrots, potatoes, blancmange powder, soap flakes, gravy browning and 'br'. Beside it lay a pencil chewed at the end. Mary always chewed a pencil while pondering the list.

'What shall we do?' I said, I kept saying, really to myself. I didn't expect any help from Osi, but I did want him with me. With the shock and the grief and the fear, too many things, too strong, to feel, I was hardly feeling anything at all. 'I don't know what we're supposed to do,' I said, hearing as if from outside myself the pathetic whimper of my voice. And then I did feel something – anger. 'There should be a parent here!' I said. 'This is not fair! Now we're all alone, what are we supposed to do?' The rage was a relief; something definite. I stamped my foot. 'How can they leave us like this? What are we going to do?'

'Is Victor coming back?' Osi asked.

'How am I supposed to know?'

I was thinking. This was Sunday. Mr Burgess would be here tomorrow. Could we leave her till tomorrow? And Victor might return, he might be back at any moment. And then he'd drive to the village for the doctor. I thought with a shudder of Mr Patey, and his dead wives. If Mary had married him, she'd be yet another to add to his list. Mr Patey, the conscientious objector and his trail of death. It was her blessed head. *It'll be the death of me.* She'd said that often enough.

If only there was a telephone – Arthur had talked so often of installing one, but always 'next time we're home' and naturally he never had. Of course we must send Evelyn and Arthur a telegram; that's what you do in emergencies. Mr Burgess would help us with that, even if Victor didn't return, and then they'd have to come home. In spite of everything, I felt a little leap of pleasure at the idea. This was so serious that they would surely have to come home and not leave us again, not without Mary. There was a gulp stuck in my throat like a rock that wouldn't move. *Without Mary*. We had never been without her in Little Egypt. Osi was staring at me, waiting for what I would say or do.

'I suppose the police must know,' I said.

'They might take us away,' he said.

I was so unused to him considering practical things that it was a surprise when he spoke sense.

'There's probably something wrong about children living on their own,' I agreed. 'Not that we're quite children any more. They'll simply have to come home.'

I picked up Mary's frayed pencil to compose the telegram. I remembered from telegrams in the war that each word cost a fortune and didn't you have to put stops in? Since Mr Burgess was already owed money again, we'd have to keep it short. *Urgent stop Mary dead stop come home stop?* Did the stops cost anything? Did we need them? I found that I was chewing the softened end of the pencil, woody flecks coming off between my teeth. I spat them on the table, thinking of germs, of Mary's germs and remembering with a jolt that she was actually upstairs dead. That this was real. I swallowed hard but the rock in my throat was lodged tight.

It would still be ages till they got home. How could we bear to wait till then? 'I'm sure Victor will be back soon,' I said. 'He'll take charge.' The lid of the porridge pan lifted and clanked with the steam and I got up and stirred. 'We should eat,' I said, surprised by a wisp of hunger stirred up by the oaty smell.

The porridge was lumpier even than Mary's most angry porridge, but I dished it out, and put milk and sugar on the table. Osi shovelled his down as usual.

'You should get properly dressed,' I said. 'And I do wish

you'd shut your mouth when you eat. It will put any lady off,' I bothered to add, I don't know why. Although there was hunger in my stomach I could hardly squeeze the porridge down my throat. I made cocoa for us both and loaded it with sugar, flinching against the ghost of a voice: *that don't grow on trees*.

Osi drank his cocoa while it was still too hot for me to swallow and then he got up.

'Don't leave me alone,' I pleaded, and then, pulling myself together, 'I mean, you need to help today. You need to help me in the kitchen.'

He looked at me, eyes wide and green as grapes. 'Later,' he said. I heard him sneezing as he went upstairs. I guessed he would go back to his work now, as if nothing had happened. If he were thinking about Egypt, nothing else would be in his head. I was almost envious. There was nothing *I* could concentrate on so fiercely and completely. I cradled the hot cup in my hands and sipped my cocoa. While we waited for our parents' return – which would be weeks – what should we eat? I'd have to do a list and I'd have to learn to cook properly quick smart.

I sat in Mary's chair beside the stove and started a new shopping list. *Cheese*, I wrote, *eggs, potatoes, chocolate, sugar, bananas, candles*. I added the items Mary had put, wondering about the 'br' – brawn? Brisket? Brandy? I should get some for Victor anyway. And with that thought I dropped the pencil, drew my knees up to my chest and allowed myself to cry. I sobbed and groaned and tried to pray. If it were the other way round, Mary would pray for me. I thought I should go up and see her, pay my respects in some way, take her a flower – though nothing outside was blooming – not leave her up there, cold and alone. But I didn't dare. I scarcely dared to leave the kitchen. Cleo crept onto my lap and we huddled together until the morning sun had passed the windows. Every now and then an icicle snapped like a bone and crashed past the glass.

Eventually I had to get up to visit the WC. And then, in order to finish my list, I checked the pantry. There was not much bread, though plenty of flour and yeast. The kitchen was plenty warm enough for proving, so I thought to try and make a loaf.

I struggled for hours with the mixture, my tears dripping into the bowl and salting the dough. Mary's strong hands and arms would knead and stretch and slap the dough about and if she was in a fanciful mood she'd make plaits of bread or even – when we were smaller – sheep and flowers and funny bun people with currants for their eyes. I realized how puny the muscles in my own arms were as I stopped to rest and scrub my wet face with a floury hand. But it was good to be doing something real and helpful, and after all we had to eat. I could just hear Mary saying that. My head clamoured all day with things she would have said.

While waiting for the dough to rise, and then the loaf to cook, I went outside and fed the birds. I put on Victor's greatcoat and stood with sparrows and finches hopping on my hands and shoulders, smelling the change in the air. The sky was already flushing with the start of sunset. The packed and frozen snow was wet and slithery, and there was a symphony of drips and tinkles, cracks and scatters, as snow and icicles descended from the roof and from the trees.

I fed the ballroom birds, averting my eyes completely from the mirrors, and then I shut myself in the kitchen once more, played patience, and read old newspapers, boring things about

Germany defaulting on its reparations, more interesting things about fashions by Chanel, even sweaters can be chic, and a list of the sumptuous treasures from Tutankhamen's tomb. I screwed that paper up and shoved it in the stove.

By the time the bread was steaming on the rack, the sky was dark. The loaves were so good, so well risen, so golden and crusty, they made me cry again. Mary would have said they were humdingers. I cut the end off one, even though you should leave bread to cool before you cut it, slathered it with butter and found that I could eat now, in fact that I could hardly stop myself.

I called Osi down but there was no answer. It took a vast effort of will for me to venture back upstairs, keeping my eyes averted from the door to the attic. I tried the nursery door, but he had pushed something against it.

'Osi,' I called. 'I've made bread.'

'Not hungry.'

'Come down and have a warm then. What's in the way of the door?'

But he wouldn't come out. I could have forced the door open but I didn't want to go into that cold, depressing room. 'Busy,' was all he that he would say.

It might seem that Osi was unfeeling, but I knew he was upset about Mary. He might even have been crying in there, not wanting me to see. And keeping busy always was his way.

'Osi?' I said again. 'Are you warm enough?' But my voice sounded so small and lonely and the gloom of the house engulfed me so that I hurried back down to the warm kitchen and stayed there, reading and eating – I believe I finished a whole loaf – and vainly straining my ears for the sound of Victor's car, until it was evening. I felt shivery and my throat was growing scratchy, as Osi's cold got into me. I made a hot water bottle and, much earlier than usual, carried it, with a stock of candles, up to bed.

On the way, I tapped on the nursery door again. 'Are you all right?' I said. 'Osi, you need to come out and eat something.'

'I will,' he said.

'Are you all right?'

Silence.

'Please Osi, come out and eat something and come to bed.'

It was as if on both sides of the door we were holding our breaths and then I heard him blow his nose.

'I hope you're using a hanky,' I called, and losing patience, went into our room and slammed the door.

I lay, fully dressed, between damp sheets, my feet burning on the bottle, chilblains itching, head filling up with cold, listening for the sound of Victor's car, or for Osi to emerge from the nursery, but I heard nothing except an occasional owl screech and the sorrowful murmurings of the house. Cleo scratched at the door and I let her in. I often did, though Mary hated it, but now it didn't matter, and that was awful. Cleo curled up at my side and comforted me with her purr. I left three candles burning. I could not stand to be in the dark. There was no moon or starlight, only the dark out there.

26

WHEN I WOKE, the sky was light, the window whited
out with frost again and Osi absent. His bed was undisturbed.
It was freezing, and utterly still. And now my head was thick
with cold. I was baffled by a sense of unease or the taint of a
bad dream – and then, with a lurch, remembered. I lay stunned,
frozen as the day for a long silent stretch before I was able to
force myself from bed.

No one else would see to the stove or make the breakfast or
be ready for Mr Burgess when he came.

In my drawer was a pile of handkerchiefs, ironed into lovely
squares by Mary. I blew my nose, put my coat over my crumpled clothes, a pair of socks over the stockings I'd slept in. I
didn't look at the door to the attic as I passed it. *No use dwelling*. That's exactly what she would have said, in fact I could
almost hear her. *Just buck up and get on with it*. And that's
what we had to do, *best foot forward*, just send the telegram
and keep ourselves alive till Arthur and Evelyn came home.
Why should we not be able to do that? We were not helpless;
we were not babies.

Once our parents (or even Victor) had returned, Mary

would not be our responsibility any more and then I could be, would be, properly, normally, sad. But I must hold it at bay till then or everything would fly apart. It felt like an actual inner manoeuvre, holding the pieces together by sheer force of concentration and will.

'I'm making porridge,' I called as I passed the nursery door. I went along the corridor to tap on the door of the Blue Room, and when there was no answer I pushed open the door with a tiny flare of hope – but the bed was empty and untouched since last I'd looked.

Down in the kitchen, I opened the vent on the stove. To my amazed relief, it contained a glowing heap of ash – enough to coax into another blaze. I put a couple of sticks in, as I'd observed Mary doing, carefully balanced little coals on them and shut the door. I pressed my ear against the warm iron to listen and soon, sure enough, there was the crackle and catch of flame. I felt an odd little sensation of satisfaction that despite all and everything, one thing had come out right at least. I noticed that there was a scatter of salt on the table and that the cutlery drawer was lolling open. Last night it had been shut. So Osi must have been down and eaten something, and that was good.

When I went outside to fill the coal scuttle, I found the ground littered with broken icicles. The air was thin as glass again, too cold to breathe. The snow, in its melt, had slid like lazy eyelids over the windows and frozen there, as if the house itself had given up and gone to sleep.

Back inside, I poured oatmeal into the pan, adding water and a handful of raisins from a jar, as Mary had done sometimes for a treat. And I stirred the porridge this time, to stop it getting lumpy, and when it had glugged and thickened I pushed the pan off the hot plate and went upstairs to fetch my brother. This time I would not take no for an answer. He had to eat and I must make sure of it. Although only minutes older than him, I was the big sister, I was the capable one; I would be responsible until I was relieved.

I noticed water on the landing floor, not water but drips of ice. I followed them to the bathroom. The door was open and the bath was full of half frozen water. Scattered on the floor was more salt.

Passing the door to the attic stairs, I saw it was ajar. The nursery door was shut. I stopped outside. The handle was made of brass, so cold under my hand that it made my fingers ache as I hesitated, building up my resolve. I had to see what I would see though I longed to run to my bed and bury my head beneath the covers. I turned the handle and pushed hard enough to move the chair that he had jammed against the door. As the door opened I saw my brother kneeling on the floor, looking up at me – and even he seemed shocked by what he'd done.

I shut the door against the sight, and stared at the paint, pale blue as on all the doors, chipped at the edge with nibble shapes as if a mouse had been at it. I breathed in and out three times watching the airy feathers bloom and vanish before I opened the door again.

'Stop,' I said, though he did seem already to have stopped. I could see the long pale blur of nakedness at the edge of my vision and also blood, roses of it, on the carpet.

'I'm preparing her for her journey,' he said.

'No!' I shouted and now my eyes went to the body, the arms and legs jutting at stiff angles, the hard blue bosoms, the cut that gaped up the left side of her abdomen. Osi stood up. His hands were bloody. 'I've done it wrong,' he said, 'you're supposed to remove the lungs and the intestines and . . .'

'No,' I said, my voice odd and wobbly. 'No, you're not.'

Osi held his fingers apart and stared at them. Would the blood freeze onto him? Does blood freeze like water? By his feet was a heap of something dark and sticky.

'I can't find her liver. I don't know which thing is which.'

The light in the nursery was dim from the overhanging snow and yet it sparkled with a cruel clarity. I struggled to keep my voice level. 'What you have to do is come and wash your hands and have your breakfast.'

He blinked as if he'd just woken from a trance and looked down at Mary and at his hands and then at me, pupils stretched so huge his eyes were black.

Someone might think he killed her, I thought. That's what it will look like. No one normal could possibly understand this. *Or even that we killed her together*. Despite her gaping abdomen there was still a slit of shine in Mary's eyes, one open a bit more than the other, and between her lips there was the glint of teeth.

'There isn't enough salt,' he said.

'Stop it, Osi.'

'I need to find her liver.'

'*Stop!*'

A long shiver travelled from the soles of my feet to the skin of my scalp. I took a deep breath, the air rasping my sore throat, and a strange dream-like species of calm settled on me. I went into the bedroom and pulled the counterpane from Osi's bed and then I covered Mary where she lay.

'Come and wash.'

I stood outside the bathroom door and watched him run his hands under the tap, red water becoming pink, becoming clear. 'And empty the bath,' I said. The gurgling was loud as the water ran away in a prolonged and greedy gulping, leaving splinters of ice, and a nest of Mary's curls tangled in the plug hole.

I dished up the porridge, put two dishes on the table, sat down and indicated that Osi should do the same.

'Now eat.'

I took a mouthful, warm and sweet with a sudden juicy squelch of raisin between my teeth – I flinched at the sensation. Osi ate steadily as always, almost mechanically. Spoon in, pause, and swallow. Spoon in, pause, and swallow.

'You know it's wrong, don't you?' I said.

'Why?' He put his spoon down. He seemed revived by the porridge.

'It's against the law,' I said.

'Whose law?'

'British Law. The law of the land.'

'How do you know?'

I stared at his red, crusted nose.

'It's what happens, Osi. Dead people have funerals and are buried in graveyards.'

'Soulless affairs,' Osi said and I recognised Arthur's voice getting into his, 'the so-called decent Christian burial. I want to do it the proper way, otherwise,' and just in time, before I lost my temper, his voice became anxious and his own again, 'otherwise she'll end up in the next world with *nothing*, Icy. She has to be preserved. She needs her *things* with her.' He looked up and met my eyes. 'But I've made a mess of it.'

He put down his spoon and swallowed. I heard the hard click in his throat, and then he pushed his chair back and went out of the kitchen, and I listened to the creaking as he went back upstairs. I didn't know what to say or do. He was only doing what he thought was best for Mary, I understood that, and knew I should not to blame him, though it made me sick.

At that moment I could easily have hated him. If he hadn't looked so scared I would have hated him. He had ruined everything. He had ruined the rest of our lives, though I didn't understand that then. All I knew then was that this would have to be kept secret, if Osi wasn't to end up in asylum, or both of us in prison. I sat staring at my porridge as it congealed.

Mr Burgess had a toothache, his jaw muffled in a tartan scarf. He stepped into the kitchen smelling of eucalyptus, with a dewdrop on the end of his nose that trembled as he went on about the night he'd had of it. Everyone had the cold, he told us, it was going round like wildfire and what with this weather, we should be bally grateful he could do his rounds at all. He put the box of groceries on the table and looked around for Mary.

'Chew a clove,' I said. 'It's what Mary does for toothache.' I winced as I spoke her name. 'Do you want one? She's gone to her sister's.'

He looked at the kettle, moustache drooping glumly, but

I only handed him the list. The dewdrop fell from his nose onto his scarf.

'I don't know nothing about a sister,' he said.

'Could you send the telegram please and add it to the bill.' My mind was flocking, with what I could put. Not Mary dead, of course, not now. 'A telegram to my parents,' I said.

'Saying what?'

'I'll write it.' I picked up the pencil. *Mary gone stop*, I put, *immediate return vital stop*. I was pleased with the concision. Surely they would take notice of that?

I held my breath as Mr Burgess took in my words. 'She went away unexpected then?' he said.

'Her sister was taken poorly,' I said. 'Very poorly.'

'How did she get word? I don't recall a letter.'

I stared at him. A new drip was gathering. 'Someone came for her,' I said.

'It's rum that she's never mentioned a sister,' he said. 'I seem to remember her saying she had no one in the world, besides you two.'

'They didn't speak for years,' I improvised. 'Some falling out – and then they . . . fell back in again.'

He was looking at me suspiciously. 'Who was it came to fetch her then?'

'Goodness!' I said. 'What does it matter? The fact is, she's had to go, so you see we need to telegraph our parents.'

'When's she coming back then?'

'I don't know,' I said. 'She's very cross, you know, about not being paid and so on.'

He believed that, at least.

'She might not ever come back.' My voice cracked and I

had to look hard at the table and crunch my teeth together to keep from wailing.

He stared at me with his bleary eyes. 'Will you manage on your own?'

I sniffed and got my voice under control. 'Uncle Victor's coming – with a lady,' I said. 'We'll be right as nine-pence.' I forced a smile. 'And Ma and Pa will be home before you know it.'

Mr Burgess glanced wistfully at the kettle.

'That'll be all then,' I said.

'She left no word for me?'

I shook my head.

'Well, when you hear from her send her my . . . best regards,' Mr Burgess said. 'Oooch.' His hand shot to his jaw.

'Sure you don't want a clove?'

He shook his head and tightened his muffler. I waited till he was out of the door and then ran up to our bedroom, scritched a space in the frost with my fingernails, and watched his van blur into white.

27

AND THEN, DRAGGING my feet, I went to find Osi. It took all my will to push open the nursery door, but he was not there. Mary was; I'd had a wild magical idea that she would somehow have gone, but she lay as we'd left her, covered with the counterpane, a pale puff of curls escaping from one end. So cold and stiff, *chilled to the marrow*, she would have said, and now that was really, literally true.

I found Osi sitting up in bed, shivering, arms clutched round *The Egyptian Book of the Dead*.

'I've done it wrong,' Osi said, voice cracking. 'I've messed her up.'

He'd lost his nerve. I understood; he had always dreamed of mummifying a human being and had woken from the dream to the reality of Mary dead and himself, a childish amateur with a knife, expecting a neat diagram of a body rather than the loose, unruly, stinking thing it is once you cut through the skin.

I slumped down on my own bed and blew my nose. I longed to be warm. I longed not to have to think. In truth, I longed to climb into bed and stick my head under the pillow and not come out till this was all over. But it would never be over. The idea of running away flashed through my mind. But I had no money and no idea, really, how to go *about* running away, especially in such bitter cold. Running away with Osi in tow would have been impossible – and leaving him even more so. I was his sister and I was responsible, and despite all and everything, I did love him. Not a love that I had decided on, but a deep and visceral tugging in my guts and in my veins. Osi needed me and always would.

His eyes were fixed on m, waiting for me to speak. At that moment I had the sensation of something, some sort of guard, falling away inside me as I admitted the thought that we would have to complete the process; that it was the only thing we could do. We could not, after all, undo it. We could not put Mary back together. We could not call police and doctors and all the normal things that people do when a loved one dies.

It would be the best thing to get her neatly wrapped, rather than to leave her loose and oozing. She would be more comfortable, more complete, stupid to even think it, but somehow *warmer* that way; cared for, at least. *Tucked up. Snug as a bug in a rug.* And it would be something that Arthur and Evelyn would understand. They could scarcely be angry with Osi, or even surprised, that after all their encouragement he'd taken to behaving like an ancient Egyptian.

And I thought it must be good for him, better for him, to complete the process he had started. I didn't want him to feel that he had failed. Failed himself, failed Mary, just *failed*. So I told him he would have to finish. At first he refused, said he could not do it. I had to pull him out of bed and force him to get dressed. I could still make Osi do things in those days. And then I dragged him to the nursery.

Jars and more salt was what he needed – though there
wasn't any more salt – and he'd need hundreds of bandages,
which we didn't have. He said he could not, would not, do it
and so I locked him in the nursery with Mary. It sounds cruel,
but it was the best thing for him. He didn't bang on the door
or shout like a normal person. He would carry on the process,
I knew he would, it would be only thing he'd be able to think
of to do.

And the best thing.

Dizzied with disbelief at what I was making happen, I went
down to the pantry. He was right that there was no salt. Mary
had wondered why we got through so much and now I understood that Osi had been purloining it for such an opportunity
as this. I emptied out currants and tea and split peas for the
canopic jars. I took the best linen sheets, beautifully ironed and
folded by Mary, out of the press and all day, till my hands were
raw, I cut and ripped them to ribbons. White mounds grew
around me on the kitchen table, tumbling onto the floor, to be
trampled on and nested in by Cleo into great bandage tangles.
I didn't know how many we would need, but I spared only
the sheets that were on the beds, becoming hypnotised by the
sound of tearing cotton.

It was the time that Mary would have sat down with a cup
of tea and put her feet up for five minutes, before I went up
to check on Osi's progress. When I unlocked and opened the
door he stood up. There were great bruisy shadows under his
eyes and he looked sick, desperate and dazed.

'Are you done?' I kept my eyes averted from the figure on
the floor.

'Nearly.'

'Come then.' I led him downstairs and sat him by the stove.

He stared at the heaps of cotton that were like a snowdrift in the kitchen.

'Will there be enough?' I asked. 'You need something to eat.' I buttered him a piece of bread that he stuffed whole into his mouth. 'It's the right thing you're doing,' I said. 'You look tired. Should we wait till tomorrow to do the wrapping?'

'No. Tonight.'

I put two big potatoes in the stove for later. Osi stood and stretched and I heard the popping of his vertebrae. He roamed around the kitchen gathering grave goods. Flour and sugar and currants wrapped in twists of paper; her rolling pin; a silver spoon.

'We have to make some shabtis,' he said

'What?'

'Servants for her, little people, so she doesn't have to work her fingers to the bone.'

Our eyes met when he said that, sounding for an instant like Mary herself.

'Like dolls?' I asked.

He nodded.

'From what? Pegs? I could make peg dolls. Or she could have my old dolls.'

'The more she has the better – and get things from her room. Her treasures. Anything she'll want to take with her.'

I was pleased that he'd regained his energy for the task, but it was with reluctance that I left the warmth of the kitchen to go up to the attic. I lit a candle, and keeping my eyes from the dip in her pillow, I snatched up her wedding photograph, the little album, her brush and mirror set, her powder compact. There was a string of peeling pearls that she wore on high days and holidays, her photographs, a desiccated iris, a felt hat and a dangerous looking hat pin with a bumble bee design. As I gathered these items it was as if someone was behind me, breathing coldly on my neck, and once my hands were full I bolted down the stairs.

On the landing I stopped. There was the sound of an engine outside. I threw Mary's things on my bed and ran downstairs. Victor had come in through the front door and was standing in the dim light of the hall. He looked vast in his coat and driving helmet.

'Dear little Icy,' he said, voice blurring drinkily.

'Have you got a lady with you?' I asked.

He shook his head and I gulped with relief.

'Come into the kitchen and I'll make you something,' I said.

'Where's Mary?' He peered behind me.

'Still poorly.'

He staggered and pulled a face. 'Must be bad.' He pulled off his gloves, scarf and helmet and threw them on a chair.

'It's her head,' I told him. 'And we've both got fearful colds. Mr Burgess said it's going round like wildfire.'

'Poor little Icy. We must make you a hot toddy.'

He followed me into the kitchen where there were still mounds of sheeting strips on the table and tumbling onto the floor. 'What the devil?' he said.

'Cut up for dusters,' I said, which was ridiculous, you don't dust with skinny rags like that, but he was not domesticated and anyway, too drunk to care. It gave me an idea, if I could get him even drunker he'd fall asleep and we could continue.

While Victor shucked off his coat, I poured him a big glass of brandy.

'I should go up and see Mary,' he said. 'Mary, Mary, quite contrary, what a contrary minx she is.'

'She's sleeping now,' I said quickly. 'I just went. She'll bite your head off if you wake her.'

'She is a firecracker, that one,' he agreed. 'What's for eats?' He sat down at the table and shoved some ribbons out of the way.

'I'm making potatoes in their jackets, but they won't be ready for ages. I'm only doing two, but we can share them. Where've you been?'

'Oh . . .' He swallowed his brandy in one gulp and grimaced. 'Poor show. Get Mary to order Cognac next time. Around and about, don't you know? I posted the letter.'

It took me a moment even to remember what he meant.

'Do you know,' he said, wrinkling his nose at his glass, 'what I'd really like is a cup of tea. Any cake?'

I shook my head. 'You look tired,' I said. 'Have you come to stay?' My eyes kept going to the door; any moment Osi might come in and give the game away.

Victor sipped his drink and nodded. 'Thought I'd put up here for a day or two.' Elbows on the table, he sagged his head into his hands. He looked grey, exhausted, scoops of shadow under his eyes and the light gleaming on the bony ridges of his eye sockets and the thin bridge of his nose. He looked uncannily like Osi had done as he sat in the same chair an hour before, shattered by his gruesome task.

I filled the kettle and put it on the stove.

'I'll just get these out of the way.' I scooped up armfuls of bandages and carried them upstairs. I kicked the nursery door till Osi opened it, and shoved them into his arms.

'Victor's here,' I said. 'Don't come down. I'll bring your food up. We'll have to wait till he's asleep. I'll keep him busy till then.'

He darted me a startled look before I shut the door.

Victor was absorbed in reading one of the old newspapers. He'd moved nearer the stove, and I was glad to see he'd topped up his brandy. I watched his eyelids grow heavy and the nod of his head as he kept approaching the precipice of sleep, but always he pulled back. When the potatoes were ready, I slavered them in butter, pepper – there was no salt – and shared them between three plates. I took a plate up to Osi, and watched Victor shovel his down. He left the skin, as usual, and I put on more butter and rolled it into a delicious tube. I thought it quite a marvel that part of me could stay hungry and normal when I knew what was going on upstairs.

'Cup of tea, Icy?' Victor asked. I'd managed to deflect him so far, afraid that tea might perk him up, but now I had an idea. Some of Mary's headache powders were on the kitchen windowsill. She rarely took them since they knocked the stuffing out her, she said. I bleated feebly as the horribly apt expression entered my mind.

'What's funny?' Victor asked.

'Nothing.' I waited till he'd looked back at the paper before I unfolded a dose of powders and sprinkled it into his tea. I wondered about giving him two, to make sure, but didn't want to kill him. And then I filled a hot-water bottle.

'Why don't you get cosy in bed?' I said. 'You can take your tea up. You do look tired, Victor, what you want's a good night's kip.'

He was sitting forward in such a way that he could lean his weight on his jumping leg, and he looked up at me with a weary twist of humour. 'Quite the little housekeeper, aren't you, Icy? When you're not going round spreading slander.'

It was as if I'd been slapped. 'I said I was sorry,' I muttered.

He got to his feet with a stagger. I put the hot-water bottle into his arms and he carried it upstairs, while I followed with his cup of tea.

On the landing, beside the attic door, he paused. 'Perhaps I should go up and see Mary,' he said.

'She won't thank you,' I told him. The tea was spilling into the saucer with the tremble in my hands. I could sense Osi frozen by our voices behind the nursery door. 'Have your tea first,' I urged. 'Honestly, she just wants to be left alone.'

The tea cup rattled on its saucer as he stood swaying, unde-cided, on the landing.

'I'll pop up later,' I said. 'Bed for you.'

To my enormous relief he shrugged and followed me to the Blue Room, where I turned down the sheets and put the hot bottle where his feet would go. My eyes were darting round looking for the key so that I could lock him in. He'd never know; I'd unlock it before morning. But there was no sign of the key. He shucked off his outer clothes and in his long wool underwear collapsed onto the mattress. I pulled the covers up and as I tucked him in I was overcome with a convulsion of grief as I remembered all the times Mary had tucked me in *snug as a bug*, all those times, and now she was no *no, no, no.*

I doubled over as if someone had slammed me in the stomach. But *pull yourself together* she was saying, her voice lodged inside my head where it always was and where it has stayed. And I did pull myself together. I took a deep breath and straightened up and turned back to see that Victor was oblivious.

'Drink up,' I said and watched as he propped himself half upright to take a sip of tea, screwing up his face at the taste.

'It's a new blend Mary chose,' I said. 'Don't you like it?'

'It's cold,' is all he said, swigged the rest of it back and handed me the cup.

'There,' I said. 'Now you'll sleep the sleep of the just.'

'Just what?' he said with a weary smile. He yawned and lay down. 'Night night, Icy.'

'Night night,' I said. 'Bugs bite and so on.'

'Indeed.'

I would have been curious to wait and see how long it took him to get to sleep, but I crept out and shut the door firmly behind me. The brandy and the drug would surely do the job of a key, and keep him there till we were finished.

28

THE NURSERY LIGHT was poor and dim, draining everything of colour. I drew the curtains across the frosty black of the windows. Osi was kneeling by the corpse, trembling, his face grey. He looked almost elderly.

'We wrap the head first,' he said.

The body was messily sewn, with wiry stuffing poking between the stitches on her abdomen.

'What's that?' I asked.

He nodded at his little armchair and I saw he'd pulled some of the horsehair stuffing out. 'It should have been salt,' he said.

'Needs must,' I said in Mary's voice, and winced.

Her eyelids were held down with coins and her face was quite blank as if she had no opinion about what was happening to her. She was drained of any Maryness, but for the wild spring of her hair. I tried to get a brush through it but it was too snarled and I could not bear the thought that all the snagging and tugging would cause her pain.

'Come on then,' I said.

He knelt by her head and lifted it, quite tenderly, while I passed a ribbon of sheet underneath and wound it round.

'Tighter,' he said. 'It must be firm.' My instinct was to be gentle. I didn't want to squash her nose, but I obeyed him and pulled it tight, finding myself grateful as the features flattened and disappeared. Together we wrapped the head until it was a blank wad of white, a landscape hidden under snow, and once that was done the task grew easier, except when it came to her hands.

I chose the thinnest sheeting, for the delicate business of wrapping the fingers – strong, scarred and so familiar they might as well have been my own. As I wrapped I remembered all the things they'd done: the stroking of hair, the patching of grazes, the drying of tears, the wiping of noses, the pinching of pie crust, the podding of peas, the loving of Gordon Jefferson – and perhaps of Mr Patey.

By the time we'd moved onto the legs and body I'd almost stopped thinking and we were working together in a smooth, efficient rhythm. Osi kept up a murmur of Egyptian spells and I kept my lips pressed together tight, concentrating on making Mary safe and neat. Between the layers, Osi slipped pictures of amulets to make Mary safe on her journey, a journey in which I was almost starting to believe.

I became so engrossed that I didn't hear Victor moving about and it was too late to hide what we were doing when the door flew open.

'Icy,' he was saying, 'where's the –' and then he stopped. He looked at the part-wrapped body on the floor and at Osi and at me. He took in the canopic jars and the pile of grave goods and the blood-stained rug.

'It's Mary,' Osi said and I actually thought I saw the hairs rise on Victor's head, as his eyes stretched wide and his hands went to his mouth and he began to scream.

'Uncle Victor,' I jumped up, my legs all cramped from kneeling for so long, and tried to get hold of him, but he flailed away from me. He would not stop screaming and staring so wide and hard that I thought his eyes would surely fall from their sockets. It was the scream from his nightmares, only now he was awake and what could be worse for his nerves than a waking nightmare? It seemed to wake me too from the strange lull I'd entered and all the energy ran out of me. I wondered feebly if I could get him back to bed and we could pretend it was all a dream, but that would be impossible.

'Please, Victor,' I said. 'Please, come on, let's get out of here.'

Eventually he calmed down enough to allow me to hold his arm and guide him out of the nursery. I shut the door behind us with my foot.

'What have you done?' he said. 'I can't believe my eyes, I . . .' His head was doing the spastic jerk and his entire body shuddering. '*You*!' He recoiled from my attempts to hold him, and ripped his arm away from me. '*You* Isis, *you*!'

'You're cold,' I said, making my voice as level as possible. And I found that I was shivering too. Strange how I had been suspended from my own discomfort during the wrapping of Mary and I had lost track of time – hours must have passed. I ran to the Blue Room and fetched his medication, came back and handed him a pill. He stared at it, before he sighed and swallowed it in a dry gulp.

I started down the stairs. 'Come on, Victor,' I said. 'If you're not going back to bed, let's get you a stiffener.'

He stood at the top of the stairs looking down with a dull space where his eyes should be, awful twitching spasms running through him. There was an animal stench of fear.

'Come on,' I urged and at last he did follow me down and into the kitchen. I poured a brandy and wrapped his coat round his shoulders. I fed the greedy stove, and then I knelt before him, held his hand and explained what had happened.

He listened quietly at first, but then the horror rose in him once more. 'Blood and guts,' he yelled. 'But this is *here*.' He waved his arm wildly. 'Not in *here*.' He punched himself on the side of his head so hard I thought he'd knock himself out.

'Don't.' I grabbed his head and held it tight and looked into his eyes. 'I'm sorry. You shouldn't have seen it.'

'Shouldn't have *seen* it!' He spat out a laugh.

'What could I do, though?' I said. 'I thought if anyone saw her like that they'd think Osi killed her. I have to look after *him*.'

I let go of Victor and he folded in on himself, rocking and mumbling. Cleo was sitting by the door, eyeing him warily and when I opened it she fled into the scullery. Victor hadn't touched the brandy and I took a sip of it myself and felt a calming as it ran hotly through me. I put a hand on his shoulder to let some of the calm stream down my arm and into him, and I do believe it soothed him, just a bit. It was four o'clock in the morning, I noticed. I had never been up at that time before.

'Do you see?' I said.

'*Mary*,' he murmured. 'Lovely Mary.'

'I *know*.' I had to brace myself against a fresh flood of knowing that this was *real*: that that thing upstairs was really Mary.

'Poor Mary. Poor *dear* Mary.'

'Don't.' I took my hand away. 'I can't be properly sad, don't you see? I can't let myself be properly sad till it's all over and dealt with.'

'How hard you are,' he said. And that is the cruellest thing that anyone has ever said to me. But I could not deny it. If being hard is keeping your emotions in control, keeping yourself under control, then I was hard. A softer person could not have endured my life.

'Please go back to bed now,' I urged. 'Shall I bring you some warm milk?'

'They might think it was me,' he said. His eyes were too terrible to meet and I turned my back, pouring milk into a pan. I wanted something else to eat, bread and milk, which is what Mary would sometimes make when we were little – bread softened in warm milk with a little crunch of sugar. Eating something comforting and babyish would help, I thought, would help to carry me through the night.

'They already suspect me of . . .'

'But I've told the truth now. Soon as they get the letter they'll know.'

'There are other things,' he said, so quietly I could hardly hear. 'Misunderstandings with women. I will have some warm milk, Icy.'

'Bread and milk?'

'Evie will think it was me.'

'No she won't. No one will. Because no one will ever know.'

'But Mary has gone.'

I cut a thick slice of bread. Soon I'd have to bake some more. That was good; something to hold onto, something wholesome I could do.

'We can simply say she went away. She was never paid properly, after all. Nobody would blame her.' I tore the bread into chunks and when the milk began to froth up the sides of the pan I poured it onto the slice and, nervy as I felt with

Victor behind me, I watched mesmerized, as the bread softened and lost its edges. I sprinkled sugar on top and we ate in silence. The bread was clammy, sweet and simple, dissolving between my teeth, making Victor's lips gleam white.

'This was a treat for Mary when she was a girl,' I said.

Victor put down his bowl and hid his head in his hand. His leg was going and his head.

'Go back to bed,' I said. 'Try not to worry.'

He looked up and gave a wild and nasty sort of laugh.

'*Please* go back to bed,' I said.

He stood and stared at me and I found myself looking around for something I could hit him with if necessary, the coal shovel would be the thing, but then he sagged and nodded and turned and left the room.

Daylight was leaking round the edges of the curtains by the time we'd finished Mary. When every inch of her was wrapped carefully separate – each finger and toe – Osi bound her legs together, and her arms to her sides, and then we wrapped the whole in the sheet from Mary's own bed, her final shroud.

'Later I'll decorate it and make the grave-mask,' he said. 'And you must make the shabtis.'

I stood up and tottered, a little giddy. I have always been someone who needs her sleep and it was the first time I'd ever stayed up all night. Osi looked dreadful, grey and drawn, and so like Evelyn, in the bony structure of his face, so like Victor, even in the cloudy absence in his eyes. And then I looked down at the tight white bundle that was Mary. She did not look so frightening or so cold now. Perhaps it was not a bad thing to have done. She did look, as Osi had said she would, complete.

We went to bed at the same time – we hadn't done that for years. It meant I could turn the key and be sure to be safe from Victor. Without speaking, and for the first time in years, we climbed into the same bed to keep each other warm. I lay curled into the heat of him – our bodies slotted together like two parts of a puzzle, our womb shape – and I lay listening to him breathing, and snoring because of his cold, and I pretended we were babies again, tucked snug in our cot by Mary, and in that way I drifted off to sleep.

29

I SLEPT TILL NOON. Beside me was the neat impression of Osi's head on the pillow. It seemed oddly light. In a daze I went to the window and parted the curtains. The sky was a pure, pale blue and the sun was shining. There was no frost, the snow had fallen away from the window, and the view was clear.

And then I remembered what had happened.

'You are so hard,' Victor had said.

I looked down at my hands, the fingers chafed from all the wrapping. In the bathroom I splashed my face with chilly water and watched the drips run down the hardness of my cheeks. I saw a woman not a girl, and not a pretty one. The roundness was falling away revealing not the swan I had hoped for but a perfectly plain duck. Plain and hard. The curse had started and I knew how to deal with it and I would have to deal with it myself. More blood, more rags.

Victor was already in the kitchen and the kettle was rising to a boil. His face was bleared with stubble – and in fact I don't think I ever saw him cleanly shaven again. The crinkled mix of fox and grey softened his mouth and the thin jut of his jaw,

273

but was ugly beside the scar, the shiny puckered rasher shape, where no hair grew.

'Where will you put her?' was his greeting.

'Good morning,' I said. The bowls from our bread and milk were still on the table, dried and crusty. I didn't know whether to prepare breakfast or go straight on to lunch.

'I've been thinking. It might be possible to get away with it,' he said, in a flat, dead voice.

I pressed my palms on the table and spoke without quite meeting his eye. 'She got in a right old tizz about her pay and upped and left. Bags and baggage and all. And who can blame her?'

He looked at me queerly. 'I do wish you wouldn't ape her speech like that.'

'Well it's her as brought us up,' I said.

The kettle squealed. I tipped out the old leaves and made a fresh pot. There was scant tea in the caddy. I would have to learn to pay attention to such things. More coal, too. Victor could go to the village and enquire about that.

'The icehouse.' I eased the felted old cosy down over the handle and spout of the pot. 'That's where he puts his other . . .' I didn't know how to put it. 'His birds and kittens and so on.'

He considered. 'And if anyone comes looking you can say she went off in the night. You didn't hear a thing. I wasn't even here.'

'It's more or less what I already told Mr Burgess.'

'Does she have a beau? Anyone who might come looking?'

'She did,' I said, 'but she fell out with him.'

'Good. What about her family?'

'Just a sister in Bristol. And she's poorly,' I said and then remembered that was not the truth but my lie to Mr Burgess. I must keep things straight. The milk in the jug, left too near the stove, had curdled. I went and fetched the last of the fresher milk from the pantry, and as I passed him, saw the effort with which Victor was pressing down on his leg, knuckles fisted white.

'When Evelyn and Arthur get back, they'll know what to do,' I said. 'And they will come back,' I reassured us. 'They should have the telegram by now. And Mary can stay in the icehouse till then, at least.' I watched the tea leaves clump together in the strainer as I poured.

Victor banged his hand down on the table so hard it made me jump. 'I've just thought – they won't get the bally letter before the telegram! If they hare straight back they'll miss it.'

He was right. I had already thought it and hoped he wouldn't. I kept my voice soothing as I said, 'Well, as soon as they get back, I'll tell them. Better face to face, anyway. I'll tell them it was all a mistake in that bally tomb. Some kind of delerium or something, I was feverish after all. I'll tell them you are blameless, make them see it. I *promise*. '

Victor stared at his tea for a long moment before he took a sip.

'They *will* come back, won't they?' I said.

As his eyes met mine, they flinched. 'Of course they will,' he said.

Victor drove to the village to order coal and fetch some groceries from Mr Burgess.

I'd gone through the pantry, deciding all we'd need for the next few weeks and making a long list. I wanted to feel secure that whatever happened next we'd at least have plenty to eat. I thought seeing Victor in person would reassure Mr Burgess and stop him quibbling about the account. And Victor could make a business of fussing about how Mary had gone and left us in the lurch, in case the grocer was still suspicious.

I made some shabtis by drawing faces on clothes pegs and wrapping them in scraps of tea towel. I made six and then forced myself to go upstairs to the nursery. I hadn't seen Osi all morning and didn't want to. I never wanted to go in that room again. I found him kneeling staring down at the dog's dinner he'd made of painting Mary's shroud.

'It's difficult to paint on cloth,' he said. 'It's supposed to be her.'

'It's good,' I lied, looking at the dabs and smears, and handed him the shabtis. He glanced at them and nodded. From the toybox I unearthed my old doll Madeleine, with her shabby china face and flaccid limbs. She looked a hopeless type – not liable to be much use to Mary in the Afterlife, but Osi said we should still put her in. There was a tin pony and a leather camel, both of which we added to the pile of grave goods.

'I wish we had a sarcophagus,' he said. 'Something wooden or stone that I could paint properly.'

'Well, we haven't,' I said.

He stood up and with his fists rubbed yellow smudges round his eyes. 'She must begin her journey as soon as possible.'

'It's nearly over, Osi,' I said and reached out to put my arms round him. It was strange and awful to feel his thinness, his exhausted quivering, and breathe the stench of blood and paint.

I had thought that making him complete the process was the right thing to do. That it would be good for him.

But I don't think he ever got over what he'd done.

Between us we struggled her downstairs. She wasn't heavy. Osi held her head and I her feet. He was muttering prayers or spells all the way through the kitchen and out and down the garden, through the orchard where I stumbled and we almost dropped her. Resting for a moment under the plum tree, I looked up through the winter branches at the thin blue of the sky and noticed the first swelling of the leaf buds. It seemed unbelievable that nature was going on as if nothing had happened, that the seasons would turn as usual.

We carried her down the steps to the icehouse and gentled her onto the ground outside the door. He took a key from his pocket, unlocked the padlock and swung open the door.

'How will we get her down there?' I stepped in and peered into the darkness of the ice pit. The black, musty stink of the place got in my nostrils and made my heart beat fast, wings of panic fluttering at the edges of my vision. I stepped out quickly, tripping over Mary in my haste to breathe fresh clean air.

'Mind out,' Osi said, breaking from his Egyptian muttering. 'Will you go and fetch the grave goods and the jars?'

Gratefully, I hurried away towards the house. The thunder of a train reminded me that this was just a day among other days. I didn't know what day it was. When the train went past, it had meant that Mary would be preparing luncheon. She would be in the kitchen making a soup. I stopped and let my head fall back to stare into the clear, pure blue above me and felt dizzied by the depth of it as if I could fall upwards and away, plummet through all that blue.

It took three trips to bring the things we were sending along with Mary and though I didn't believe in the journey, still I went into our parents' room and took a pair of jet earrings from Evelyn's jewellery box and a silk nightdress from her wardrobe. Evelyn didn't much care about such things and would understand. She would want Mary to have them. The worst things to carry were the jars that held bits of her innards. They were stoppered earthenware kitchen jars labelled *raisins, tea, and sugar* in Mary's own neat hand and smeared now with her blood.

I put the jars and all the things outside the icehouse. I could hear Osi inside muttering his incantations and I ran away. I could not be there when he put her down into the cavern of the icehouse. I should have helped but I was sickened by the close dark space, and the harshness of the Egyptian words that seemed to whisper and breed in that dankness. And I was sickened by Osi, by myself, just sickened to my soul.

I went to swing on the gate as if I was a child again, waiting for the distraction of a car. I was hoping for Victor, but the road was quiet. Nobody would be calling me for lunch or telling me to wash my hands or to change my frock. Victor would want something to eat when he got back, unless he stayed in the village. He liked the pub, where they made their own pork pies – and I expect he liked the landlady, too.

I went out of the sun into the kitchen, such a mess of dirty plates and dishes, Cleo winding round my feet and crying for her food. How Mary had managed for all those years, all alone, to keep it warm and tidy, to keep us well fed and in clean clothes, I do not know. Now I picked one of her aprons from the back of a chair and tied it round my middle. The floor was in need of a sweep and a mop. The table was strewn with crumbs and cat hairs and streaks of dried-on food. I was overcome with a wave of helplessness thinking of the filth in the nursery, the growing mounds of laundry – though there were hardly any sheets left to wash, at least – all the dirt and mess swelling and growing, and I understood so well, so much too late, Mary's crossness. In fact, I thought it a wonder she was ever cheerful at all, with all she had to do and then me on top, pestering her for company, for games of cards, for *love*.

There was hot water from the stove and I grated soap into the bowl and set to washing up every plate and bowl and cup we'd used. Osi came in and stood staring at the empty table.

'All done?' I said.

He nodded and met my eyes for just one bleak moment.

'I gave her Bastet,' he said.

'Good.' I wiped my hands on my apron in a Mary gesture and fetched bread and jam for us. I was hungry too and must make more bread, must think of a meal to cook for later – Victor was supposed to be bringing back fish, milk, sugar, cheese, chops, butter, and Mr Burgess would deliver the rest on Monday as usual . . . my mind went sliding along the tracks Mary had left. And she had even found time to make us cakes. Arthur often said she was a wonder, and he was right, and again I almost doubled over with the sudden punch of missing her. I had to keep my mind away from the slight and shrouded thing we'd carried down the garden, and from the silver padlock, big as a bath bun, locked now and that would stay forever locked.

'Ma and Pa will be back before you know it,' I said, and though we never called them that, it felt the right thing to say and he nodded as if comforted. We ate our little lunch in silence and then Osi went upstairs to sleep. I felt sleepy too and allowed myself five minutes with my feet up beside the stove, before I got out the bowl and prepared to make the bread.

I SAT AMONGST THE flattened shrubs by my poor Osi for I don't know how long, hearing the ebb and flow of traffic roar, the important racket of the trains. A blackbird came and sang his song, and I could hear its beauty though it didn't touch me. Other birds arrived, a silly chitter of them, and a chaffinch landed on Osi's arm. What would the birdies do when they brought in their bulldozers and all? Whatever would my spudgies do?

I wasn't cold; oddly *it* wasn't cold, though Osi was, chill and absolutely stiff. The shadows were more solid than the light. There was a secret language in the creaking and the clicking of the shrubs trying to right themselves after the catastrophe, and the bush that Osi broke breathed sourly from underneath him. Nine came picking through the shrubbery to see what was happening, sniffed Osi's scalp, marbled her eyes at me and stalked away, tail lifted in eloquent disdain.

And then I heard 'Sisi,' and a battering in my chest swept away my breath, until he called again and I recognized the voice as Spike's. I got up, so stiff, chilled after all, sitting in the damp for hours, perhaps, I don't know, time gone strange and slippery.

Spike was on the other side of the gate. Rust on the bars, you could taste it on the air, reminding me of the old gate where I used to swing – that would be right in the middle of the dual carriageway now – the ghost of a girl swinging, longing for a motorcar to come, as the traffic ploughed right through her.

'I came to say I'm going home,' said Spike.

He looked different in some way; I couldn't place it. In the bright light I could see a spot beside his mouth and a sprouting of young blonde whiskers.

'Home?'

'The States. Are you OK?'

I looked down at my filthy self, crusted white with bird all on my clothes and Lord only knows about my face and hair.

'You are an angel, dear,' I told him.

He looked a little shifty, embarrassed. 'Thank you, Ma-am.'

'Is there anything you want?' I said. It was the stud on his eyebrow that had gone, all the studs taken out, leaving him punctuated with tiny holes.

'See.' He bit savagely at his thumbnail. 'See, I wondered if, you said I could take anything I wanted from the house, well if you had something I could sell, then I could buy my ticket home.'

I was touched that he asked. He could have taken anything. Stolen anything from me. You hear the vilest things on the wireless. Talking to him through the bars it seemed as if one of us was imprisoned.

'I don't want to ask my folks,' he said.

I could see that, after all his anarchist bluster, to have to crawl back with his tail between his legs would have been humiliating.

'I've got a little job for you, and in return you can take anything you like,' I said. 'There isn't a fat lot left of value, but there's still some pieces, some jewellery of Evelyn's – my mother's, that is.'

'Pleased to oblige,' he said. His hands were curled around the bars of my portcullis.

I went into the house to get the key. My legs were soft, knee jagging viciously, hot while the rest of me was cold. Everything takes so long now. Oh how I used to flit about when I was a girl, everything working without having to give it a thought. Moving around now is like operating a complicated machine, one that grows stiffer with every passing day.

'It's Osi,' I told him as I opened the gate.

He blenched but said, 'Sure, no problem.'

'Come on,' I said.

Without another word he followed, and took my arm and helped me struggle through the undergrowth. I don't know what he must have been expecting, but when he saw Osi flung face down in an attitude of flight he gave a startled yelp and dropped to his knees.

'He flew,' I explained, deciding that he might just as well understand the logic of it. 'Horus rescues Osiris from death, you see, the falcon, see his beak.' As I spoke I saw the paling of Spike's lips and added swiftly, 'Of course, *I* know he is a man, really, but that is what he thinks, thought, I'm sure of it, so you see for him it was a good end and not as bad as it might appear.'

His lips moved silently.

'So you see, it's quite all right,' I added.

After a few moments he gathered himself enough to ask, 'Have you called the cops?'

'No dear, no need for that. You see, I know what he would want me to do now.'

It was difficult to convince him that there was no need to bring any authorities in. It took time. I was surprised how law abiding he was deep down. But with the promise of items to sell to fund his journey home, he overcame his scruples. Though he was slightly built he proved strong. I could not look or take part while he shouldered Osi and took him down the garden.

It took us hours to uncover the icehouse door, or took Spike hours, it was too much for me. Brambles had grown over the icehouse like a crown and what a shame it seemed to rip them up, disturb the creatures: a hedgehog, centipedes, birds' nests and all manner of scuttling, buzzing creatures; quite a little world destroyed. And Mary's resting place. The padlock was still there and still locked, but the wood of the doorframe had rotted and Spike managed to prise it open. No bad smell came out, I'll have you know, only the scent of earth, of darkness; breath of the end.

I could not be there when he put Osi inside and it took all my flagging strength to carry things out of the house and down the garden ready for the burial: three tins of paté, some Dairylee, there were no cream crackers left so I brought oat-cakes. I brought the tin opener and a gravy boat that might be silver. I lugged out some of his more portable artefacts and a few books, including *The Egyptian Book of the Dead*, which would surely be useful. Hastily I cut a row of hand-holding shabtis. I brought out soap and a pair of Arthur's cuff links, silver with a greenish stone. I put these offerings on the ground while Spike worked away, ripping his forearms on the brambly thorns.

During the work he stopped every hour or so to smoke a cigarette, rolling a big one and adding herbs to it. Each time he stopped I offered to make tea, but he would drink nothing except water from his own bottle. His eyes were red, and dusk was falling by the time Osi was safely tucked away down there with Mary and Dixie (I did not stay to watch for that) and all his grave goods with him.

For Osi to join Mary in the Afterlife (*his* Afterlife, I want no such thing) is *correct* and I know it from the peace that settled right through my bones when Spike had hauled the brambles back across the icehouse, obscuring it from sight.

He'd worked all afternoon and I was touched by the scratches on his arms and cheeks, the leaves caught in his snaky hair, his *breathlessness,* and all on my behalf. You see, Spike was like an angel, to me, setting me free. And once it was done he consented to stay for tea, though insisted, while he was rinsing his hands, on washing some cups and plates in readiness. I endeavoured not to take offence. We dined on blackcurrant tarts, feta cheese, spicy peppers from a jar and, as well as tea, drank gin and tonic, ready-mixed in handy tins. I lit the lamps and the candles to dispel the gloom and it was a pleasant and melancholy little wake we had in all the flickering. I didn't want him to go. I didn't want to be alone in the house, not that Osi had been any company at all, but still he had been *there.*

'Go upstairs,' I told him, and described where he would find Evelyn's jewellery box, in the bottom of her wardrobe. He was rather reluctant to go upstairs in the dark, what with the pigeons, but went off with an oil lamp and I heard a creaking to tell me he was upstairs and he was up there long enough for the house to start up its whining and wingeing and for tiredness to roll over me in waves. There were tears like beads of wax stuck in my eyes but they wouldn't melt till I was alone. My knee throbbed and the house throbbed along with it as if it was the centre, the heartbeat, and Mary was there, scolding me for something with that flick of dimple and when I was a girl I used to hold pencils to my cheeks, digging hard in to train dimples in, but all I got was graphite smudges.

Spike drove Mary away by coming in surrounded by a cloud of bird stink, bearing the leather box in his arms like one of the three kings, I thought, *bearing gifts from Orient are* and the tune of that got in my head. When Grandpa was still alive and all the servants, there used to be a Christmas party in the ballroom, oh that fox with the feathers in his mouth, oh my poor dear spudgies.

In the box were necklaces with glittering stones, a scarab brooch, a bracelet that looked like diamonds, but surely not? Rings and earrings, pearl and jade and amethyst. Evelyn rarely wore a jewel but for her plain gold wedding band and where had that gone? Stolen by some Egyptian devil, I must suppose. Victor's medals were in the box too, tarnished against their stripy ribbons.

We spread the treasures on the table amongst the crumbs, and in the waxy light they glittered and gleamed. Nine sprang up to look and sat, neat chinned as an Egyptian cat, as Bastet, eyes aslit, tail tidied round her legs.

'Are you sure?' Spike picked out a pair of dangling ivory earrings.

'Take them and that and that,' I said. In truth I didn't care; the things were jabbing and pricking and pinching at my memories of Evelyn and her distance; anyway, she never liked them very much, only wore jewels when she dressed up and that was seldom.

'My mom would love these.' He was dangling a smaller pair, garnet and gold, shaped like tiny birds, up to the light.

'Your mom?' I repeated, and oh, he looked so young then, such a silly baby boy run away from home. 'Give them to your mom, by all means,' I said, 'but take something else to sell for your ticket. This, maybe?' I held up the bracelet. What if it was diamonds? Surely Evelyn would have sold it to fund her wild goose chase.

'Tell me about your mom,' I said. What a sweet little bob of a word. Evelyn never even let us call her mother and that was mean of her, when we, or I at least, so wanted to. 'Mother,' I said now.

'Pardon?' said Spike.

'Tell me about her,' I said. 'Your *mom*.'

Spike shook his head, making the snakes dance. 'Oh she's OK, she's cool,' he said, and looked as if he might be fighting tears. I averted my eyes to allow him to compose himself. He took a sip from his tin before he continued. 'It's my pop that's the prick, excuse me, Ma-am.'

'Prick,' I repeated and laughed.

'He sells white goods,' he said. 'Washers and dryers and dishwashers. Kitchen stuff. Iceboxes, microwaves. Wants me to join the firm.'

'So you ran away.'

He looked abashed. 'Didn't go home,' he corrected. 'And fought with my brother who's all like *yes sir, anything you say sir.*'

'Make it up,' I said. 'You need your family.'

He had blackcurrant in the corner of his mouth and a blurring in his eyes. 'OK if I take these?' He lifted the bird earrings and the diamond-effect bracelet.

Stephen had told me that once I'd signed over Little Egypt I'd never need another penny in my life. U-Save would take care of all my bills, all my living expenses. I didn't need this stuff. 'Take it all,' I said, then changed my mind, 'I'll keep the scarab,' I decided. It was carved from a dark stone inlaid with carnelian, jasper, lapiz. If I'd known that it was there I would have sent it off with Osi, but too late. And Osi had flown away on falcon's wings.

Spike put the other jewels in his haversack. 'They'll think I stole them,' he said.

'If anyone says that, refer them back to me.' I liked the grand sound of that.

He fingered Victor's medals.

'My Uncle Victor was a hero.' I told the story of how he'd tried to save his whole battalion and risked his life, but sustained such terrible injury to his mind. Spike listened, rapt as a child. And Victor was there in the kitchen, nodding at the lie. I could see the bony structure of his nose, the hollows of his temples, the length of his thin lips. The scar was sizzling on his neck. And Mary was shaking her head at him, that exasperated smile, the spring of curls, that raising of her blue eyes to heaven. Osi came in, a child again, hair in his eyes; Mary stretched out her hand.

'Are you OK, Sisi?' Spike was saying. 'What are you looking at?' His hand was on my arm, warm; I hadn't even felt it.

'Tired out,' I told him. 'Only tired.'

'You want to sleep?' he said.

I nodded. Oh I was so tired it caught me suddenly in its folds so I could scarcely speak.

'I'll go,' he said. 'Thank you, Ma-am.' He patted the pocket in his haversack and hoisted it on his back.

'Thank you,' I said, 'for being my angel, for being my friend.'

The night was long, peopled with ghosts, deep pits of sudden sleep, a dream from the womb, the packed-tight squirm of twinnish flesh. And, of course, I cried, I roared and all the eyes blinked open in surprise because you should not make a fuss nor make an exhibition of yourself. The tears were hot wax and with the flame in my knee I was the candle that showed myself up in a transport of grief and it was like a transport or a transfer as it was my last night, would be, must be, my last night in Little Egypt, all the fabric of the house aching round me. My last night in the kitchen among the litter and the traces of the people, even Mr Burgess there, the ghost of a damp moustache, but never Arthur, never Evelyn, who I don't remember in the kitchen ever. Never Mother.

30

VICTOR DIDN'T RETURN till after dark. Osi was sleeping, breath smooth, only a trace of stuffiness left from his cold; I was in the bedroom, peering out, waiting to see, praying to see, the headlamp of Victor's car – and at last there it was, swinging up the drive. From the way it swerved through the dark I could tell that he was drunk again but I didn't care; I was so pleased that he'd returned. I ran downstairs to greet him. He came crashing in through the front door – ripping off his helmet and untangling his scarf.

'Where's the food?' I said, noticing his empty arms. 'I was waiting to do the chops.'

'Never mind the chops.'

My heart sank at the slurring of his speech. I followed his blundering to the kitchen where he threw himself down on a chair and let his head sag on the table.

'Pull yourself together,' I snapped.

'Oh, Icy . . .' Eyes shut, he reached out a hand for me to take, but I didn't take it.

'Is the food in the car?' I said. 'I've been waiting for the food.'

Slowly, he hauled himself upright and blinked round the kitchen as if he was surprised to have woken up and found himself there.

'Mary?' he said.

'Done.'

'How am I going to tell you?' he said.

I wanted to slap him. 'What?'

He fumbled in his pocket and brought out a screwed up telegram.

'Surely they haven't found their bloody king?' I said, though he was clearly not the bearer of good news. This was not the telegram we'd been waiting for. I snatched it from him and read:

You are advised of the disappearance of Captain and Mrs AHP Spurling. Await instruction and payment for services rendered. Mr AB Ali.

I stared and stared and though I could read the words perfectly well, my mind refused to take them in. Disappearance? How could they *disappear?*

'You'll have to go and find them,' I said. 'They can't simply disappear!' I walked round and round the kitchen. 'They will have run because they couldn't they pay their bills or pay Abdullah,' I decided. 'That loathsome man, I never trusted him.'

'Don't, Icy,' Victor bleated, lifting his head and peering at me as if through fog. 'Keep still. You're making me dizzy.'

'We'll have to find them we can't just –'

'Odds are they'll turn up,' he slurred. 'Make me a cup of tea. I reckon you're right, they'll have got themselves in too deep and scarpered.'

'Well, what shall we do?'

'Make a cup of tea, or coffee better still,' said Victor.

I stood with fists clenched looking at the useless husk of a man as he began to sob.

'She won't have got the letter, Icy, now she'll never know it wasn't me.'

I turned my back on him and filled the kettle.

I had been wrong. It was possible for our parents to disappear. Eventually Victor pulled himself together, went to town and made calls; he spoke to persons at both the British and the Egyptian embassies, but there was nothing. No news and nothing useful that we could do. I wanted Victor to return to Egypt and search, but he said he wasn't well or strong enough. I wanted the police set on Abdullah. He had been questioned, Victor was informed. Abdullah's story was that one morning Captain and Mrs Spurling had vanished into thin air, owing him a considerable sum of money – the police found nothing suspicious in that. And as far as owing the money went, neither did I.

A few days after the telegram, a postcard arrived from them, a view of Karnak and the message in Evelyn's spiky hand: *Still awaiting our concession, but the excellent Abdullah keeps our spirits up. Keep well dear beasties and keep warm, Evelyn,* with a kiss, and underneath in Arthur's neater hand, *chins up, much love, Arthur.* It was dated a month ago, before they would have got either my letter about Victor, or the telegram about Mary. We were never to learn if they received either. The card with its dingy avenue of sphinxes had been posted in Luxor, but held no other clue. Their motorbike and side-car turned up a few months later in Alexandria and that was the last of them.

Weeks passed by and all three of us hung suspended, waiting for them or news of them. Anger alternated with grief and sometimes my mind fell into a dull, blank trance, for which I was most grateful. The longer we heard nothing the more likely it became that they were dead, out in the desert, perhaps, buried in the grit, or picked clean by vultures, or shut up in a tomb, but I had to steer my mind away from tombs – even the word caused sourness to rise in my throat and frantic wings to beat.

Osi simply refused to countenance the fact that they would not come back, nor even that they would not succeed in finding Herihor. He seemed to continue as normal, though I'm sure he worried for them – as I'm sure he grieved for Mary – in his own unfathomable way.

Victor stayed with us. He was, it turned out, in serious debt and so he sold Berrydale and came to live at Little Egypt. In *loco parentis* was his phrase, though the way he lived with us could scarcely be described as that. He tried to find a maid, but it seemed no one wanted to be a maid by that time, at least not for the amount he'd pay, and most of the domestic work was left to me, which, curiously I took some comfort in. I discovered that I really liked to cook. I enjoyed the swish of sifting flour, the fleshy give of dough, the bubble of roiling vegetables, the spit and scent of roasting meat. In the kitchen I found peace and a sort of communion with Mary who stood beside me as I worked, whispering advice into my ear – *give it five more minutes, cut them smaller, try a dash of vinegar.*

The spring passed in a queer disconnected manner and by the time the lilac was blooming, we, at least Victor and I, agreed to assume that Evelyn and Arthur were never coming back. And so, after what seemed a lifetime of waiting, there was nothing left to wait for. Osi withdrew further into himself, into a sort of blinkered stupor from which I don't think he ever truly emerged; I think he spent the rest of his life awaiting our parents' return.

After the first few months, Victor began to go away again, drinking and gambling and chasing ladies. There was one he brought back more than once, Ivy her name, a lady with freckles on her arms, lovely and young and cleanly scented and I had a hope that he would marry her. Perhaps she'd come and live with us, I thought. But Victor ruined it with all the drink, and soon it was just us again.

It was years later, I think, time all gone into a smear, when one particular night I was woken by Victor's bellowing, and lay with the moonlight washing bluish across my bed. It must have been spring, he was always worse in spring. There was nothing unusual, only my own response. I made no decision that I recall, still befuddled as I was by sleep and dazed by moonlight, but climbed out of my bed and, barefoot, walked to the Blue Room door.

Between his screams he was talking, as if to another person, saying, 'Richie, Richie take the . . .' I could not make out what, and sobbing. I couldn't bear the fear in him, those awful wrenching sobs, worse than the screams. I tapped at the door but he didn't hear or answer, so I opened it.

He was not on the bed but crouching against the wall in his pyjamas, cowering, hands protecting his head. I walked across the room and touched his shoulder, and he jumped and yelled. The moonlight stained his face and I could see from the dark holes of his eyes that he was not awake. I took his hand and felt how he was quaking, how cold with sweat he was, and I pulled him towards the bed.

He let me lay him down and cover him, juddering and sobbing. I took a shirt from the floor and wiped his face. He was shivering so hard he made the bed shake. I got in to hold him, to steady and warm him. I moved him onto his side and I hugged him. I could feel the thin branches of his ribs through the clammy cotton of his pyjama jacket. I stroked his back, and made soothing, mothery noises close to his ear, like Mary would make if ever I awoke frightened in the night.

Eventually, he quietened down and one of his arms came round me. It was such a beautiful feeling to be held like that after no tenderness at all for years. The rigidity of his terror went out of him, and he was soft in my arms, relaxed, his hand stroking my back, a part of me that had never been touched by another hand, since Mary had washed me when I was small, and I wanted to arch my back against the movement of his hand, to purr like Cleo. He started to push his knee between my legs and I let him and I let my legs open but then he stopped, stiffened, shoved me off the bed.

He sat up, wild haired, wild eyed in the moonlight. 'Icy?' He peered at me as if I was something from his nightmare. 'Icy?'

I sat on the edge of the bed and reached for his hand but

he would not take it, he backed himself right up against the bedhead, arms wrapped round his legs. 'Go,' he said. 'Leave, leave, leave,' and he kept on saying it until I left the room.

Back in my own bed I lay and thought. My heart was thudding with a particular kind of excitement, but there was a sick lump of something in my throat. It should have been shame. I tried to make it shame. But it was disappointment.

Next time I heard the screaming, I got up and went to his room. But the door was locked. Whether he had locked himself in or me out, I don't know. I stood by that locked door with my heart thumping and my cheeks flaming, and then I went back to my own bed. I never tried again.

Next day he was as normal. Neither of us spoke about what hadn't happened. And we continued just as we had done since Mary had gone and our parents vanished. After supper in the kitchen, Osi would go up to the nursery and Victor and I would clear the table and play cribbage or rummy, we'd read to each other, or together we'd do a crossword puzzle. Sometimes he'd go away for a week or so, but would always come back, and seem glad to be home.

But one day he came back raggedly drunk. He was at his worst, shambling and stinking and he lurched towards me in the kitchen, holding out his arms. 'You're a bad girl,' he said, his voice all skewed and slurred. 'You want it though, do you, you want it, that's why you told those lies, that why you ruined me?'

I had been trying to darn one of his socks. I threaded the needle through the grey wool and put it down, before I said, in my calmest voice: 'No. Stop it Victor, pull yourself together.'

'Your *fantasy*.' He grabbed hold of me and I inhaled the

staleness of his clothes, felt the rasp of his beard. I didn't fight, only stood limply saying, 'Stop it, stop it.' I knew what kind of a drunk he was; I knew he would sag and stop any moment. I wasn't frightened, only repulsed and pitying and ashamed for him, for us both.

'I'll make some tea,' I said when I felt the energy leave him.

And he let me go. 'I wish Mary were here,' he said, as he slumped into her chair by the stove.

'*Don't*,' I said. There was still tea in the pot and I put the kettle on to refresh it.

'Good name for you, *Icy*,' he said.

I sliced bread and slathered it with the last of Mary's apple butter. Out of the corner of my eye I could see the jumping of his leg.

'Can't stay here,' he said. 'You're grown up now. I can't . . .' He focused on me blearily. He was drunk, but it was a sober truth he spoke: 'You should never have come to my bed.'

I turned away from his eyes, waited for the kettle to whistle, poured water into the stewed slops in the pot. 'You mustn't go. Please don't. I only wanted to comfort you, like Ivy and Mimi and Melissa.' As I spoke my words revealed themselves as thin and silly. 'I only wanted to make the horror go away.'

His jaw dropped and a sudden shocking jag of laughter leapt out. 'Make the horror go away! Make the horror go away! You think that's possible?'

My hand was shaking as I poured his tea. 'Don't,' I said. I tried to hand him the plate. 'Eat,' I said, but he swiped his hand through the air and sent the plate flying to smash against the stove, the bread landing sticky side down on the hearth mat.

'That's pathetic,' he said, 'make the horror go away!' He gave another mirthless laugh and when he turned his head to look at me again I saw an awful and familiar deadness had come into his eyes. 'When you've seen how easily they come apart.' He pressed his fist against his leg.

'*Don't,*' I pleaded.

'Bodies,' he said. 'Legs and arms, feet and hands, heads. And it's my fault.'

'No,' I said, '*please, Victor.*'

'It's like a nest of snakes in here.' He smacked his hand against his own abdomen. Under the skin everyone is a nest of snakes just waiting to burst out.'

I put my hands over my ears. 'Victor, *don't*. It's not your fault. Listen! The war was *not* your fault!'

'You don't know.' He was breathing heavily. 'If I had kept my head they'd be alive,' he said. 'They might be.'

I stared.

'My lads. I sent them the wrong way, into danger, then kept my own bloody head down.'

I sat down at the table, warming my hands round his cup of tea.

'No,' I said. 'That's not right, is it? Think; *remember*. You got the MC'

'Shouldn't have accepted.'

'No, Victor, no,' I said.

'I lied. It was all a cover up. Those poor bastards.'

He kept on talking and then pacing round the room and talking madness and so much ugly awful stuff I had to stick my fingers in my ears and hum just like I used to do to shut out Osi's rubbish, and then the door banged and he was gone.

I sat and listened to the crash of doors, the roar of the engine, and then, when it was quiet again, I picked up the pieces of the broken plate, and the bread from the floor, took up the sock and resumed my darning.

HE LEFT THE house for a week and came back with a lady of sorts. Deirdre, I think she was called, or Flo? I lost track. Sometimes they would stay for days, sometimes just one night. Sometimes they were friendly and would play cards, even tinkle on the piano in the ballroom, with the birds skittering madly round, and sometimes they ignored me. Sometimes they shouted out their joy in the middle of the night, and sometimes they were silent.

Victor and I never really talked again, though he was friendly enough, calling me 'Dear little Icy' and playing cards in the evenings, treating me like a child, but never again did he look me in the eye.

When we'd run through Victor's money, he sold the land for the road, so big and noisy when first it was built, it seems like nothing now, compared with the dual carriageway. We lived on that money for years. Victor stayed with us most of the time, sometimes he went away, and sometimes brought a woman back. When he was alone, he still occasionally screamed at night, and I pulled the pillow over my head.

And then one morning I found a farewell letter on the

kitchen table. It was formal, impersonal, almost. He had made arrangements with some solicitors – he must have been sober to do that – to deal with all financial matters, to sell a further parcel of land – the nut grove – the money to be invested, which would keep us in funds for the foreseeable future. Groceries would be delivered; the house would be looked after . . . it was all about practical arrangements. He must have been planning for ages to leave us, and to leave us looked after, but he'd never said a word.

Where he went or what became of him, we never knew. I used to wonder if he'd done himself in, but I don't think he would have had the nerve. He will have gone off and drank and lost himself in his affairs with women, that is what he will have done.

Victor could not bear his own mind; I can understand that. If it was true that he was no hero, then how could he bear it? He couldn't bear it that Evelyn died believing he did something to me in the tomb. And that is my fault for lying. At least I think it was a lie. When I try to send my mind back now, all those years, I don't know what the truth was. Was it one of the Arabs? Or was it anything at all? There was one I took a fancy to, and you might say I gave him the eye; his name has gone. I can't even recall if he was there that day. Everyone else at the scene will be dead by now, or extremely ancient. And what does it matter now? Traffic under a bridge.

There's a memory buried somewhere on the West bank of the Nile. Beneath that rocky desert there are cells of colour – still to be discovered – of gold, of hope, of love, of riches, of belief, of shrivelled bodies, desiccated sludge in jars, of painted eyes and gods and goddesses all invisible in the dark, under the sand, under the rock, under the pressing sun. Forever and ever a horse gallops across that desert, followed by a faithful whiskery dog, nose down, hunting.

When Osi came down for his supper, I showed him Victor's letter. I watched his face as he read and there was no change in his expression. He had the beginnings of a beard by then, I remember, thin and scrappy, but it gave him the look of a man, so much like Victor, with the thin bony angles of his face. I smiled, though it almost made me ache to look at him.

'The nut grove?' he said, when he had finished reading. 'He sold the nut grove? But what about the foxes?'

'The foxes?' The smile died on my face. Victor had left us and his concern was for the *foxes*.

'Don't you realize we might have to stay here forever?' I shouted. 'Because of Mary. Because of you. We can never leave this house. We'll have to stay *forever*.'

Foxes!

I couldn't bear to be near him. I ran upstairs and lay beneath my eiderdown. *Forever*. Because of Osi and what he'd done to Mary we'd have to stay forever in Little Egypt.

But as I lay there, a memory crept back, a picture of the earth scraped bare round the foxes' holes. A deep stink hung in the nut grove, and sometimes you'd find a scatter of bones and rags of fur or feathers. One evening when we were tiny, we were gathering cobnuts with Mary, when she caught my arm and pointed. I turned to see a vixen, frozen, one foot in the air, snout lifted and quivering. 'Keep still,' she whispered. 'Shhh.'

We stood as still as the trees and the fox never saw or smelled us. Next thing a tumble of cubs nosed up from the earth, three of them, and Osi and I clutched each other in delight and fear – you could see the sharp glint of the vixen's teeth as she guarded the rolling, tumbling snarl of her cubs at play. And Osi and I were joined for that moment in our pleasure.

Light was coming through the clots of stuffing in the eiderdown. I pushed it back, anger leaking away. Perhaps he'd remembered that evening and how close we were in the moment of the foxes; perhaps that's why he cared so much about the nut grove. Overcome with a surge of love, I jumped out of bed and ran downstairs. He had just finished his breakfast and was getting up from the table.

At first he quailed when I hugged him, gathering all the bonyness, the *awkwardness* of him, tight in my arms.

'We're stuck here now,' I said, 'together foreveranever.' I heard Mary in my head, and I echoed her: 'We must make the best of a bad job.' And then I kissed his cheek and pushed him away. He left the room then, but as he went through the door, he squinted curiously back at me, and smiled.

It's not as if he could ever have lived elsewhere, though he would have made a wonderful Egyptologist. Apart from his obsession, his almost total lack of interest in physical comfort would surely have been an asset. Think what he might have done. And if he had done that, I would have lived an ordinary life, married and had children – great grandchildren by now. I would have *been* in the world.

But how could I have left him? I was his twin, his big sister. I loved him. I protected him. And behind our portcullis I kept him safe for all his natural life. And I am proud of that.

But since he's no company, I've made friends: Doreen in the café; the various postmen who bring letters over the bridge and with whom I try to catch an occasional pleasantry, and Spike, my friend. And Stephen, of course, my charming young developer.

Today *is* Tuesday and oh the morning was so long in coming but here it is at last, strands of daylight trailing through the window. Nine jumps down from somewhere, stretches and miaows. There's cat food in a tin and I take the lid off, she can eat it from the tin, and when she can't get her face in far enough she wedges it against the table leg and dips in a clever paw.

I go straight out, no time to waste today.

Today *is* Tuesday and the water in the Ladies is hot, the mirrors gleaming, but I keep my eyes away from them. I know I look a sight; hardly need confirmation. The lavatories have such comfortable seats. Sitting, spending a penny, I lean my face against the wall. I could go to sleep again, so easily. Why didn't I think of it last night? The place is open 24 hours, after all; I could have had a warm and comfortable night sitting on the lavatory.

But still, today is Tuesday and all is well. And in the café here is *I'm Doreen how may I help you?* and despite her sour expression, I'm comforted by her presence. In truth we're hardly *friends,* but we've known each other for years and for all those years she has reliably disapproved of me, a dreadful liberty since she is working in my shop. *If it were not for me you wouldn't be here*, I've told her and she knows it. We both know where we stand.

I take my seat by the window and watch the early light picking out the roof of Little Egypt. From here it's clear the house has had its day. The time has come. Pull it down and build your megastore, and with my blessing, just get me out of there. I can't bear the sight of it.

Now my mind's made up I tremble with eagerness to do the deed and get it over with. Stephen will be, must be, here this morning unaware that today's the day he has been waiting for. I've been dangling my indecision, squirming on its hook just out of his reach, for weeks. Stephen's married to a girl called Carly and they are trying for a baby, as he puts it. If he could be the one to persuade me to 'sign on the dotted line', he confided, he'd get a bonus with which he could put down a deposit on a house with garden 'just a handkerchief would do'. They want somewhere to put a swing. He's shown me pictures of Carly all fair and pink and soundly fertile, by the look of her.

Although I know it's counter service, I sit and wait till Doreen cracks and comes across.

'It's counter service,' she says, though she knows I know and that I know she knows. It's part of a ritual we've built up over the years.

'Well, thank you for telling me, dear,' I say. 'But now you're here, a cup of cappuccino and a pain au chocolate, please. This is Tuesday, isn't it?' I add.

'It is,' she hisses as she swivels on her heel.

In the corner of my eye, a taunt from Little Egypt, the tiny waving of the rowan on the roof, but I will not turn and look.

And Stephen arrives just as Doreen is slamming my tray down in front of me. 'Espresso, please,' he says.

'Counter service only,' she says and stalks away.

'Bitch,' Stephen remarks cheerfully, not quite loud enough for her to hear.

He doesn't know it yet, but today he's getting what he wants, and so am I. Warm with relief, I study him at the counter. He's of a chunky build, dark blood in him of some variety, rather handsome, eyes so dark they . . .

. . . breath snatched away, suddenly a flash of desert, beautiful boy, beautiful boy, breath of honey, eyes like that, like ink. Was that a dream? It seems a dream now in the turquoise and orange of the café with everything so bright, wipe-clean Formica, plastic chairs, serviettes made of paper that you use once and throw away.

This is reality.

Stephen returns with his espresso in its tiny dolly's cup, (what Spike would term a 'rip off'). We always indulge in small talk before Stephen tries to force my hand, in the nicest possible way, telling me it's for the best and all. Hungry for conversation, I try to make it last as long as possible. I've become truly fond of Stephen; he is someone who will talk about himself till the cows come home to roost, and I don't mind that in a person. (He's an egoist if you like, but real and live and entertaining, and oh oh oh those eyes.)

Today, I'm impatient to get down to business, but still, I listen to him chattering on about a holiday they've booked (Carly's a travel agent and gets a discount) – a fortnight in

Dubai. As he talks I lick the delicious chocolaty foam from my teaspoon (I always think a cappuccino's halfway to a pudding) and I notice that he can't prevent his eyes from wandering out of the window and over to the roof of Little Egypt. I keep my own eyes down and grit my teeth against the buffeting of knowing that Osi isn't under it.

After stirring his sugar in, Stephen swigs his coffee in one gulp, his signal that the informal chat is over and it's time to get down to business.

'I don't get it,' he says, all sympathy and velvet eyes. 'If you sell up you'll have ten times, twenty times more money than you'll need to live in luxury for the rest of your days. Some-where warm, round the clock care – should you need it,' he adds carefully. And once again he lists all the luxuries on offer. He's found yet another place, with another glossy brochure, but I barely glance at all those grey haired, plastic grins in their plush settings because I have already made up my mind. Sunset Lodge is the place for me.

Sucking on a mouthful of pastry, I keep my smile pent up and listen. Stephen has a sweetness to him, partly youth no doubt, that works on me, in a way that the older men, the over-sympathetic business women who've tried to win me round before have never even approached. Previous develop-ers have always seemed my enemy, while charming Stephen has become my friend. He certainly deserves his bonus. Once I'm installed in Sunset Lodge, he'll visit me, he's promised, and bring along his travel agent too.

'What I don't get,' he says, gesturing towards the house, 'is why you would choose *that*, rather than to live in the lap of luxury.'

'Lap,' I say. 'Why lap, I wonder?'

He starts to frown but transforms it into a grin. He has a disarming grin, a dent at the corner of his mouth, halfway to a dimple. 'Dunno. Never thought about it. Thing is . . .' He leans closer, letting his professional mask slip, 'if you're ever going to cave, please do it for me. Carly's getting right broody and there's a little property we've seen . . .'

'With a garden?'

'Back and front. And a downstairs loo, which is always handy.'

I nod. 'Indeed. There's just one thing I need to check.'

His mouth drops open.

'Listen,' I say. I take my time. The hook is quivering just out of his reach, he strains forward, open mouthed, ready for to snatch. 'Sometimes people have things to hide.' My hand shakes as I lift cup to lip.

'Ah?' Stephen lifts both his hands in eager anticipation, ready to quell any worry I might have.

I put my cup down carefully. 'Someone told me that these big firms like U-Save and so on, that when they buy land for a project they don't let anything like . . . Roman ruins, for instance, stand in the way of progress.'

His expression falters. 'You got Roman ruins?'

'No, no, that's an example. Is it true?'

'What do you mean? Like something in the house?'

'Hypothetically,' I say. 'Or in the grounds.'

Stephen leans forward and actually takes my hand, greasy from the pastry though it is. No one has held my hand like that for years and I shut my eyes for just a moment to savour it. 'Listen,' he says, glancing furtively about, 'off the record and everything, get me?'

I tighten my fingers round his.

'All they want is to get built and trading with no hold-ups. They're not interested in what's there, they'd keep their eyes shut and get it covered over quick.'

'That's what Spike thought,' I say.

'Uh?'

'A friend.'

'Well, yeah,' he says. 'Off the record, I've heard there *is* a Roman Fort – or Bronze Age or something – under Cleopatra's – that's the big casino next to the station? Illegal, of course, not to report it, but they got the thing flung up that quick.'

I could no longer keep his hand without a struggle so I let it go.

'Can you promise?'

'Can't *promise*,' he says. 'But the likelihood of anything getting in the way of profit . . . and you've held them up that long now. They'll want to be trading by Christmas, I reckon.'

'I will sign.'

I sit back to luxuriate in his incredulity. Doreen's watching, face a study, but she snatches her eyes away when she catches me looking.

His eyes are wide. 'Straight up?' he says, hand ferreting already in his briefcase.

'As long as I can go today – to Sunset Lodge.'

'Today!' He's startled. 'Takes longer than that,' he says. 'You'll need to be assessed and that, they'll need to have a room for you. And there's the paper work.'

'Well, that's my deal,' I say. 'It's that or nothing.'

'Ready to sign?' He has the pen out of his pocket and the papers spread out before me.

I do not take the proffered pen. 'I'll only sign,' I say, 'if I can move today.' I remember a phrase of his own. 'It's a deal breaker.'

Brow furrowed, he nods. 'Hang on,' he says. 'Let me make some calls.'

He pretends there's no signal, but he's made calls from here before. Naturally, he doesn't want me to hear his negotiations.

'One other thing,' I say. 'You'll have to take my cat. Unless I can take her with me?'

'Not a problem. Another cappuccino while you wait?'

He's in a hurry now. At the counter he orders and points across at me. The look *I'm Doreen how may I help you?* flicks him as he walks away is one I'll treasure for the remainder of my days. But she does bring me my coffee. 'So,' she says. 'You're giving in?' I was not aware she was so *au fait* with my business, but then I do conduct it in her café.

'Giving in?' I ponder for a moment. 'Not a bit of it. It's simply that the time has come. I'm ready for pastures new.'

She nods. 'Well then, good luck,' she says and turns away, but not before something like a smile breaks on her face, a real one too, for the first time in all these years! Aghast, I watch her walk back to her position behind the counter and present her usual chisel face to the waiting customer, the sort she hates, the blurred type with chaotic children.

I sip my coffee and stare out of the window at the waving rowan, and I see it's not a tree at all but Mary, waving her handkerchief at me. I eat the foam. In Sunset Lodge will they have cappuccino of this excellence? I'll miss the turquoise and orange brightness, the paper serviette dispensers; I'll miss the comforting roar of the hot air dryer in the Ladies' Lavatories. And I'll miss *I'm Doreen how may I help you?*.

Although I last it for as long as possible, my coffee cup is empty before Stephen returns, all shiny and excited. 'Phew,' he said, 'I knew that money talked, but this is something else!' There's a smell of sweat coming off him, hidden behind a freshly squirted miasma of Sure or Lynx or something of that order.

My hands shake and I attempt to knit my fingers tightly but they are too stiff and knobbly, ugly stranger's hands, not my own at all. 'So?' I ask.

'U-Save's lawyers will advance to Sunset Lodge your first month's keep – just on proof of signature. You'll have to pay an extra month for urgent processing – that OK?'

I nod, loving that expression. *Urgent processing*. It seems of appropriate weight for this momentous moment.

'You only have to sign. There's a room going, nice one, front, view of the river. Hate to think who they're bumping off to get you in there,' he quips, rather tastelessly, perhaps.

'And what about Nine?'

'Sorry?'

'My cat.'

'Yeah. There's a no pets policy, but I reckon Carly'll be sweet with having a cat.' He gets out his pen again. 'Shall we, then? We need a witness.' He looks across at Doreen who's ostentatiously absorbed in doing something to her till.

My breath is short. This is it. He summons Doreen, who stomps grumpily across.

'What now?'

Stephen explains. The pencilled eyebrows rise like wings. 'No skin off my nose,' she says.

'Incidentally,' I say, 'compared to your young colleague yesterday, your coffee is first rate.'

She gives a little moué – pleased, I think.

The pen is thick between my fingers, shiny, hard to hold. My name emerges as a trembly scrawl, the signature of a half-wit. Doreen leans over and puts her name, quite neat and childish underneath.

Stephen sits back, runs his hand through his hair. 'Phew,' he says. He glows with triumph and pleasure and some of it reflects on me. 'Thank you,' he adds, to Doreen and, of course, to me.

'Is that the lot?' Doreen returns to the queue that has been building.

'Give her a big tip,' I say and Stephen extracts from his wallet a £10 note.

'Of course, there'll be lots more paperwork,' he says, 'but we can conduct all that from your new home. I'll pop in to-morrow, shall I? See how you're settling in.'

Since I am adamant that I don't want any strangers in Little Egypt till after I have left, we arrange that a taxi will meet me in front of U-Save at 2 o'clock.

'But what about your luggage?' Stephen says. 'You'll need help with that.'

'No luggage,' I say. 'I want to start anew.'

'Nothing?'

'Nothing I can't get in my trolley.'

'Fair dos,' he says and stands. He leaves the £10 on the table and, once I've struggled to my feet, he shakes my hand.

'But you need to come and get the cat,' I say.

'I'm on my way to the office . . .' he says, then shrugs. 'It'll have to wait in the car is that OK?'

'She,' I say.

I take him onto the bridge and leave him at the gate. Nine is curled as usual on the table. An old cat, shedding hairs, she's docile and droopy in my arms as I carry her out. Stephen waits on the bridge, leaning over the parapet to watch the flow of traffic. Nine stiffens and her claws come out and catch Stephen a nasty scratch on the chin during the transfer through the gate.

'See you on Thursday,' he says over his shoulder as he tussles with the hissing, struggling Nine, and oh I do feel a traitor as they go. But Stephen is a good boy and she'll be looked after. That's my last responsibility gone, except for the spudgies, and now I'll set them free.

*O*UTSIDE THE ENTRANCE *to U-SAVE's brand new HOMESTORE, a brass band plays carols beneath a sparkling giant of a Christmas tree. There's a carousel in the car park, clowns on stilts, and Santa-hatted assistants in orange and turquoise uniforms distribute sweets and vouchers.*

A taxi draws up as close to the doors as it can get, and from its window Sisi gawps. Lovely Surinder, her dedicated 'friend' opens the door and, as gently as he can, hauls her out. She's like a sack of potatoes, she knows it, fattened right up on all the lovely food, pumped up like a tyre with cream cakes every single afternoon and cocoa in the evenings to help her sleep, though sleep's a waste of time what with all the television she's got to watch. What a marvellous invention! He hauls her out to stand on the family land.

Inside the colossal structure, she tilts her head back to look up at the walls of glittering glasses, saucepans, mountains of candles and an area the size of the ballroom entirely dedicated to bedding. Surinder takes her up the moving stair-

case to where they have it all laid out in rooms without walls, where she wanders for an hour, touching fabrics, sliding open drawers, peeking inside empty wardrobes; it's rather overwhelming. There's a feeling inside her she doesn't quite recognize or like. What would Osi say? Is his ghost floating here; bewildered amongst the swatches, the choice of glossy finishes?

If Mary's here, she'll like it fine.

There's no way of calculating where the icehouse would be.

And no way of knowing if they're still there – Mary, Osi, the missing kitten. A sob rises in her. Surinder takes her arm and rubs her back, the way she likes.

'Come on, Sisi,' he says. 'You're getting tired. Let's get you a nice cup of tea.'

The café is vast, and part of it done over for children, with dinky chairs and bright plastic toys. Christmas jingles play and tinsel twizzles above the tables. They find a seat beside the window and Surinder brings her a mug of tea and a flaky mince pie with cream, which goes down well, pushing with it the lump in her throat.

Of course, Osi is not here; he's gone. As she will be before too long. As even the excited children with balloons will be eventually. And this glittering palace: one day it will be derelict and the bulldozers will do for it. And what will they put here next?

She chomps the last of her mince pie, feels energy returning and smiles. Of course it will change, it will change and change and change and go on changing until the ending of the world.

From the high window, she can see the railway line, and all at once, she gets her bearings. 'Come on, dear, drink up,' she tells Surinder. She leads him through the store. If that is the direction of the railway line, then it must be round about here. The icehouse and its contents.

They go downstairs and walk through Storage Solutions and Home Decoration into Lighting, into a dazzle of candelabras, lamps and lampshades; there must be thousands of twinkling bulbs.

'What are we looking for?' asks Surinder.

Sisi catches sight of a lampshade and squints. 'Get me that one,' she says.

'You want it for your room?'

He lifts it down and she squints closer and laughs.

'What?'

She's bending over now, and laughing in a way that's more like vomiting or crying, she can't stop the torrent of hilarity.

'Is she all right?' someone asks Surinder.

He stands uselessly holding the bloody lampshade with its Tutankhamen design, and she cannot stop the laughing and doesn't even care when pee runs hotly down her legs.

'I'd get her home,' a woman in a Santa hat advises.

'This was my home,' she says, when she can straighten up. 'You're only here because of me.'

'Come on, Sisi,' Surinder says. He holds her arm in that way he has, gentle and strong, and they take a taxi back right to the lap of luxury.

ACKNOWLEDGEMENTS

With thanks to Andrew Greig, Bill Hamilton, Tracey Emerson, Ron Butlin, Regi Claire and Claire Gilmour. And to the Society of Authors who honoured me with a Somerset Maugham Award in 1991. Without this award, which I used to visit Egypt, I would never have written this novel.